Roz Denny Fox

CHRISTMAS STAR

Harlequin Books

TORONTO • NEW YORK • LONDON
AMSTERDAM • PARIS • SYDNEY • HAMBURG
STOCKHOLM • ATHENS • TOKYO • MILAN
MADRID • WARSAW • BUDAPEST • AUCKLAND

ISBN 0-373-70672-3

CHRISTMAS STAR

Copyright © 1995 by Rosaline Fox.

This edition published by arrangement with Harlequin Books S.A.

® and TM are trademarks of the publisher. Trademarks indicated with ® are registered in the United States Patent and Trademark Office, the Canadian Trade Marks Office and in other countries.

Printed in U.S.A.

"This dude's totally awesome, Mom!"

Mom? Clay mouthed the word and did a fast double-take.

Nine-year-old SeLi tipped her head to gain a new perspective on the stranger. She gave a low whistle. "I don't know where you found him, but it's okay by me if you keep him, Mom."

"You have a daughter?" Trying to recover from his shock, Clay McLeod studied first the girl, then the woman.

Starr rushed to stand protectively beside the child. It would have been nice, she thought—though hardly typical—if SeLi had kept quiet. This stranger already labored under enough misconceptions.

"Oops!" SeLi clapped a hand over her mouth. "If you're ever gonna snag a husband, I oughta call you Starr—not Mom." Before Starr could gather her wits, the child thrust a small hand toward the man and said around a lopsided grin, "Don't worry, mister. She's not married."

"To your room, young lady!" Starr pointed. "The *gentleman* was just leaving."

"Aw, Mom! You said we could get out the Christmas decorations tonight."

"Yes, well, that was *before.*"

As Clay looked on, bemused, SeLi skipped off with a backward glance, muttering something about wishes and dads and a Christmas star....

Dear Reader,

Holidays around the Fox household are always times of celebration. We love to decorate, make candy, read Christmas stories and see holiday plays. No matter where we've made our home, the family always tries to meet and explore some of the special holiday traditions there.

In the state of Washington, we loved to watch the parade of Christmas boats all decorated with colored lights. In Arizona we enjoyed the lighting of luminarias and the traditional candle-walk down Squaw Peak. In Texas we've joined in the reenactment of Christmas at Old Fort Concho, where we saw how soldiers and their families celebrated those early Christmases on the harsh and lonely plains. In California we loved the festivities on Olvera Street and the breaking of the piñata. Our first Christmas in Hawaii, Santa arrived in red swimming trunks on a surfboard. Kansas City decorates the downtown plaza buildings with millions of tiny white lights, and horse-drawn carriages meander through the streets. Growing up in Oregon, we cut our own Christmas trees and went sledding and participated in taffy pulls.

Each of those Christmases has been special. There's something about this holiday, no matter where or how you celebrate it, that touches us in very profound ways.

It's always seemed to me that one star shines brighter at Christmas than at any other time of the year. It's the star on which people everywhere can pin their hopes and dreams. The Christmas Star.

Happy Holidays to you and yours!

Roz and Family

P.S. I'd love to hear about your favorite Christmas traditions! You can get in touch with me at 3520 Knickerbocker, #224, San Angelo, Texas 76904.

CHRISTMAS STAR

CHAPTER ONE

STARR LEDERMAN sank gratefully into the warm leather cushions of Senator Harrison McLeod's limousine. She shivered as mid-December fog obliterated the San Francisco skyline. Almost absently she brushed the moisture from her hair and watched the drops bead on the smoked-glass window, along with condensation from her breath. Beyond the window she caught a glimpse now and then of sparkling Christmas decorations. She should be making her own holiday plans, not worrying about how to combat her almost-adopted daughter's compulsive stealing.

Starr sighed. The state senator's unusual summons for lunch had come late today—the day from hell. Not only was she without her compact car, having taken it in for repair, but a sudden unscheduled conference at SeLi's school had drained her of her normal vitality. Sinking back into the comfort of the aromatic leather, she closed her eyes.

The current incident involved an influential family. The principal at this latest in a long line of private schools had more or less issued an ultimatum: one more disturbance, and SeLi would be asked to leave.

Lord, Starr thought. She was running out of schools—and options.

She opened her eyes as the driver turned off California Street onto Powell Boulevard and pulled to a stop beneath the dripping awning of a prestigious old hotel. Ah, this was nice. She'd paid little attention to where the senator had said their luncheon meeting would be.

Starr smiled at the elderly chauffeur who handed her from the back seat. Whorls of fog swooped between them, and Starr automatically flipped up the collar of her wool coat and checked her watch.

"Yikes," she muttered more to herself than to the doorman as she hurried inside. "It's later than I thought. I'd better phone Blevins." She hoped it wasn't too late to have the manager at her condo complex catch SeLi after school to send her upstairs to Darcy Donnelly's.

The sharp-eared doorman smiled and directed her to a bank of pay phones. On the way there Starr shrugged out of her camel-hair coat. Deftly she turned the lining out—to keep her linen suit dry. It was a trick she'd learned when she first moved to San Francisco.

Starr drummed nervous fingers on the phone's casing while she waited for either Mr. or Mrs. Blevins to answer. At last Mrs. B. answered and said, bless her, that she'd be happy to pass the message along. Sagging in relief, Starr thanked her profusely. This wasn't the first such favor she'd begged from the older couple.

As Starr ran to catch the elevator, she hoped fervently that Wanda Manning, the social worker appointed to oversee SeLi's adoption, never got wind of her increasing lateness. Wicked Wanda, as SeLi usually called the woman, jumped on every transgression.

The gilded elevator was old and slow, and oddly relaxing. Starr's gloom was dispelled when she stepped out into the sparkling room. A kaleidoscope of colors spilled from a beautiful chandelier and silver Christmas stars glittered on boughs of evergreen.

Busy as she'd been, Starr hadn't had time to worry about what the senator wanted. No bad news, she hoped. His secretary had been vague.

After giving her name to the tuxedoed host, Starr followed him into the dining room, thinking it'd been almost six months since she'd seen Senator McLeod. Yet in spite of a thoroughly rotten day, she didn't have to force a smile for the handsome older man who rose from a secluded table to greet her with a hug and a quick kiss on the cheek.

"Starr, if you aren't more beautiful than ever, I'll skip lunch and eat my hat. Let me look at you." Tall and distinguished-looking, the man pulled back and studied her upturned face as he handed her still-damp coat to the hovering host.

She let her eyes linger a moment on his charismatic smile, then she laughed. "Harrison, you old flatterer. Ever the politician. I'll bet you say that to every woman in your district old enough to vote. But you know, considering the day I've had, I'll accept your blarney."

He seated her at the table, then sat across from her. "Job getting you down?" he asked after the water goblets had been filled. Scanning her taut features, he murmured, "I do believe you've lost weight since I last saw you, young lady."

Starr blushed. She didn't like talking about herself. "Are you planning to make my job more interesting?" she asked bluntly. "Otherwise, why the cryptic summons?" She rested an elbow on the table, braced her chin in a palm and waited.

The senator laughed. "As if you and I would have a clandestine meeting." His amused gaze followed the water glass to her lips. "Matter of fact, I have a small favor to ask." He unfurled his napkin. "A project I think is right up your alley." Leaning forward, he lowered his voice. "The State Department needs a good, discreet biochemist. I've been asked to commission you at any cost."

"Really?" She arched a brow several shades darker than her auburn hair. "Hey—I knew this meeting wasn't personal," she said. "I was only teasing. The society pages are full of how much in love our newest candidate for governor is with his pretty wife. By the way, good luck in your campaign. Now," she continued more briskly, "about this project. It sounds... ominous." She tipped her head. "Well, at least more ominous than my eating lunch with a happily married man."

In the middle of her speech the smile faded from the senator's eyes. Instead of answering, he motioned the wine steward over and selected a bottle of Napa Valley Riesling. Then he picked up a leather-bound menu and appeared to get lost in it. When the silence stretched between them and Starr continued to study him with curiosity, he cleared his throat and said softly, "I guess I'd better tell you before you hear it someplace else, Starr. Vanessa and I are having marital problems."

Harrison's eyes, which hesitated meeting hers, were dark with pain. Starr straightened, unable to disguise her shock. "Because of the political campaign?" she asked once she'd found her voice.

He shrugged. "Certainly it's gotten worse now that I've been drafted to run. Vanessa feels she's raising our son alone. I'll admit, lately I'm practically living out of a suitcase. But what can I do? Tell my backers to chuck it all?'' His tone grew more guarded. ''They've invested more than money, Starr. And I've plowed a lot into this race. Family money, which makes matters worse.''

''Family money is always touchy.'' Starr's sympathy was genuine. Few knew her background better than the senator, a long-time friend of her movie-mogul father, Sam Lederman. The wealthy Hollywood genius tended to think he could manipulate his family the same way he could his actors—with demands . . . and money.

Harrison looked bemused. ''You know, Starr,'' he went on, ''the most ironic thing in this whole deal is that Vanessa runs to my younger brother for every little thing—whether or not I'm home. She claims Clay is *sensitive,* that he listens to her. More and more, I see him taking my place.'' His voice sounded bitter, and he fell silent as the wine was served.

When the steward had left, Starr took a sip of the chilled wine to ease a suddenly dry throat. Her voice remained thick. ''So what are you saying? Not that your wife and your brother are having a . . . an affair.'' She glanced around, lowering her voice.

Harrison's shoulders slumped. Every one of his fifty years showed in the deep lines etched in his face. ''Put like that, it sounds so sordid. But I'm afraid it's true. During our last big fight, Vanessa plainly said she wants a man in her life and she wants him at home, not running around the state handling other people's problems.'' Bowing his head, he swirled the wine in his glass. ''Maybe she's right. Politics *is* demanding. I'm torn between obligations to the state and those at home. But, dammit, she knew this when we met.''

He drained his glass and continued to talk, but his musings seemed more random, less for Starr's benefit. "If Vanessa had turned to Clay early on, I would've understood. Barclay—Clay's a nickname—is fifteen years my junior, and a handsome devil. I doubt you two have met. He dislikes the city. Anyway, he and I met Vanessa at a fund-raiser. I was used to women falling all over him. Was shocked—puffed up, really—when she showed interest in me."

Harrison refilled his wineglass; Starr covered hers, still half-full, with a palm. Apparently her silence encouraged his ramblings.

"I don't know what Van wants!" he burst out, thumping the bottle down. "She says I don't spend enough time with Morgan. Thing is, when I *am* home, she keeps him tied to her apron strings. Won't even let him play ball. Says he'll get dirty." Harrison gripped his glass so tightly his knuckles turned white. "I'm sorry for dumping this on you, Starr. Truth is, I haven't been able to tell anyone for fear it'll creep into the news."

Starr smoothed her napkin. She knew Vanessa McLeod only slightly. Though nearer Starr's age than Harrison's, Vanessa seemed older. All cool, blond elegance. Somewhat aloof. "You think it's a phase?" she ventured.

"Like the terrible twos, you mean?" Harrison shrugged. "Van *is* spoiled. Again, my fault. Something to do with my damned ego. At first I found her dependence gratifying." He settled a brooding gaze on Starr. "I wish she had your strength. Frankly I can't see my wife arguing with Judge Forbes or that hatchet-faced social worker to adopt a half-wild dock child."

He shook his head. "When you came to me for help dealing with all that red tape, I pictured Van—and didn't give you an iceberg's chance in hell of sticking it out." His smile was brief. Reluctant.

Starr wrinkled her nose. "I haven't won yet, and I didn't *want* to ask for help, you know. Backlash, I guess, from Dad organizing my life and Mother following the advice of every guru, psychic and fortune cookie in Sausalito. But I wouldn't have gotten to first base if you hadn't vouched for me at the hearing, plus leased me a two-bedroom place I could afford on my salary."

He said nothing.

"Maybe you're selling Vanessa short. I'll bet she *would* fight to take a bright, beautiful child like SeLi off the streets."

The senator seemed so despondent that Starr impulsively reached across the table and clasped his hand. Compared to what he was facing, her problems with SeLi seemed minor. "Have you talked to your brother? You're such a kind, caring man. Surely he's not so different."

Seeing his eyes blink rapidly, Starr averted her gaze. The senator's thoughtless younger brother needed a good swift kick—and she'd love to be the one to administer it. What kind of man *was* he? Having spent her childhood in Hollywood, Starr had seen her share of rats. But to think of a brother sinking so low... well, it was unforgivable—even though she knew for a fact that people who did the unforgivable rarely considered the consequences to others.

By the time the waiter brought their salads, the senator had pulled himself together. As he mixed a cruet of vinegar and oil, he said casually, "I read your master's thesis, Starr. Very impressive. Especially the part about testing the oxygen levels in the blood of bighorn sheep. Imagine. What you discovered has helped increase the breathing stamina of mountaineers.''

Her mouth fell agape. ''Why would you be interested in a thing like that?''

He speared a pimiento-stuffed olive with his fork and brandished it in the air. ''Because environmentalists are kicking the State Department's butt over opening federal wildlife preserves to selective oil explorations.'' He glared at the olive before popping it into his mouth. ''Actually,'' he confided after swallowing, ''it's a federal reversal of an old law. I initiated the movement in California. Now because some fool found a couple of dead bighorns in the San Jacinto preserve, they want to scrap the whole project.''

Starr laid her fork aside and stared at him. She barely acknowledged the arrival of a steaming platter of clams. ''Why the State Department? Why not Fish and Game?''

The senator flushed as he carefully opened a hot clam. ''I should have known you'd ask,'' he muttered, dipping the succulent morsel in butter. ''Considering how angry you were at the captain of that freighter who flushed a dirty cargo hold into the bay.'' He gave a mirthless laugh and picked up another clam. ''That little fiasco had a few state politicians in a tizzy. Those same men want you on this job. Mad as you were, you let the state handle the fines. And you didn't run to the media.''

''But...'' she began.

He leaned across the table and stuffed a juicy clam in her mouth. Starr was forced to swallow as he continued, ''Damned if you still don't look more like a

Hollywood starlet than a research biochemist. In this case, that might be a hindrance."

"What *is* this case?" Starr persisted, reaching for her wine. "Why do I get the feeling I'm not going to like the bottom line when you finally reach it?" Her quiet gaze pinned him.

"Dammit, Starr! I'm responsible for the broader picture. You analytical types only ever look at details. You only see things in black and white."

She held tight to her temper. "Well, you political types operate in the gray areas. When will you learn, Senator, that gray is where the sticky issues lurk? Listen, before this argument mushrooms out of control, let's cut to the chase and talk sheep. What's killing them?"

He shifted, glanced around, then tented his fingers. "Lower your voice, please. That's what we want *you* to tell us. We hired a naturalist who ran some blood tests, but they came up negative."

She straightened, all business now. "A virus? Some new bacteria? No, blood tests would've shown that. What *are* you doing in there, Senator?"

Harrison took a sip of wine, then leaned closer. "We, uh, we've sunk a petroleum test well. That's all." Brow furrowed, he met her flush of anger head on. "The team from Calexco swears their well isn't to blame."

"And I'm the Wizard of Oz," she scoffed.

"It's God's truth, Starr." He shoved a hand through his salon-styled hair. "The bottom line is... I can't afford to have environmentalists or wildlife advocates get wind of this and go off half-cocked. They'll kick my ass from Sacramento to Washington and back again."

Starr frowned. Her brain was stalled on Calexco—a huge oil conglomerate that had been in environmental hot water before. Somehow they always came out looking clean. She drummed her fingers on the pristine tablecloth. "Since I'd class myself as an environmentalist, Harrison, I'm not sure what you expect from me. I'd advise handing it over to Fish and Game. Anyway, Christmas is too close. SeLi's never had a real Christmas. I intend to make it extraspecial for her."

He snapped back a crisp white cuff to look at a wafer-thin watch. "If you've finished lunch, perhaps we can discuss this further in the privacy of my car. It's obvious I need to tell you more."

Starr refused to respond to his practiced smile. Nice as Harrison was, he was still a politician. In her position with Fish and Game, she dealt frequently with politicians whose regard for the state's wildlife was less than noble. Rising with him, she said, "Just so you know up front, I'm nobody's patsy. And don't think you can trade on your friendship with my dad. You know how I feel about his misuse of power." She paused, frowning. "In the case of that freighter, your state committee handled the violations faster than I could have. It was that simple. If I agree to help you, it'd only be to save those sheep."

Harrison signed the check. "I understand. Believe me, your wish is my command." Smiling, he dropped a socially correct kiss on her cheek. Then, hand at her waist, he guided her out, all the while filling her ear with promises.

Starr knew he was pulling out all the stops on his considerable charm. She found it comical—until he stopped to collect her coat and she suddenly felt as if they were being watched by unfriendly eyes. A quick glance over her shoulder turned up nothing but guests involved in eating.

She and Harrison resumed walking. It was probably nothing more than his cloak-and-dagger attitude, she thought. Except that the feeling persisted, and Starr didn't protest when he draped an arm casually around her shoulders as they waited for the elevator.

AT A TABLE cleverly hidden behind a group of potted ficus, Barclay McLeod sat and watched the progress of the vibrant redhead. As she swept toward the exit with his older brother, she garnered male interest from every table. Tall and leggy, she exuded a sexual energy that left him practically drooling into the plants.

The younger McLeod took a moment to catch his breath. He'd come into town late last night, driving up from the ranch to see for himself why Harrison was shirking his husbandly duties. Well, he'd sure enough gotten his answer. In spades.

His temper returned. No wonder it had taken near subterfuge to worm the location of this lunch date out of a secretary who knew good and well that he was the senator's brother. And why the maître d' had refused to lead him to Harrison's table. Now, considering the touching scene he'd just witnessed, Clay was glad.

Uncoiling his six-foot-plus frame from the uncomfortable Victorian chair, he snatched his new felt hat with the cattleman's crease from an adjoining chair, peeled out enough cash to pay his bill and dropped it on the table. He spared a brief glance for all the three-piece suits around him. Even in his expensive leather sports coat and boots polished to a high sheen, Clay felt out of place here.

Once, Harrison would have, too. Apparently the older brother he used to idolize had changed. A lot.

Sad—and angry—Clay stalked past the maître d', pulled his hat low on his forehead and unleashed his pent-up fury on the elevator button.

How long, he wondered, had Harrison been fooling around with that babe? Irritated, Clay jabbed the button again. He and Harris kept up business matters over the phone, but they hadn't seen each other since—when? A year ago Thanksgiving? Had it been *that* long?

Vanessa and Morgan often came to the ranch of course. Without his brother. To think of all the times, such as last Christmas, he'd stood up for the son of a bitch. Clay recalled assuring Vanessa it was affairs of the state that prevented her husband from coming home on such an important family holiday.

Ha! Now, as he thought back to all the times Vanessa had cried on his shoulder about Harrison's waning attention—and how he'd continually made excuses for his brother—Clay wanted to spit. What a fool he'd been.

The elevator opened. He strode into the car, oblivious to the crowd of people who had to part to make space for him. Nor did he care that his ferocious scowl stopped talk, allowing the car to glide all the way to the lobby in silence. Clay emerged in time to see Harrison help his babe into a long black limo, then climb in himself. When the door shut, the two of them were out of sight behind conveniently dark windows.

Clay fumed. Gross misuse of a state vehicle if ever there was one. More than annoyed, he yanked his hat brim until it all but sat on the well-defined bridge of his nose. Perhaps some taxpayer should give the senior state senator a lesson—in marital fidelity, among other things.

Well, the senator's brother just might be the man for the job. Did Harrison know—or care—that at this moment his wife was at their apartment packing stuff into Clay's carryall? Apparently not.

Striding to the curb, Clay grabbed the first cab. He leapt into the back seat and ordered the driver to follow the limousine.

SECONDS AFTER HARRISON gave his driver Starr's address and closed the partition, Starr returned to the subject of the sheep. "Save the smiles for your constituents, Senator. I'm immune. Do you have any idea how few bighorns are left in California? San Jacinto is finally rebuilding its herd after rangers caught that poacher out of L.A. The guy'd been sneaking hunters up the face of the mountain for months to take the big rams."

"Then maybe it's something totally unrelated to the exploration." Harrison's troubled brown eyes met hers squarely. "I mean, you just brought up another possibility. What if the guy had disgruntled relatives?"

"You mean someone's poisoning the sheep? No, the naturalist's blood tests would have shown it."

"I suppose. But I swear to you, darlin', I'm as anxious to get to the bottom of this mess as you are." He shifted to face Starr and placed an arm along the seat behind her head. "I trust you to keep this under your hat. Truth is, Starr, the state is going broke. We need this oil strike bad. For the jobs and the revenue."

"Oh, God!" she said, slumping against his arm. "I thought that was only rumor."

In a taxi behind the limo, a scowling man made note of the darker shadows in the limo's back window and formed his own opinion about what was going on. His growl was loud enough and surly enough for the cabbie to shoot him a wary look.

But nothing was going on, except that Starr was reassessing the situation. "I want to do my part of course. But the timing is terrible. SeLi's gotten herself into trouble again at school. If you could find someone else—"

"We want you, Starr," Harrison cajoled. "Can you imagine the panic if any of this gets out? Besides, with your background in sheep, I doubt you'd need a week. Take the kid with you. A change of venue might do her good," he urged. "Cloud Haven Ranch lies in the valley below the preserve. It'd be perfect for your home base and a great place for SeLi to explore."

"I know that name. You grew up there, right? My father lived down the hill at Willow Bend. But... I thought your parents moved to Florida."

"They did. Clay runs the ranch now. My shares are temporarily in trust. In addition to breeding top bulls, Cloud Haven has some of the best quarter horses in the state. You ride, I presume? This time of year the preserve is only accessible by horseback."

"Clay runs the ranch? Clay, as in the brother who's fooling around with your wife?"

Harrison flushed. "It takes two to fool around," he said darkly. "And maybe if you and SeLi are there, Van might think twice. I can almost guarantee Clay won't impede your progress if we feed him the story I've cooked up for your boss—that the university wants you on loan to do some genetic studies on the sheep."

The senator let those words sink in, then said, "My brother's soft on kids and animals. But you can't mention the explorations. I'll need your promise on that, Starr. Consider what's at stake. Your job—millions of jobs. My political future. My life," he added dramatically.

The limo stopped outside her building as Starr switched mental gears. She contemplated SeLi's Christmas break; this trip would not only allow her to help save the sheep, it might give her a chance to reach the root of SeLi's problem. Starr wanted to be able to keep her nine-year-old daughter in a private school where class sizes were smaller. SeLi had been steeped in all manner of unsavory elements on the docks. And old habits died hard. Already they'd gone through three schools. Starr was at her wits' end. A few days in the bosom of Mother Nature might be just what they needed.

Harrison cut into her thoughts. "I'd be willing to call Judge Forbes and arrange for you to take SeLi out of town. What do you say, Starr? Can I start the ball rolling?"

She opened the car door and stepped out, in spite of a fine mist that was turning to rain. "And bypass Wanda Manning, who already resents the way you intervened? No. If I agree, *I'll* deal with her and my boss. And with Dr. Ellsworth."

Harrison's driver left the car running and hurried around the vehicle to hold an umbrella over Starr. She bent to speak, never thinking the senator would scoot out on her heels. He nearly bowled her over.

His quick action in grasping Starr's shoulders kept them both from taking a tumble. "Who's Ellsworth?" he asked as he took the umbrella from his driver and sent the man back into the limo. "He's not your boss."

Starr saw that his tie was knocked askew and reached to straighten it. "Dr. Ellsworth and I are colleagues. Stanley's a brilliant biochemist. But he sort of fancies himself my...mentor." She smiled. "If you were to ask SeLi, she'd call him a nerd. Preferable, I might add, to what she called him last week in public at the science fair. Would you believe 'Stanley Stud'?"

Harrison threw back his head and laughed. "Ah, Starr, that child's something. I don't envy you. Although," he said, suddenly sober, "at times, I wish Morgan showed a bit of her gumption."

Starr suffered a twinge of sadness. It was so obvious that Senator McLeod loved his wife and child. Her own parents, a Hollywood producer and actress, had had a stormy marriage. Starr's childhood had been rocky—one reason she so badly wanted to give SeLi stability.

"Senator," Starr said impulsively, placing a hand on his arm, "I'll go. But I won't stay at *Judas* McLeod's ranch. Dad's filming in Japan. He has a motor home in storage, and I'm sure his staff will give me the key. There are campgrounds near the preserve—Idyllwild, for instance—so hookups shouldn't be a problem. What's the weather down there doing now?"

Harrison shifted the umbrella and gave her a quick peck on the lips. "I'll find out. But please stay at the ranch. We've got two concrete pads with hookups some distance from the house. I'll be more comfortable knowing you're there—and I'll be able to reach you. Not that I can be visibly connected, you understand. Oh, by the way, I've taken the liberty of setting up a special number for messages." He pulled a piece of paper from his breast pocket.

She felt a moment's unease at the fact that he'd done all this before she'd even agreed. And she'd have to cram her Christmas shopping into two weeks. Was she crazy? Then she visualized the dying sheep and knew she had little choice—she was the best person for the job.

He pressed the paper into her hand. "Be careful, Starr. Until you mentioned poachers, it never occurred to me some nut case might be involved. If anything happened to you, your dad would... Well, don't do anything foolish."

She nodded, lifting a hand to brush raindrops from his lapel. "This is silly, standing out here in the rain. Besides, you're beginning to make me doubt my decision."

"Think of it as your patriotic duty," he said, crawling back into the limo. "I'll touch base with you tomorrow. Do you need anything?"

"No. Stanley will get me the equipment I'll need." As she bent to close his door, she said with feeling, "I'm sure you and Vanessa will work things out. How could she *not* recognize that you're the nicer brother?"

Grinning, he rapped sharply on the partition, signaling his driver to leave.

Starr turned and raced toward the entrance of the luxury condominiums. Blevins appeared out of nowhere to open the door, and Starr ducked inside, paying no heed to a cab that sat idling across the street.

"Miss SeLi is upstairs with the Donnelly twins," said the gray-haired man who held the door. "Shall I have Mrs. Blevins let them know you're home?"

Starr shook droplets of water from her hair. "Give me a minute to change clothes and unwind. It's time for another heart-to-heart with my little charmer, and I need to rehearse my speech."

The portly Englishman nodded. "Mrs. Blevins remarked last night that you deserve sainthood, taking on that pistol."

Starr stepped into the vacant elevator and laughed. "SeLi does keep me on my toes." As she pushed the third-floor button, her attention was drawn to a man hurrying toward the glass door.

She stared at his black cowboy hat, then let her gaze roam down his lean body to a pair of highly polished, square-toed black boots. For no explainable reason, her pulse quickened. She was vaguely disappointed when the elevator door slid shut, blocking him from view.

It was the dark hair curled slightly over the collar of his black leather sports coat, she decided. She was a sucker for men with that slightly disheveled look. Did the stranger also have a mustache? She wasn't positive about that, but for sure the part of his face not shadowed by the hat was tanned a healthy bronze. She envied him the tan. All she'd seen in San Francisco for weeks now was fog and rain.

Her reverie ended when the elevator bumped to a stop. It wasn't like her to get carried away about a man—a cowboy yet. But cowboy-types were oddities in the city. Idle curiosity—that was all it'd been. Even so, as she dug out her key, Starr wasted a moment wondering why he was here. Just needed directions? Or was he visiting someone in the building?

Or maybe, she mused, letting herself into the apartment, he was a millionaire come to rent the penthouse. As far as she knew, it was the only vacancy in the building. A damned expensive place, too.

As she hung her coat to dry, her more immediate problems edged out her speculations about a man she never expected to see again. Proceeding into the bedroom, she kicked off her shoes, removed her suit and unbuttoned her blouse. Pausing, she mulled over how best to start the discussion with her daughter.

Starr had thought SeLi understood that she no longer needed to steal. Recently, though, she'd had to let SeLi know she couldn't have *everything* her heart desired. But why on earth would she take another girl's purse when she had two of her own?

Someone pounded on Starr's door. Standing there in her slip, she suffered a moment's panic at the thought of company catching her half-undressed. Then, just as quickly, she relaxed. SeLi was forever losing or misplacing her keys.

The hammering grew louder.

"All right, hold your horses, young lady!" Starr yelled. "I'm coming." She snatched her silk robe off a hook and raced toward the door. Lord, where had the time gone? She wasn't half-prepared. SeLi had a way of closing out the world when she didn't want to talk, and Starr wasn't looking forward to weaving her way through the girl's defenses.

Out of breath, one arm still groping for a sleeve, Starr muttered a few impatient words as she yanked open the door. An unfinished epithet died, a small "Oh" on her lips, to escape a moment later in a soundless scream as the dark-haired stranger she'd glimpsed downstairs pushed his way in and slammed the door.

"Who are you? What do you want?"

She scrambled into her robe, her hands shaking. In all her life no one had ever looked at her with such loathing. Stunned, she somehow found the courage to take command. One hand clutching the robe over her breasts, she pointed the other imperiously toward the door.

"Get out," she ordered, her voice not quite as strong as she'd like. "Leave this instant or I'll call the police."

One corner of his mouth lifted in a smirk.

Starr made a dash for the phone in her living room.

For an unbridled moment Barclay McLeod savored the full beauty of the woman he'd come to buy out of his brother's life. That she was even more exquisite up close than she'd been at a distance didn't really surprise him. Harrison had always had an eye for beauty. What Clay had in no way expected, however, was the sudden stab of lust that set his own heart racing.

Starr Lederman, the manager had said. A fitting first name he thought—for a call girl. For that was all she was, Clay reminded himself, as he leapt to block her path. Bought and paid for with McLeod money and who knew how much from innocent taxpayers. Especially as the manager's wife—the bookkeeper—mentioned Lederman held a state job. No doubt something Harrison had set up.

Clay had needed only a quick peek at the ledger to identify the token monthly payments for this place. She was a kept woman, plain and simple. His brother's mistress, housed in luxury. Only she was *his* property, as well. McLeod property.

"Don't hurt me." Starr shrank from his touch.

Clay would be damned if he'd be sucked in by her outraged-virgin act. He yanked her back flat against his chest. Spinning her around to face him, he suddenly found her trembling lips far too close and far too attractive. His fingers flexed in the soft flesh he could feel beneath the silky material. Unable to help himself, he pulled her closer as he stared into her wide aquamarine eyes. Eyes darkened with what he assumed was a desire to match his.

The simple truth was, he wanted his brother's mistress more than he'd wanted any woman in a long, long while.

A heartbeat before Clay indulged in what he'd thought would be a mutually satisfying kiss, it registered in his addled brain that she might *not* be willing, that she was, in fact, trying to scratch his eyes out. Horrified, he broke away. Reining in his runaway lust, he drew back, trying not to breathe in her intoxicating scent. His scowl grew blacker. Partly because of the way she'd flattened herself against the wall, acting for all the world as if she thought he planned to rape her. But mostly because the damn woman looked sweet as sugar candy.

Sweet? Ha! Sweet women didn't have afternoon tête-à-têtes with married men. Clay had a very clear picture of what went on in this apartment after dark, on nights when Vanessa thought Harrison was out of town. Adultery was neither sweet nor innocent.

Disgusted, he stepped back and pulled from his jacket pocket the check he'd already made out. He recounted the zeros scribbled after the ten. Considering how close he'd just come to compromising his own principles, Clay McLeod was very glad he'd decided to be generous. A woman like Starr Lederman probably placed a hefty price tag on every favor she chose to dispense. And judging by the pricey artwork on her walls, his brother had enjoyed plenty of favors.

CHAPTER TWO

STARR KEPT HER BACK flattened against the wall. Her heart beat furiously. In spite of her panic, she saw him take a paper from his pocket, put it back and pat his pocket as though satisfied. Rape instructions? She almost laughed hysterically, but swallowed, instead, as he swept off the hat she'd admired earlier and tossed it onto her coffee table.

He studied her again and she felt his renewed anger. It created a nameless dread in her. Moments ago she'd have sworn he intended to kiss her. Had the circumstances been different, had they at least met before, she might have let him.

Now what? Her gaze tracked him as he prowled the room. His eyes came to rest on her, and Starr automatically tightened her grip on the robe. Apparently without need. Something about her living room had made him frown again.

Starr frowned back. There was nothing wrong with her furnishings. Everyone said she had good taste. Twin Wedgewood blue chairs were comfortable, as was a large, overstuffed burgundy-flowered couch accented artfully with the same blue tones.

Perhaps the brass-and-glass tables were too modern, but they didn't intrude. Ah—the signed Monet prints that had belonged to her grandfather. Starr relaxed—a little. So, he was nothing more than a common thief.

Common, but discriminating. She felt the urge to laugh. What would her thief say if she offered to pay him to take them off her hands? She'd never liked the muted pastels or their god-awful gilt frames. It was her mother who'd insisted they be hung.

Actually Patrice Lederman had brought her decorator of the month over to do the job.

Picturing the dramatic fit her mother would pitch when she swept through on one of her rare visits and found them missing did make Starr laugh.

Her laughter drew the stranger's angry gaze.

By now, however, Starr was pretty confident that if he'd intended her bodily harm, he'd have already done it. Trying but failing to control her relief, she waved a hand airily. "Take the paintings. Please. I'll give you a head start before I report them stolen."

"You think I'm a thief?" Clay's jaw tightened. "I was simply calculating their worth—wondering how a...civil servant can indulge such expensive tastes. But then, we *know* how, don't we?"

The news that he'd poked into her personal life galled Starr. Trying to shake up his arrogance, she said, "Well, maybe I have a sugar daddy."

"Do tell."

He'd obviously missed the sarcasm. "Hey—that was a joke." She gripped the back of the chair defensively. But the way his eyes raked her, she felt as though she'd been tried and convicted of something slimy. Moving back, Starr clutched her robe again. "I'm serious about the prints. Take them and get out. I'm not likely to give you a proof of purchase for the IRS."

"Cute. Very cute. And since you brought it up, how does your tax form read on these little—what do you call them?—perks."

Starr blanched. Was this about taxes? Oh, Lord. She had to wait until she was thirty—a year from now—to get her trust fund. Her grandfather had set it up for her through his bank, so she'd thought the fund's administrators had paid the inheritance tax. Maybe they hadn't....

"Are you from the IRS?" she demanded, all levity gone. "I mean, am I being investigated?"

"I'm not from the IRS, sweetheart, but I fully intend to have you investigated. You know, you amaze me. Don't you feel a shred of guilt, knowing your 'sugar daddy' is a married man?"

Starr closed her eyes. Good grief, the man was a full-blown fruitcake, after all. Wanting to appear casual, she edged toward the phone. If she could punch in a one-number code, Blevins would summon the police.

"What's your name? Do you have ID?" she asked, trying to buy time. Her smile felt wooden. But crazies responded to smiles and gentle voices, didn't they?

Suddenly her heart froze. What if SeLi came down into the middle of this? Terrified, Starr made a wild lunge for the phone.

Clay read her intent and with ease fenced her against the wall.

Their eyes locked. Starr was the first to look away.

"All you need to know," he said, his tone dangerously soft, "is that I'm someone who plans to throw a monkey wrench in the senator's little game."

"Senator...McLeod?" Starr's mind raced, though her voice squeaked. "Oh, my goodness!" Her gaze again tangled with the stranger's ice blue glare. All at once things fell into place, and Starr felt less of a personal threat.

"Who sent you?" she asked. "Wildlife advocates or environmentalists?"

Clay fought her attempt to throw him off track. God, but she had that look of innocence down pat.

"Don't BS me, sugar." Clay dug the check out of his jacket pocket and waved it under her nose. "I think this should clarify my position."

Starr had to cross her eyes to see what he was holding. It looked like a check. But he didn't keep it still long enough for her to be sure.

"I trust this is enough to get you out of the senator's bed and out of town. A long, long way out of town," he drawled.

It was indeed a check, Starr saw now. A very big check if she'd seen all those zeroes correctly. And seeing her name on the line beside them made her gasp. Her gaze flew back to his. Heat clawed its way to her cheeks. This arrogant cowboy was offering her a bribe.

"You snake," she hissed. "How dare you try to compromise Senator McLeod in such a sleazy manner!" Forgetting that her robe wasn't secured, Starr drew back a hand to slap the smirk off his face.

Clay saw it coming. Without effort, he blocked her swing and pressed her hand to the wall.

The air between them crackled like a live wire. For a moment the only sound in the room was their combined breathing.

Clay moved a fraction of an inch back. "It's a waste of breath to deny it. I followed you two today and saw everything."

He'd followed her? Starr raised her chin haughtily. "You saw nothing, you baboon. Our lunch today was business."

Clay threw back his head and laughed. "Yeah, right. A state senator always does business with low-level state employees. I suppose the kissy-face when he dropped you off was business, too?"

"Let me go!" She tried kicking him. What she wanted to do was throw him bodily out of her apartment, but he was too big. Too big and too solid. And she was shaking in fury. "What rock did they turn over to find you?" she spat, twisting to and fro. "Even if you have no regard for the senator as a politician," she panted, "think of what smear tactics like this will do to his family. I suppose you took incriminating pictures, you louse!"

The moment the words left her lips, Starr had another terrifying thought. Harrison's family wouldn't be the only ones hurt by such muckraking. If the people responsible for sending this thug went to the press, Wanda Manning would have SeLi out of here in a wink.

She quit fighting. Maybe they could bargain. But, no. His eyes were cold. Starr thought then that both the senator and she were doomed.

"Have you no shame?" He forced her to look up. Damn, he wanted to see her eyes, to see her contrition, if only for a moment. Except that when their eyes met, Clay wished he'd paid her and left. Her lips, now a scant inch from his own, looked exceedingly soft and kissable. And her eyes—they were huge and dark with something other than remorse.

Desire? Clay slid under her spell. Lord help him, but he could see why his brother transgressed.

He felt himself sinking. "Forget the senator," he growled. "Let's talk about you and me."

Starr nodded, although she hadn't the vaguest idea what it was she was agreeing to. Being this close to him made rational thought impossible.

Suddenly Clay had visions of carting her away from the life she'd fallen prey to. He had visions of helping her turn her life around. Damn Harrison. Charming and rich, he'd blinded her. Led her astray.

"I'm not without influence," he said. "Give me a week. I'll find you a real job. How about in San Diego? You can start over."

Starr watched a range of emotions streak through the electrifying blue eyes like fruit flipping through a Vegas slot machine. Earlier she'd seen fury on a short leash. Then she sensed an intense internal struggle. Now, underneath, something she couldn't quite identify.

He clearly thought the offer should please her.

A job, he'd said. But he knew she had a job with the state. A shiver of fear danced up Starr's spine. *Harrison's project...*

Oh, God. Starr tensed.

He did the same, and they both waited.

For what? Starr was drowning in a sea of confusion. His eyes did that to her. Looking into them was like staring into a lake. Hypnotic, deep. And they did funny things to her insides. "Uh...could we sit and discuss this, uh, job?" she ventured, feeling her knees caving in beneath her.

Clay tried to disconnect from her, but his body wouldn't obey. At the restaurant he'd thought her skin had been made up to look youthful and dewy. Up close it gleamed like satin cream. Freckles dusted the bridge of her nose, and a few more traced the lush valley between her breasts.

Clay shivered. No, he couldn't completely blame Harrison. As if from a distance Clay heard himself ask, "This check plus how much?"

"Pardon?"

He gestured with the check, then forced it into her hand. "You know, what will it take?"

"Take to what?" He was talking in riddles. She gripped the check, finding the crinkle of paper comforting.

"Help me out, please," he asked nicely, then felt foolish. "Hell, I've never done this before. I'll offer the same deal you have with Harrison. Better," he hastened on seeing her frown.

He looked so boyishly embarrassed and sincere that Starr wanted to smile. She and the senator hadn't discussed salary. But no way was a week of research worth this kind of money.

"Do you two have a contract or what?" he asked.

Starr felt the term *contract* like a slap in the face. What was she doing? Maybe this man was killing the sheep. She shoved at him and was appalled when she accidentally scratched his face.

Clay touched a finger to the welt. "Wildcat, huh? Look, if that was too blunt, I'm sorry. I don't know the protocol for relocating a mistress."

Mistress? Suddenly the truth dawned. Starr didn't know when she'd felt so murderous toward another human being—if indeed he *was* human and not some subspecies. She'd thought this was about the senator's project. Surely this dolt didn't think that she and Harrison . . . that they . . . Her mouth dropped open. That was *exactly* what he thought.

Purple with rage, she waved the check beneath his arrogant nose before she ripped it to shreds and flung the pieces in his face. "Get out!" Her body shook. "You're despicable. No, you're worse than despicable." Her voice rose hysterically right before it cracked. "Get out!"

Pieces of the check drifted over him like snowflakes before Clay gave vent to his frustrations, caught her arms and pinned her slender body to his.

Both were breathing hard. "Dammit, woman, when I tell Harrison everything I know, he'll leave you cold. You'd be wise to listen to me."

Before Starr could kill him, or at least do him major bodily harm, the door flew open and in rushed SeLi Lederman on a whirlwind of motion. Her long-sleeved plaid shirt was only half-tucked into slim jeans, and her twin, jet black braids snapped against the shirt's hem like whirling dervishes.

The man abruptly released her.

Starr read a host of questions in SeLi's lively almond eyes. Eyes that took in her normally conservative adoptive mother's disheveled state, then moved quickly to assess every inch of the tall dark stranger who'd had her mother wrapped in his arms.

Starr knew how it must have looked. Her choked protest was lost, however, in SeLi's unladylike whistle.

Clay flinched and took several steps back.

Starr made haste to escape. "Ah, SeLi, you're home," she said inanely, giving a nervous toss of her auburn curls.

The child skidded to a halt near one of the blue chairs, where she nonchalantly dropped her bright purple book bag. She continued to regard the male in their midst with frank curiosity.

Clay refused to be intimidated. Instead, he challenged the girl's amused gaze. She was, after all, just a kid.

"Totally awesome." SeLi tipped her head to gain a new perspective. Another low whistle. "I don't know where you found him, but this dude beats Stanley Stud hands down. It's okay by me if you keep him, Mom."

Mom. Clay did a fast double take and said aloud, "Mom?"

Starr rushed to stand protectively beside her child. Of SeLi's two pet names for Stanley, Starr couldn't help wishing the girl had chosen Stanley Stupid this time. Not that either was acceptable, but they were working on the problem. It would've been nice if SeLi had kept quiet altogether. Lord only knew why, but this stranger already labored under a mountain of misconceptions. And somehow, some way, he was tied to Harrison's proposed project.

"You have a daughter?" Trying to recover from his shock, studied first the girl, then the woman.

"Oops!" SeLi clapped a hand over her mouth. "Didn't I say if you're ever gonna snag a husband, I oughtta call you Starr?"

Before Starr could gather her wits, the child thrust a small hand at the man and said around a lopsided grin, "Don't worry, mister. She's not married."

A growling sound gurgled from Starr. "To your room, young lady." She pointed. "The *gentleman* was just leaving," she said, doubting the man had ever a passing acquaintance with the term. "I know you have homework."

"Aw, Mom. You said we'd get out the Christmas decorations today."

"Yes, well, that was before I had an unexpected chat with your teacher."

Sullen, the girl buried her hands in her back pockets.

Starr knew that look. But she could be stubborn, too. "You heard me, SeLi. And not another word."

Starr might as well have saved her breath, because SeLi obviously wasn't finished talking to their uninvited guest. "Judge Forbes said I could use Starr's last name till the 'doption's square. 'Cause it will be... soon." She paused to shoot Starr a troubled gaze.

Starr smiled and touched one of the girl's shining braids. How could she not show encouragement? As usual, though, when she gave SeLi an inch, the little rascal took a mile.

"Jeez, mister." SeLi gazed up at the man. "I know boyfriends get antsy 'bout kids from another marriage, but she ain't been. Married, I mean. She don't even date much, 'cept for nerdy Stanley." The girl shot a sly grin over her shoulder at Starr.

Starr groaned. She didn't *date* Stanley—not that it mattered. Maybe this was nothing more than a hideous nightmare. But no, she knew it was real the moment the stranger jammed his hat on so tight it rode the crest of black brows that met over the bridge of an impossibly aristocratic nose.

"I called you a wildcat," he snarled. "Alley cat might be more fitting. Allowing yourself to be a kept woman is one thing. Having your kid solicit is quite another. I imagine the child-protection service would be interested."

Starr wondered where to begin unscrambling this awful mess.

"He doesn't work for Wicked Wanda, does he?" For the first time SeLi showed alarm.

Starr wanted to assure SeLi that he wasn't with the county adoption agency, but at the moment she couldn't be sure of anything. In the midst of a helpless shrug, her gaze fell accidentally on a piece of the check, which had stuck to the sleeve of her robe. A bold, black signature leapt out at her.

Barclay McLeod.

This lowlife was the senator's brother?

Anger welled from the tips of Starr's toes. "You have some nerve," she said, tossing the piece of check against his broad chest. "How dare you threaten a nice man like the senator. How dare you threaten me!"

Her sudden offensive caught Clay off guard, and he backed toward the condo's entrance.

In steady pursuit, Starr reached around him and yanked the door open.

Clay stumbled backward across the threshold.

The moment Starr saw him safely outside, she regained enough control of her senses to deliver a scathing lecture.

Entranced by the fiery halo of her hair under the skylight, Clay missed half her tirade—until she wound up by shouting, "I suggest you clean up your own backyard, Mr. McLeod, before you start on mine!"

The door, en route to closing in his face, jolted Clay back to reality. "What do you mean, clean up my yard?" He wedged the toe of his boot between the casing and the door. If he wasn't always left to mop up his sister-in-law's tears, he might find this woman's last-ditch efforts amusing.

"It means," Starr said, gritting her teeth, "ask yourself where the senator's wife has been for the past few months."

"At my ranch." The thrust of Clay's jaw dared her to make something of it.

"I rest my case."

"So that's Harrison's angle. The oldest ploy in history. A poor, misunderstood husband. Well I hate to ruin your day, sugar, but he lied."

"Don't call me sugar!" Starr tromped on his toe. When he yelped and jerked it back, she slammed the door in his face and slid the bolt home. For just a moment she leaned against the cool surface, and held her breath. Did he think she'd fallen off a turnip truck? *She* knew who'd lied.

Lips pressed in a disapproving line, Starr crushed the piece of paper that bore his name and stuffed it into her robe pocket. She still wasn't sure why he'd come. Were he and Harrison's wife looking for someone on whom to hoist the blame for their infidelity? In meeting Harrison for lunch, had she played into their hands? Or did Barclay McLeod have a different reason? After all, Harrison had said his brother was "soft" on children and animals—like bighorns.

Maybe he did and maybe he didn't. Starr rather thought the man cared for no one but himself.

At any rate, she had to let the senator know right away about this visit. On her way to the phone, Starr bumped into SeLi. The child's face was pale and her eyes wide.

"Holy shit, Mom. What'd that dude do to make you so ticked off?"

"Watch it, little lady. You're already in hot water up to your ears. I don't think we need swearing added to the list."

"I, uh, sorta forget now and then," SeLi said. "Wasn't he neat? If I had a dad like that, Buffy Jordan wouldn't dare spread her dirty ol' lies. Her dad's an old fart with big ears. Jug ears." She giggled.

"SeLi!" Starr closed her eyes and massaged both temples. "Stop it. We're never going to see that man again. Now put your backpack away and let me make a call. Then we'll talk."

"Uh-oh," SeLi muttered, skipping across the room. "I can see you're gettin' all tense again. I'll just go do homework like you said."

Starr nearly jumped out of her skin as the bedroom door slammed. She glanced quickly back at the more solid door that closed out Barclay McLeod. Tense was much too tame a word for how she felt, Starr decided. Homicidal was more like it.

At least she knew now how he'd gotten past Blevins. He was the Clay in Harris-Clay Enterprises, owners of these condominiums. Good grief! Harrison had given her a break on her rental payments, because otherwise she couldn't have hoped to adopt SeLi. Starr fervently prayed the senator's brother never learned about that.

The fingers that dug through her purse in search of the number Harrison had given her weren't quite steady. She dialed, but connected with a machine. After stressing that it was important and hoping she didn't sound hysterical, she asked him to call. Then she returned to her bedroom to don jeans and a sweatshirt. Had it really been only half an hour since she walked in? It seemed like a lifetime.

Now to tackle the problem with SeLi. It hadn't escaped Starr's notice how her daughter had neatly avoided admitting there even *was* a problem. Which meant it was roll-up-the-sleeves, get-down-in-the-trenches time. These sessions always took a lot out of her. Out of them both. Was she losing ground? When had SeLi decided she needed a father—and Starr a husband? If SeLi made remarks like that around Wanda Manning...well, it didn't even bear consideration. Starr's single status was the social worker's strongest argument against finalizing the adoption. SeLi knew it, too.

Starr thought she and SeLi had come to terms about all of that. Perhaps not, though, if SeLi felt compelled to broach the subject with a perfect stranger.

Correction—Barclay McLeod was far from perfect. Starr couldn't imagine anyone less likely to be good father material; obviously SeLi wanted a father badly. Was Wanda Manning right, then? Did SeLi need to live in a two-parent family?

Starr shook off her doubts. Adoptions of nine-year-olds were rare. Rarer still when the child came with an attitude. And boy, did SeLi have an attitude. Girding herself for the task at hand, Starr knocked on her daughter's door.

SeLi's CD player was on too loud for her to hear.

Starr cracked the door and stuck her head inside. Across the room the girl swayed to the beat of some current rock tune. Starr felt like more of a mother upon realizing she didn't have a clue what the tune was. After a brief hesitation she decided to get everything right out in the open. Marching to the bed, she sat down and snapped off the music.

"I want us to talk about the visit I had today with the principal and your teacher, SeLi."

The little girl froze. She whirled, her dark eyes snapping. "So what'd old Prissy Polly have to say 'bout me? Nothing good, I'll bet."

Starr's lips tightened. "Your teacher's name is Mrs. Bergdorf. She's a nice lady who is very concerned about your behavior." Starr patted the bed in invitation for SeLi to sit, but the youngster stubbornly remained standing.

Starr kept her voice and gaze neutral. "I've heard what Mrs. Bergdorf and the principal had to say about an item belonging to another child turning up in your desk. As you denied taking it, I'd like to hear your version of the incident."

Almond-shaped eyes glittered for a moment, then hardened in a way Starr hadn't seen since the time she witnessed SeLi lie point-blank to a dock vendor. The child had taken an orange—for her ailing mother.

At first Starr thought SeLi was going to keep silent. Would she be defeated before they'd even begun? Suddenly, though, the girl sat on the floor to inspect a nonexistent spot on her sneaker and announced at large, "If I'd taken Buffy's purse, do you think I'd be stupid enough to leave it in my desk?" SeLi raised her eyes defiantly. "I hate Buffy Jordan! She and Heather Watson think they're such hot shit. They make up stories about me and get the other kids to laugh."

All at once a sly grin replaced the hurt that flickered across the youngster's taut features. "Wednesday I got even. I dropped a spider on Heather's lunch tray when she wasn't looking. She screamed real loud and flung her tray. Food flew all over Mr. Hood, and Heather got

in trouble. It was only a bitty old spider, too.'' SeLi
tilted her chin smugly. Her braids brushed the carpet.

Starr glanced away to hide her smile. SeLi was such
an imp. Starr tried to place Buffy Jordan, but dainty
and blond were the only details that came to mind. She
knew the Watsons, though. Heather wore frills and
bows and never had so much as a speck of dirt on her
at the end of a school day. Mr. Watson owned an im-
port firm backed by old family money. As the school
mostly catered to the rich, Starr assumed both girls
were cut from the same upper crust. Until she came
into her own money a year from now, Starr had to
scrimp to pay tuition.

Parkwood Academy was far from her first choice. In
fact, she'd had to trade liberally on her father's name
to get SeLi registered. But darn it, this was the third
school since September. SeLi had managed to get herself expelled from each of the others for either bad
language or stealing—or both.

Feeling helpless, Starr voiced a question that had
been troubling her. "What do the girls tease you about,
Skeeter?" Her deliberate use of an old wharf nickname was aimed at breaking down barriers. Sometimes it worked.

SeLi steepled her fingers, studied them, then let her
hands fall loosely into her lap. "Just stuff," she muttered, ducking her chin.

"Like what?" Starr probed gently.

SeLi shrugged noncommittally, blinked and tried to
wipe away unwanted tears. "Stuff about my real mom
coming to California to find my dad and him not
wanting us. Buffy said her mother doubted anyone
even knew who my dad was. And I couldn't say I do,

'cause I don't.'' Her delicate chin trembled. But she refused to let the tears fall.

"Oh, SeLi, honey.'' Starr's heart melted, and she reached out to gather the forlorn child into her arms. At the same time, anger flared at the mindless cruelty of adults who should know better. Adults who discussed a child's painful history in front of other children. Rocking her gently, Starr tried to think what she could say to help ease SeLi's sense of hurt and betrayal.

"I know your mother traveled all the way from Thailand to find him, Skeeter. There are people who say he was a sailor. I heard he died in some kind of accident at sea, never knowing you two had arrived.''

Starr framed SeLi's face with her hands. "Let me tell you something, SeLi. Any man worth his salt would be proud to be your father.''

"Really?'' SeLi asked. "*Any* man?''

"Of course.'' But Starr didn't like the fact that Barclay McLeod's ruggedly handsome face abruptly intruded. She lost no time shaking the vision. "SeLi, are you saying those girls set you up because you don't have a father?''

"Uh-huh. Before lunch Buffy showed family pictures. Everybody did but me. Later Heather told Prissy Polly she saw me take Buffy's purse and rip up Buffy's pictures. She lied. I wanted to, but I didn't.''

Starr hugged the child tight. "Don't you fret, Skeeter. I'll go see Mrs. Bergdorf again. We'll get to the bottom of this. And tomorrow I'll have a copy made of your mother's passport photo. If you want, I'll give you a dozen pictures of me. Now dry those eyes. How about if you do your homework and I'll order in Chinese food for dinner?''

"Cool. Can I have pictures of your mom and dad, too?"

"Sure. I'll go find some."

SeLi started to turn away, then stopped and glanced back at Starr. "Sometimes . . . I take stuff, but I don't mean to. Not like Buffy's purse," she rushed on, "but outa people's pockets. You know, to make sure I still can. Trader John said if you don't practice, the touch might leave when a body needs it."

"You won't ever need to pick pockets again, SeLi. Not for any reason." Starr paused. "Honey . . . you don't keep any of the stuff, do you?"

"N-no. Mostly I put it back."

"Well, then, there's nothing to be upset about. You won't do it again, and now that we've had this discussion, in the future it won't be an issue."

SeLi fidgeted as if she wanted to say more. "But—"

Starr rose from the bed and smiled in spite of the fact she always felt drained after one of these talks. "No buts. There is *no* reason to steal from people. Now go on. Scram. Do your homework. I have some news to share with you about my job. We'll talk at dinner."

SeLi trailed Starr to the door. "Does your news have to do with the macho hunk?"

Starr grabbed the door casing. "Definitely not," she said sternly. "I told you, we'll never see him again." She shivered. "Never would be too soon, believe me."

SeLi buried her hands in her pockets again, and her face fell. "Never?"

"Absolutely. Now hit the books, kiddo, or I'll eat your egg roll."

SeLi still looked gloomy. "Don't get that hot stuff." She had to raise her voice, because her mother had moved down the hall.

"Szechuan?" Starr called back. "If I hear you starting homework by the time I reach the phone, I'll leave it out. Otherwise it's buyer's choice."

Starr held off until she heard scurrying feet and the scrape of a chair, followed by what sounded like books tumbling to the desk. She grinned. It worked every time.

Glancing out the window, Starr saw it was still raining. As she picked up the receiver to dial, she noticed a cab pulling in. Barclay McLeod climbed into the back seat. Even at this distance he looked formidable. What had he been doing so long at the complex? She had a terrible sinking feeling that she hadn't seen the last of him at all.

CHAPTER THREE

BLEVINS BROUGHT the Chinese takeout upstairs, grousing good-naturedly as he always did about the smell driving him wild. Starr gave him money to pay the delivery man and on impulse mentioned Barclay McLeod. "To what do we owe the visit from Mr. Barclay McLeod?"

The portly gentleman smiled. "Such a nice young fellow. So polite. Mrs. Blevins is still in a swoon." He winked. "Just joshing. Actually it was good to discuss outside maintenance with someone who can get things done. I send letters, but I'm never sure they get read. That last storm did some roof damage. Mr. McLeod said he'd take care of everything. He paid a visit to every owner before he left. Said he'd be back, too."

Starr's heart plummeted. So he'd visited everyone, had he? Clever man. Who would believe his talk with her had been any different from the others? It'd be her word against his. "Why will he be back?" she asked. "I mean, won't he hire a contractor to oversee the work?"

"No. He said he's a hands-on kind of guy. Hey, your food's getting cold. The delivery fellow's waiting, and Mrs. Blevins'll give me what-for if I'm late for dinner." He waved and ambled toward the elevator.

Starr stood in the doorway a moment. "McLeod's hands-on, all right," she muttered, stepping inside to securely lock her door. Yet try as she might, she couldn't say his touch had been offensive. His offer, yes, but not his touch. Her mouth went dry, remembering. No, definitely not his touch.

"Yum-yum. Thought I smelled food." SeLi stood in the kitchen archway and rubbed her stomach. "Hurry, Mom. I'm so hungry I could eat the carton."

"Not so fast, young lady." Starr lifted the still-warm bag above the child's head. "Wash your hands and set the table."

"Wash? I washed before I started homework. My pencil wasn't dirty."

Starr placed the bag on the counter, and when SeLi started to open it, she shooed her away. "Don't you dare let the heat out before the plates and napkins are ready. Just because you like cold fried rice doesn't mean I do."

The child grumbled but did as her mother asked. When the individual cartons had been opened, each of them grabbed her favorite.

Sweet-and-sour sauce dripped onto the plate in front of Starr. She stuck out her tongue to catch the overflow, and the two paused and grinned at one another.

SeLi had chow mein spread from ear to ear.

Starr smiled. "Don't let Mrs. Manning know how often I order in food, instead of cooking well-balanced meals, Skeeter. I have a feeling that's the kind of stuff she's documenting."

SeLi reached for a second helping of chow mein. "Darcy feeds Mike and Kevin takeout when Joe's out of town. Nobody cares what she gives her kids."

"Mike and Kevin are Darcy and Joe's natural children," Starr said, referring to the Donnelly's, who lived upstairs and, besides the Blevinses, were her only friends in the complex. "You and I have six months before the court finalizes the adoption. The thing is, SeLi, adoption by singles is still being studied. That's why they're so careful."

"Studied how?" SeLi asked.

"Specifically as it pertains to us? Well, Mrs. Manning fills out a report each month. If I don't measure up as a parent to the set of objectives they have, the judge may decide you'd be better off in foster care." She toyed with her rice and frowned. "That's why I harp at you so much on manners and all. They double-check everything."

SeLi rolled her eyes. "You mean like not fighting at school and not swearing? That kinda stuff?"

At Starr's reluctant nod, SeLi smiled and helped herself to the last egg roll. "Bet it'd help if you got married. If I had a mom *and* dad, Wicked Wanda wouldn't have those stupid 'jectives, right?"

Starr choked on a noodle. She quickly gulped down some iced tea. "Don't call her Wicked Wanda. That's the kind of things I'm talking about, SeLi. Please don't label everyone you meet."

Softening her reproach a bit, Starr reached over and poked the girl playfully in the ribs. "Who would you have me marry? Stanley?"

"Ugh! Stanley's worse than Wicked Wanda 'bout junk food. He's always preachin' at me to eat nutri... nutritiously." SeLi stumbled over the unfamiliar word.

"That's how parents are, SeLi. Mothers *and* fathers. Having two parents isn't always hunky-dory. Sometimes they fight and you're caught in the middle." She stared off into space.

SeLi looked thoughtful. "You're talkin' about yourself, aren't you?"

Starr gave a guilty start. "I . . . well, yes."

"Your mother smells good, but she's kinda weird. Is that why your dad split?"

Starr shrugged. "Not weird. If Nana Patrice lived on the docks she'd be considered weird. With her money, it's called eccentric."

When SeLi seemed confused, Starr smiled. "Forget I said anything. Hollywood marriages simply aren't the best examples of lasting love," she said cynically. "My mother's made three unsuccessful trips to the altar, and she's worse than you are about trying to find me a husband. I tell her the same thing—I enjoy my independence." Star chuckled. "Look at the practical side, Skeeter. There's no room in my bathroom for another toothbrush."

Diving for a fortune cookie, SeLi broke it open and passed Starr the fortune. "Is the Christmas star out tonight, do you think?"

Starr glanced up from unfolding the bit of paper. "You mean the North Star?"

SeLi propped her chin on her elbows. "Nana Patrice called it the wishing star. She said she wanted a baby real bad, and one night before Christmas, she saw the brightest star. The Christmas star. She wished on it and her wish came true. Didn't you know that's how come she named you Starr?"

"Honey, my mother believes in rabbits' feet, Ouija boards and four-leaf clovers. She won't go out of the house without consulting her guru."

"So?"

"So, don't take her stories as gospel."

"Well," the child said firmly, "she didn't name you Clover. Or Bunny." SeLi giggled. "I'm gonna look for that old star." She jumped up.

"It's raining, SeLi. There aren't any stars out tonight."

The girl didn't look convinced, so Starr gave a quick lesson in weather and felt vindicated when SeLi sat back down.

"Read my fortune, then."

Starr read, "'Something you want very much is within reach.'"

She frowned as SeLi clapped her hands and said, "Now read yours."

Starr cracked open the cookie and nibbled on a piece as she read her fortune. "'You will meet a tall dark strang—'" She threw it down. "Oh, for heaven's sake. These are silly. They print ten thousand of these sayings."

SeLi only grinned wisely as she snatched up the fortunes and tucked them into her pocket.

Starr reached across the table and tugged one of SeLi's braids. "You haven't asked about my surprise." Rising, she gathered the cartons and placed the leftovers in the fridge. After trying to stuff the empty ones in an already overflowing garbage can—the emptying of which was on SeLi's list of chores—she said, "Do you remember Senator McLeod?"

SeLi sat back, burped, then clapped her hand over her mouth, her dark eyes dancing. "Not bad manners, just good egg roll. Trader John says good beer, 'cause when he drank, he really belted out the burps."

"SeLi." Starr curbed her exasperation and informed the girl, not for the first time, that it was polite to say, "Excuse me."

" 'scuse me," SeLi parroted dutifully. "What about the senator? He's a cool dude. Old dude, but an okay head."

Starr sighed. "He's the one who hired me to work on the wharf. You know—when I met you and your mom. I was doing a special job, trying to isolate an organism that was making folks on the docks get sick. Senator McLeod pulled a lot of strings so I could take you to Nana Patrice's that first night when we thought your mom had the bug worse than the other people did."

"First time I ever had a bed all to myself," SeLi mumbled. "That part was neat, even if I was scared. Mom and me always shared a mattress, you know. She was sick at her stomach lots."

Starr sat down again and traced the pattern in the bright tablecloth. "Yes, so we learned later. At first the visiting nurse didn't realize your mother's illness was different from the food poisoning that was affecting everyone. If only she'd asked for help earlier—before her appendix ruptured."

"Can we talk about your surprise? Talking about her makes me sad."

"Of course, honey." Starr touched the child's face. "At lunch today the senator told me some wild sheep in the San Jacinto mountains are sick—sort of like the people on the docks. Only, the sheep are dying. The senator wants me to see if I can find out why."

"You... you're gonna go away?" The little girl's lower lip trembled and tears sprang to her eyes. Stoically she dashed them away.

Starr hadn't expected a tearful reaction.

"No, silly! Well, I am, but not unless you can go, too. That's the surprise. Over Christmas break, if Wanda says it's okay, we'll take my dad's motor home to the mountains for a week. I won't have to work all the time. We'll play in the snow and explore. What do you think?''

The dark eyes cleared and the sparkle returned. "Oh, wow!" Seli breathed. "I've never seen snow. Will we see deers? Or bears? Won't Woody and Trader John just split a gut when I tell them? I bet they've never been to the mountains." She bounced wildly in her chair.

"Whoa! Calm down." Starr rested a hand on Se-Li's arm, ignoring her dock talk this time. Some would call them bums, the two derelicts SeLi referred to. Granted, she'd picked up some bad habits from the old coots, but they'd also protected her from those who would harm a child. They'd been SeLi's family. Not exactly the influence Starr would prefer a child to have, but she recognized a need to wean the girl from them slowly.

"Remember," she cautioned, "I have to get this approved. We don't want Wanda reporting that I've run off with you." Starr gazed into space, speaking more to herself than to the child. "I can't imagine that she'd object."

SeLi's face fell. "Do you have to tell her? Wicked Wanda hates me."

"Not you, Skeeter." Starr saw no point in making an issue of the fact that *she* was the one the social worker disliked, not SeLi. Starr wished she knew why. "Tell you what, SeLi. If you can't go, I'll turn the job down. The senator will have to get himself another biochemist. Deal?"

SeLi gave her a thumbs-up and grinned. "De-al," she drawled. "But don'tcha think Senator Dude can pull those strings again? Buffy and Heather'll crap in their pants if they hear where I'm goin'.''

"SeLi Lederman! Young ladies do not say 'crap.'"

"I thought you told me young ladies didn't say 'shit.'"

"That, too," Starr said.

"So what *do* young ladies say?" SeLi demanded.

"Why, uh, they..." Starr floundered for a moment, then in a no-nonsense voice said, "They simply don't speak of bodily excrements."

"Well, gol-ly. That sounds boring. Why be one? Young lady, I mean."

At a loss for a comeback, Starr was exceedingly glad when the telephone rang, providing her with a reprieve.

"That's probably the senator now," she said in a rush. "If you've finished your homework, you need to take a bath and get ready for bed. I'll come say good-night when I finish here."

"Okay. Don't forget to tell him you're gonna ask Wicked Wanda first thing tomorrow."

"I will, I will," Starr promised, snatching up the phone on the third ring.

The line crackled. "Starr, it's Harrison. I know it's late, but I just got your message. Have I caught you at a bad time?"

She thought he sounded exhausted. "It's fine. I'm glad you called. This'll be hard for you to believe, but your brother paid me a visit."

"I know."

"You do?" That stopped her. "Then I imagine you set him straight about our relationship," she said, after recapping what'd happened. When she finished and encountered silence, Starr felt her cheeks grow hot.

Maybe she hadn't explained things well, but somehow, she'd expected sympathy. "Hello? Are you with me, Senator?"

"I'm here. I guess I'd better explain. You see, when I got home, Vanessa was packing. Said she was leaving me for good. I would've begged her to stay, but Clay showed up. Without so much as a hello he started lambasting us for having an affair—you and me, I mean."

"That's what I was trying to tell you," she burst out. "I denied it. But he wouldn't listen. I hope you made it very plain."

"I'm afraid I didn't."

"*What?* Why not?"

"Because Vanessa looked so shocked—and she acted jealous as hell. Kind of tells me how much she cares, if you get my drift. So I didn't correct their mistaken impression. I didn't come right out and confirm it, either, mind you." He hesitated. "I just didn't deny it."

"How could you not?" Starr asked angrily. "You'll be ruined politically. And what about me? When this hits the newspapers, Wanda Manning will see to it that SeLi's taken away."

He chuckled.

"Frankly I don't see anything funny," she said.

"Now, Starr, you're making mountains out of molehills. Clay isn't going to let this leak. I told you—deep down, he has a soft spot for family."

"No, you said kids and animals."

"Well, I should've included women, and women and kids spell family. He certainly has a soft spot for animals, too. Which brings us back to business. I don't know how he stands on the oil explorations. At first he was violently opposed. You'll have to guard what you say. I can't take a chance on him stirring up trouble down there."

"Really? Well, I can't take a chance on him stirring up trouble *here*. Senator, I need to give your proposal more thought."

"Now, now. Don't get yourself in a dither. Trust me. Clay will escort Vanessa to Cloud Haven tonight. Way I see it, she brought this on herself by always running to him. A taste of her own medicine will do Van good. Let her stew for a few days, then I'll call and throw myself on her mercy."

"Sounds risky to me. Or should I say *for* me?" Starr twisted the telephone cord around her finger. "You didn't see the way your brother looked at me—as if I was sewer sludge."

"Naturally. He's trying to be Vanessa's hero."

"How can you defend him after what you said earlier—about them carrying on an affair behind your back?"

"Ahem, I, uh, could've been wrong. My son, Morgan, let a few things slip today. Enough to make me think Clay and Van may not be sleeping together—not yet, anyway. I love her, Starr, enough to go to any lengths to get her back."

"Yes, well, I can't help wishing those lengths didn't involve me."

"Believe me, they'll be halfway to the ranch by now. Put it out of your mind, honey. I did. Listen up—I've had someone at the university call your boss. You're cleared for a two-week leave. That'll give you a week for me and a week to do the Santa thing. I'm sure I don't need to remind you that secrecy is imperative." He paused. "If you run into trouble getting equipment, let me know. Otherwise I'll call again tomorrow night."

At once the line went dead. Starr clicked the receiver. "Hello?" She heard a steady hum and glared at the phone, not believing he'd simply hung up. But after returning the receiver to its cradle and waiting for a ring back, she decided that was precisely what he'd done.

Amazing. Politicians—they all had colossal egos and played silly little-boy games. Starr had a funny suspicion that the senator didn't know his brother well at all.

Put it out of your mind, he'd said. All right. She'd go tuck SeLi into bed, write up a list of the equipment she'd need, then soak in a hot tub. After that she would crawl into bed and forget anyone by the name of Barclay McLeod existed. By morning all would be rosy again.

STARR SHOULD HAVE KNOWN from experience that the morning wouldn't be rosy. It rarely was in the Lederman household. She liked to sleep until the last possible second, and as a result she and SeLi were often late. Never one to eat breakfast, Starr had been forced to change her ways when she became a mother. More accurately, she'd seen a need to change when she caught SeLi hoarding food under her bed. That, and Wanda Manning's checklist, with three nutritious meals a day right at the top, had been strong motivators.

These days, though, SeLi usually ate anything put in front of her.

Not today.

"Why me, Lord?" Starr exclaimed to the kitchen clock. Last night hadn't been too good. Sleep had evaded her. Not because she was worrying about her encounter with Barclay McLeod, but because she'd been plotting into the wee hours how best to approach Wanda with this outing. Her uncharacteristic lack of patience with Seli definitely reflected her loss of sleep.

"This is lumpy," wailed SeLi, expression militant. "Why can't I just eat cold cereal like kids on TV?" Her spoon made ragged craters in a bowl of steaming oatmeal porridge as she picked out lumps and plopped them on her napkin.

"SeLi, stop that. Oatmeal is good for you. It's *supposed* to have a few lumps. I always ate hot cereal when I was a kid. Especially when it was cold and rainy out." Starr bent and gave SeLi a coaxing smile around the hair ribbon she held in her teeth as she attempted to French-braid SeLi's hair.

"Ouch!" The girl jerked away. "You had a cook— Nana Patrice said. I bet no cook ever fixed yuck like this." Plop went another lump, only this one flew and stuck to Starr's chenille robe.

"Darn it, SeLi, watch—" The doorbell rang sharply, cutting off the rest of Starr's lecture. She swiftly tied a bow at the end of the braid, then settled her hand on SeLi's shoulder to keep her seated. The girl had leapt up to answer the door.

"That'll be Kevin and Mike," SeLi said in the tone of one seeing a reprieve. "You're not really gonna make me finish this junk, are you? The school van won't wait," she warned. "Yesterday the driver told Darcy you'll have to get up earlier or he'll leave me behind."

Starr scraped at the cereal embedded in her robe. "Sit. If it's the van, it's early." She checked her watch. "Fifteen minutes early. He'll just have to wait."

Starr was determined SeLi wouldn't wriggle out of eating this morning, even if she had to drive all three kids to school herself. "Eat half. I'll invite the boys to wait in the living room."

"Bro-ther." SeLi sat and picked up her spoon.

On her way down the hall, Starr gloated a bit over this minor triumph in the clash of wills. Yesterday the principal had recommended that she dig in her heels on some of the smaller issues. He said the larger ones would follow. It sounded logical. After all, SeLi had had free rein a long time.

Well, no one ever said motherhood was easy, Starr thought as she opened the door and stepped behind it to conceal her ratty robe. It was comfy and warm, but not fit for any neighbor who happened to be in the hall to see.

"Come in, guys. SeLi will be with you in a minute. Have a seat in the living room. I guarantee you won't be late for the van." Starr nearly choked on her last word as the door swung fully open to reveal the last person she'd expected to see. Barclay McLeod!

It took a moment for the shock to pass. When it did, she snapped her open mouth shut so quickly she bit her tongue. The moment she was able to speak, she asked icily, "What do you want?"

"Not a morning person, are we?" Clay shrugged and doffed his black Stetson. The action drew Star's eye to his Western-cut suit, white shirt and tie. He looked impeccable—and very handsome, she admitted grudgingly.

A spark of vanity made her feel a bit embarrassed about how she compared in her rumpled state.

"How did you get into the building?" she demanded, transferring her anger to its rightful place.

Barclay McLeod again stepped uninvited into her home. "In answer to your first question, I seem to have misplaced my wallet. I thought perhaps I'd dropped it here. The answers to question two seems obvious, but I'll explain in case it slipped by you. As property owner, I have a master key." He seemed amused by her attempt to hide behind the door.

Starr held on to her temper by a thread. "There is such a thing as a tenant's right to privacy. Since you've already invaded mine, by all means, retrace your steps. Look for your stupid wallet. You won't find it here."

"Thanks, I will. It contained a fair amount of cash. Enough for someone needing a quick getaway," he said pointedly.

"Good. When you find it you can get out of Dodge." Why was he still here, instead of heading south as Harrison had said? Starr thought it was ironic that a man so drop-dead good-looking could be such a jerk. Today he looked civilized, too. Yesterday he'd been more appropriately dressed in satanic black.

She lingered by the door while he knelt and looked beneath her couch and both chairs. Her gaze was caught by the sprinkle of dark hair on the wrist of the arm reaching to feel beneath the furniture. Suddenly very warm, Starr shifted from one slippered foot to the other and nervously retied her robe. Why, the two times he'd shown up, did she have to look as if she was heading for bed? Especially since he thought she made her living there.

When he rose and glared at her, she willed her features to remain passive. Instinct warned her not to let him see how nervous he made her. "You obviously left your wallet someplace else. Did you check under your sister-in-law's bed?" she asked sweetly.

Before he could react, the doorbell rang. No doubt Darcy's twins this time.

"Hi, fellas." She waved the pair in and the man out. "If you don't mind," she said to her unwanted guest, "I have a busy morning ahead."

Mistakenly she'd thought he would leave. Instead, he introduced himself to the twins.

"Excuse me," she said, "I'm going to check on SeLi's progress. I won't object if you're gone when I come back."

Staring at her coolly, he turned back to the boys. "Do you kids go to a neighborhood school?"

Mike, the more outspoken twin, answered as Starr hastened into the kitchen. "Nah," he said. "We go to a private school, 'cause our mom thinks we'll learn more. Why? You got kids?"

"No. But my nephew moved in upstairs last night. He's been home-schooled. But I think it'd be good for him to have friends his own age."

Starr had returned with SeLi in tow just as Clay made his big revelation. Did Harrison know? she wondered, unable to hide her dismay. She was startled by SeLi's squawk. The girl stopped right in the middle of thanking her for the family pictures. "What's he doin' here, Mom? You said we'd never see him again!"

"He lost something, honey," Starr said absently. In the next breath she asked Clay, "Do you mean the senator's son, Morgan?"

He smirked. "Yes. Cozy isn't it? Luckily I noticed a vacancy when I checked the books. Perfect for Morgan and his mom. But then, I'm sure his parents breakup isn't news to you."

It wasn't of course. But obviously the estrangement was more permanent than Senator McLeod realized. Or at least more than he wanted to think.

SeLi sidled past both Starr and Clay, then ran for the door. "C'mon guys, the van's waiting. Mom, you're still gonna go see Wicked Wanda, aren't you?"

In the process of digesting Clay's news, Starr glanced up and nodded at the departing child. "This morning," she murmured.

Clay frowned. "How is it you have a job but don't ever seem to work? And who's Wicked Wanda?"

"Wanda Manning. SeLi's case worker." Starr broke off suddenly. What had struck her in the midst of her preoccupation was the odd way her daughter was acting toward Clay. Yesterday she'd all but had Starr married to him. Today she couldn't seem to escape the man fast enough. Fear gripped Starr's heart.

"Please leave," she told Clay. "I have to run. I—I forgot to give SeLi lunch money."

"Fine. Vanessa promised me breakfast in exchange for helping her move."

Tight-lipped, Starr acknowledged this new information with nothing more than a nod. She didn't want to hear about his breakfast arrangements. Or his sleeping arrangements. Right now she needed to stop SeLi. It would be a touchy situation, but if she didn't ask the girl about Clay's missing wallet, she'd have this knot in her stomach all day.

Not caring that she still wore her bathrobe, Starr ignored the elevator and ran down the three flights of stairs. She caught up with the children as they were about to leave the building. Asking the boys to hold the van, she motioned SeLi back.

The girl's guilt showed in her reluctance. Starr's heart spiraled downward as she realized the time for finesse had passed.

"Do you have something to tell me about Mr. McLeod's wallet, SeLi?" she asked gently.

SeLi ducked her head. "I was gonna tell you 'bout it last night. Till you made such a big deal over Buffy Jordan's purse." Defiant eyes rose to meet Starr's troubled ones. "I didn't take her old purse."

"Forget Buffy's purse for now. What about Mr. McLeod's wallet?"

Narrow shoulders shrugged. "He didn't even have it buttoned in his pocket. Somebody downtown coulda heisted it easy."

"But they didn't, did they, SeLi? It was gone before he went downtown, wasn't it?" Starr ignored the van driver's impatient honking and smoothed back strands of dark hair that had already escaped SeLi's braid.

"It's under my mattress," the girl mumbled. "Can I go now?"

Starr sighed, stepped back and gathered the lapels of her robe beneath her chin. For a moment she closed her eyes. This compounded yesterday's theft at school. It was serious business, and she didn't know what to do.

"I didn't take any of his money," SeLi stated defensively as she ran toward the van.

Starr's eyes sprang open. "I sincerely hope not," she said, even though SeLi probably didn't hear her as she boarded the van. Once it was under way, Starr turned leaden feet toward the elevator—an elevator on its way down from the top floor and the penthouse where Barclay McLeod was no doubt about to enjoy breakfast.

Oh, Lord, she hated the thought of facing him! She hadn't the foggiest idea how to go about returning his wallet. But Starr knew she'd go to any lengths to protect SeLi. With all her heart she believed permanence and stability in SeLi's life would ultimately erase her compulsion to steal. All Seli needed was a chance to prove herself.

But if Wanda got so much as a hint of this, SeLi would be instantly whisked away. To keep that from happening, Starr would face ten Clay McLeods if she had to.

CHAPTER FOUR

STARR RAN UPSTAIRS, went inside and straight to SeLi's room. She found the wallet tucked beneath the mattress, as SeLi had said. She handled it gingerly, like a hot potato, even though the smooth black leather was cool. She placed it on the kitchen counter while she cleaned up the breakfast dishes. But the wallet bothered her; it seemed to mock her efforts as a parent. So Starr took it to her bedroom and stuffed it in her purse until she could decide what to do.

The simplest and most expedient approach, she decided as she showered and dressed for work, would be to march upstairs and hand it to its owner. And tell him what? *That* was the tricky part.

She straightened the collar of the navy blue, nononsense suit she'd selected with an eye to visiting Wanda Manning. It made her look less youthful, more conventional. So did the gray eye shadow.

In the midst of this brief self-assessment, Starr made up her mind—she would simply return the wallet, saying SeLi had *found* it. And once he had his wallet back with its contents intact, why should he doubt her story?

The closer she got to the penthouse, the more her resolve, and her knees, seemed to waver. Twice she reached for the doorbell before finally pressing it. And what would she would say if Vanessa answered? As it turned out, she needn't have worried. Clay himself appeared at the first ring.

He'd removed his suit jacket. His shirtsleeves were rolled to the elbows of muscular, suntanned forearms; he clutched a hammer.

Starr winced. She'd just as soon not face him when he held a blunt object. But what choice did she have?

"Mr. McLeod." She spoke first, hoping for some softening in the hawkish features. There was none, unless one considered the curl of dark hair that drooped appealingly over his left eyebrow.

Bravely she cleared her throat and plunged ahead, "I, ah... It seems SeLi found your wallet. The kids were in such a hurry to catch the van this morning it completely slipped her mind until I ran down to ask if she had lunch money." Not used to lying, Starr felt her palms grow damp. To hide her discomfort she dug in her purse for the offending item. Finding it at last, she held it out, suspended lightly between her thumb and forefinger.

His steely-eyed inspection began at the top of her carefully contained curls and roamed downward to the tips of her low-heeled pumps.

"I've gotta hand it to you," he said grudgingly. "I'm not easily duped. How many men are tempted by your delectable wares—only to be parted from their money without a sample?" He took the wallet from her hand, opened it and fanned through a sheaf of bills. "You're good," he grunted, "Very good. So why blame the kid?"

Starr's temper flared. "I didn't *blame* anyone. Nor did I come here to be insulted. You'll find every last cent there. I trust this will be the last we need see of each other." Heat stung her cheeks and she shifted her raincoat to the other arm.

Clay McLeod laughed as he slid the wallet into his back pocket and buttoned it in place. "Come now. This is a small intimate complex. There's no doubt we'll meet again." He paused. "Unless you're not neighborly. Is that it, hmm? Afraid people might find out what you really do?"

Starr's steps faltered. She went on the defensive. "I'm a biochemist, Mr. McLeod. For the state of California. And a darn good one."

"Is that where you're going dressed like a corporate VP? I thought chemists wore long white coats. Or is that only on TV?"

"We do wear lab coats at work," she informed him. "Not that it's your business, but I have an appointment downtown."

He stiffened. "I'm making everything you do my business. I've moved here for the express purpose of becoming your shadow."

Starr's jaw went slack. "*You* moved ... here? I thought you said *Vanessa and Morgan* did."

Clay shrugged. "It's a big suite. Two complete wings. No reason to rent downtown when I have a great view of the condo entrance from my bedroom here. I can see everyone who comes and goes. Mention that to my brother, will you?"

Her fingers curled around her purse strap until she realized she was playing into his hands and relaxed her grip. "You've got it wrong. *If* the senator visits, it won't be to see me. After all, his wife lives here. *And* he owns the building."

"Technically not. When he chose politics our joint holdings became mine, at least on paper. Did he mention all leases are up January first?"

So that was it. Harrison had agreed to let her catch up on the rent when the trust was turned over to her. Both she and Mrs. Blevins kept a running account of how much Starr actually owed. Now it sounded as if the senator's brother wasn't aware of that—and intended to change things. Well, Starr would be darned if she'd beg.

"Go to hell, Mr. McLeod." Whirling, she walked away.

Clay dropped his hammer in the hall, closed the door and followed her to the elevator where she was angrily punching the button. He leaned against the wall and slowly rolled down his shirtsleeves. "Does that mean you won't reconsider San Diego?"

"Look, enough already. Take this up with your brother. He agreed in SeLi's court hearing that we'd have this place until the adoption's final. That's six lousy months." Seeing his frown, she threw up her hands and headed for the stairs. "Oh, what's the use?"

Clay mulled over the curve she'd just thrown him. What did Harrison have to do with her adopting an Asian child? *Amerasian,* he corrected thoughtfully. And the judge in their case was a longtime friend of the McLeods. "Uh, how are you getting to work?" he called. "Blevins said your car is in the shop. Is my big brother providing a limo? If so, you won't be hard to follow."

Starr's steps slowed—although if she kept going and slammed the heavy fire door, she wouldn't have to listen to him. "I use public transportation, Mr. McLeod," she said in a tone so sweet it dripped honey.

"Bus number 1203. We make twenty-two stops between here and my office. Feel free to count them. I hope you choke on the diesel fumes."

"Hey," he yelled seconds before the fire door slammed. "You want a lift? May as well, since I'm going your way."

Starr almost never swore, but she did so now, succinctly. She'd been wrong about the door; it didn't block sound as well as she'd thought, judging by the thoroughly masculine laughter that chased her down the stairwell.

Ordinarily she hated waiting for a bus in the rain. Today she welcomed the cooling drizzle. Except that while she stood in the doorway struggling to open her stubborn umbrella, bus number 1203 zipped past without stopping. *Blast and damn!* It only ran every fifteen minutes. In addition to having a perfectly wretched morning, now it appeared she'd be late to work, as well. *Fantastic.*

Without warning, the stupid umbrella opened with an unexpected *whish.* Starr stomped out into the downpour but had barely reached the bus stop when someone honked. Glancing up, she saw Clay McLeod parked at the curb in a big dark Blazer. It figured he'd drive a tank. Starr ground her teeth and ignored him.

He rolled down his window and leaned out, seemingly undisturbed by the slanting rain pummeling his Stetson. "No need to get wet while you sulk. The mature thing to do would be to let me drive you to work."

Her back teeth all but cracked. Didn't he just love seeing her shoes getting soaked! Not in a million years would such a jerk expect her to take his offer. Which was exactly why Starr decided to accept.

"You're absolutely right," she said amiably. "Never let it be said that a Lederman doesn't know when to come in out of the rain." Jumping over a large puddle, she marched toward him. "San Francisco traffic is dreadful when it rains. I trust you're a good driver, Mr. McLeod."

Clay made a quick recovery from his surprise. At least enough of one to jump down, slog around the vehicle and gallantly open her door.

By then, though, Starr was thinking maybe she hadn't been so smart—she'd seen the height of the step and compared it to her slim skirt. Ready to reverse her decision, she turned and met his knowing smirk.

"Problems?" he murmured seductively.

Starr squared her shoulders and shook her head. She laughed, deciding to be honest. "You know I do, darn it. By any chance, does this contraption have a portable step?"

"Afraid not."

His little half grin irked her. "A gentleman would lace his hands together and make a lady's first step easier," she said.

"Now, you know. I'm no gentleman." A wicked laugh lurked just below the surface of his words. Then without warning, Clay slid his large hands beneath her coat and spanned her waist. Taking his own sweet time, he boosted her up and into the cab.

Starr felt her skirt slither to midthigh. Unfortunately she had her purse, her lunch and a half-open umbrella to dispense with before she had a hand free to yank it down. She could well imagine the back view she presented for Barclay McLeod's pleasure.

"Mmm," Clay murmured as he let go and thumbed his hat back on his head.

Dropping her things, Starr gave a sharp tug on the back of her coat. She treated him to her best glare and plopped down onto the seat. But she'd forgotten he was so tall. Sitting placed her nose at level with his very white, toothpaste-ad smile.

Without warning, Clay leaned forward and brushed a cool kiss over her lips. Then he stepped back and calmly shut her in.

Shock waves ricocheted clear to Starr's toes. Her entire body bucked as the door's latch engaged, cutting off any chance of escape. Dazed, she watched the outline of his broad shoulders through a window speckled by rain as he circled the hood and slid beneath the steering wheel.

"So," he said without a hint of inflection, "which way? And don't give me the bus route," he said over the sound of the engine. "I'm not about to make twenty-two stops." Casually he removed his damp hat and dropped it on the seat between them.

As if in slow motion, Starr faced front and broke the all-too-compelling connection with his gaze. Every nerve in her body was functioning on overdrive.

She desperately wanted to appear controlled. Better yet, bored. The very last thing she wanted was to blurt like some ninny, "Did you kiss me?" Yet that was exactly what came out of her mouth.

Clay's dark brows arched to meet a dark curl that refused to be tamed. "Sugar, when I *kiss* a woman, she doesn't normally ask if I did. Now, about that route? I hate to press, but we're in a bus zone and one of those stretch models is stopped back there at the light."

"I meant . . . you *did* kiss me. Why?"

With a steady hand, he injected a CD into a state-of-the-art system that promptly filled the cab with a bluesy country tune. "I couldn't have you thinking my curb service is less...satisfactory than Harrison's, could I?"

"You are the most desp—"

"Despicable man," he finished. "I know, but it won't matter in a minute 'cause, honey, we're gonna get creamed if you don't give me some directions."

Between the hiss of air brakes and furious blasts from the angry horn of the bus, Starr rattled off an entire set of directions without taking a breath. "Left lane for a block, left at the light, right at the corner. Go three miles on the freeway to the first exit, make a left, a right, then another left."

Clay swore and bulldozed his way into a busy lane.

Starr smiled. "Oh, did I go too fast? Sorry."

"Not to worry. I know the way to your office. I thought you were going to see a woman named Manning this morning. I assumed you meant before work. My mistake."

Starr froze. Either he had an uncanny memory or he did indeed plan to follow her everywhere. "I'm going to work," she said too fast. "I'm not sure Mrs. Manning will have time to see me today." She took care to avoid his eyes. "What with all this rain, I may even skip going."

"Really?"

"Yes. So if you persist in this silly little spy game, there's no need to drive back into town until five." She recalled the hammer he'd been holding when she'd gone to the door of the penthouse. "I'd hate for you not to finish Vanessa's carpentry project."

"Leave her out of this. I intend to check on you at lunch."

Starr dangled a brown paper bag in front of his nose. "Corned beef on rye. Another boring lunch at my desk. But, gee, if I'd known you were coming, I'd have made you a sandwich—arsenic on whole wheat.''

Ignoring her sarcasm, Clay stayed on the freeway for several miles, then left it and drove two blocks, finally pulling into the parking lot across from the building where she worked. Letting the engine idle, he reached for his hat.

"No need for both of us to get wet," she said quickly. "You wouldn't want to spoil me, now would you?" Gathering her things, Starr hopped out. The long drop jarred her teeth.

Clay's hand hovered over his hat for a moment. Leaving it, he shrugged expansively. "Suit yourself."

"Ta-ta," she murmured sweetly, shutting the door hard enough to rattle his windows. She seethed as she dashed through the rain, never giving a thought to using her umbrella.

Clay watched her join a group of women on the walkway. It surprised him to see that even at a distance she stood out. At first he dismissed it as merely her rich auburn hair, which made a dazzling crown of color among nondescript browns and blonds. But it was more than her appearance, he decided when she sailed blithely into the old brick building. Few women could have resisted taking a final peek to see if he'd gone or stayed. *She* didn't.

Starr Lederman had class, he'd give her that. Either she didn't care if he dogged her footsteps or she didn't have anything to hide. Tapping his lips with his thumb, he wondered whether to revise his assessment. But maybe the lady just played one helluva game of poker. Clay's fingers drummed on the steering wheel in time to the hammering of rain on the roof of the Blazer. She was up to something. He'd bet his last dime on it.

Question was, what? Yesterday his brother had acted damned odd, too. Where most men would have denied an affair if confronted, Harrison seemed almost pleased. Was he covering some greater sin?

Maybe he should pay his own visit to that social worker, Clay thought. If Starr intended to call for an appointment, it might be smart for him to swing by social services now. Yes, he'd do that.

STARR STOOD at the window in her boss's office on the fourth floor and observed Clay McLeod's departure. Two fingers strayed to her lips, and as his vehicle disappeared, her stomach unknotted. Behind her, the steady rise and fall of her boss's words started to make sense. "It will reflect well on the department that the university chose you for this special project."

"Thank you, sir," Starr said before Mr. Jensen launched into one of his long-winded speeches. "I really hate asking another favor today." And she meant it, too. Yesterday when the school called, Starr had hated having to leave her desk piled high. And then her late lunch with Harrison... "I wouldn't ask for time to visit Mrs. Manning if there was any other way," she said after explaining her need to see the case worker.

The white-haired man nodded. "Go now. I'll explain to Dr. Ellsworth."

Starr thanked him again and used his phone to call a cab. The element of surprise might just work to her advantage with Wanda Manning.

Less than a half hour later Starr thought perhaps she'd been right. Wanda flew out of her private office the moment the receptionist announced Starr's arrival. Wanda even sent the receptionist on a break and sat at the woman's desk. Always before, Starr had been kept waiting for hours.

"To what do I owe this unscheduled intrusion?" Wanda asked.

Left to stand, Starr realized the speed with which she was being seen was all that had changed. "My job is taking me out of town over SeLi's Christmas break. I'd like permission for her to go with me."

"As if you hadn't already had it approved by Judge Forbes."

Starr's smile slipped. The senator must have called the judge, even though she'd asked him not to. If she'd only known, she could have saved herself a trip.

"Since you're here," Wanda said, "I want you to know that I'm opposed to everything about this idiotic scheme of yours. You think that just because you have clout with the judge, you can flit off at the last minute on a poorly thought-out vacation. To me it shows irresponsibility. I've said before and I'll say again—that child needs a stable home in a two-parent family."

Wanda's thin lips barely moved as she continued, "Frankly I'm not sure why I was assigned to this case, the way you break rules."

Starr stiffened her spine. "I'd hoped we could set our personal differences aside and agree this trip would be good for SeLi."

"Hmph!" Mrs. Manning's denigrating sniff accompanied a toss of her mousy curls. "I'm afraid you and I will never agree. Your kind thinks money talks. I am not impressed by your wealth or your association with political power. I've seen both come and go in my time. As far as I'm concerned, you are no more a fit parent for that child than her own streetwalking mother was. Which I intend to prove before this adoption is final."

Starr was taken back by the vitriolic speech. "My father has money and power, Mrs. Manning, not me."

"Oh, no? Am I mistaken about your trust fund?"

For a moment Starr didn't know what to say. Then temper kicked in. "It's true my grandfather left a modest sum that I'll get when I turn thirty. Silly me, I imagined the money would be a bonus for SeLi. To pay for things like college. Surely you don't have to like me to see the benefits!"

"Like you?" Wanda sniffed. "If you have nothing more to say, Miss Lederman, I have another, equally distasteful caller to see. It seems there's no end to the line of rich and powerful people in our humble office today." A dour look crossed her face as her gaze alighted on the door to her private office.

Starr glanced that way herself. For a moment she thought maybe Clay...but, no. She shook her head. He wouldn't come here. Why would he?

Still, the thought of *anyone* overhearing this discussion embarrassed her. Starr turned away. She couldn't wait to escape this oppressive room. But good manners dictated she at least thank Wanda for her time.

Or did they?

She paused, a hand on the doorknob. "This visit has been no more pleasant for me than it has for you. You should realize, however, that I haven't the slightest intention of letting you take SeLi away from me. You may not approve of me or my single status, but there's an important fact you've missed. I love SeLi—and she loves me. But maybe love is a foreign concept to you, Mrs. Manning. Good day."

AS THE FRONT DOOR closed savagely behind Starr, the one leading to the social worker's private office creaked slowly open.

"Rich bitch!" Wanda's fury was almost palpable, and it stopped Clay from stepping fully into a room still vibrating with it.

At last, appearing to have gained control, Mrs. Manning managed a halfway civil tone for the man who waited. "Now, how may I help you, Mr. McLeod?" Her clipped speech reflected her lingering agitation. "As I was about to say before we were so rudely interrupted by Miss Lederman's unexpected visit, your brother has already gotten permission from Judge Forbes for the Lederman child to leave the city. I have no doubt that you know the power the senator's name wields. After all," she finished sarcastically, "I am but a poor servant of the state, and this is an election year."

Clay thrust his hands deep into his pockets and rocked back and forth on his heels. Something in the way Starr went to bat for the child touched him. But he'd come here for answers. What he had was more questions.

"The walls are thin, Mrs. Manning. I heard every word of your exchange with Miss Lederman." Clay stopped short of saying the woman's own attitude had left him with a bad taste for certain representatives of the social services in this town.

"Our agency is overworked and understaffed, Mr. McLeod. Visits without appointments add to the load. Could you get to the point, please?"

Clay freed one hand and dragged a thumb across his lower lip—an action that reminded him how soft Starr's mouth had felt under his earlier. Quite a contrast to the hard determination he'd heard in her voice moments ago. Which was the real Starr Lederman?

Irritably he switched gears. The only reason for his visit today was to determine his brother's interest in this adoption. Was it political—or was it personal? While in Wanda's office, Clay had put together some possibilities. He didn't like the one that most insistently reared its ugly head.

About eight years ago Harrison's marriage had hit a low spot. It rallied briefly—until Morgan was born. Other men acted sappy over their firstborn. Not Harris. He threw himself into his work. But what if Morgan *wasn't* Harrison's firstborn? And what if his opponents knew?

Damn, suspicions of this nature were distressing. Yet he had to ask. "Uh, Mrs. Manning..." Clay cleared his throat and studied the tips of his boots. "Do you know why my brother would take a personal interest in this particular child?" God, he wanted out of this suffocating room.

Mrs. Manning's unfeeling eyes showed a spark of interest. "Perhaps *you* can tell *me*," she said curtly. "Go ahead, Mr. McLeod. I'm listening."

Clay didn't look at the woman as he began to pace. "What do you know about the child's mother? What did she do? Was she pretty?"

"Those are odd questions. Pretty is as pretty does, Mr. McLeod. She had no visible means of support, other than the usual for homeless dock women, if that's what you're talking about. Do you mind my asking what difference it makes?"

"I've only recently learned of the senator's involvement with the little girl. As his brother, I find it curious. I mean, Miss Lederman isn't related to us or anything." He stopped beside the desk, bile threatening to choke him. "As you pointed out, this *is* an election year. My brother's opponent isn't new to mudslinging. Do you follow me?"

The woman merely inclined her head.

Clay crossed to one of the room's narrow windows. With his back to the social worker, he lifted a dirty slat of the miniblind and restlessly monitored the progress of slow-moving vehicles on the wet streets below. In a low, impassioned voice he expressed the fear that had begun to fester ever since Starr had planted the seed of doubt this morning. "Is it possible that Harrison is SeLi Lederman's biological father?" There was no point in mincing words.

At the woman's shocked gasp, Clay struggled to breathe in the stale air. His fingers tensed on the slat. Apparently whatever Mrs. Manning had expected him to ask, it had definitely not been this question. That brought Clay at least a degree of comfort.

He turned and she sat forward. The old chair protested in a loud squeak. "I must say that's an interesting notion, Mr. McLeod. One I hadn't considered."

"We can't rule it out, then?" He was disappointed. Her words hadn't delivered the unequivocal relief he would've liked.

"Only Judge Forbes can do that."

Clay frowned. "Judge Forbes and my father go way back—to law school. I attended elementary and high school with the judge's son, Joel. Lost track of him when I went off to college. I heard he'd joined the navy after his mother died. Haven't thought of him in years."

"Yes, well, Joel was killed in a training mission off Alcatraz a few years back. The judge hasn't been himself since. He should retire, if you ask me."

Clay walked back across the room. "I'm sorry. I didn't know. Naturally a man would dote on his only son." Which brought him back to wondering why his own brother didn't. Morgan hardly knew his dad.

"I assume you have reason to suspect your brother," Wanda Manning mused aloud, breaking into Clay's reflections.

"Frankly you're one reason, Mrs. Manning. You seem to resent his involvement."

Her top lip curled to reveal teeth yellowed by too many cigarettes. "He vouched for Starr Lederman, who is a rich spoiled brat. Do-gooders like her are the worst. Gung ho when it enhances their image. Then, like old toys, their projects are dropped when they tire of being charitable."

Clay rubbed his neck. "She sounded pretty sincere a moment ago."

"A lot you know," Wanda said smugly. "I lived in a series of foster homes when I was growing up. One of my foster sisters could have been Starr Lederman's twin. I wasn't fit to wipe her boots. Oh, the whole family patted me on the head and threw me crumbs to show their rich friends how benevolent they were. Poor little Wanda—saved from the evils of the streets. But never quite good enough to be in their social circle. Sincere, Mr. McLeod? I doubt it. There's a well-defined limit to the good works of the wealthy."

Suddenly, as if realizing she might have said too much, Wanda pressed her lips into a disapproving line and changed the subject. "Actually, Mr. McLeod, you've hit on something that's always puzzled me—

why a man as well connected as the senator would choose to involve himself in the nitty-gritty of this case.''

"Would the girl's birth certificate shed any light?"

"Perhaps." Her fingers toyed with a pencil. "Except that Judge Forbes ordered the records sealed."

Clay arched a brow. "What exactly does 'sealed' mean, Mrs. Manning?"

"It means no one has access. Oh, SeLi can petition to see them when she turns eighteen, but no one else."

"That's it? There's no other reason to *un*seal them?"

"Sometimes in a rare instance. If an adoptee should need an organ transplant or has severe psychiatric problems—those types of things."

"Well, I guess that's that." Clay was almost relieved by the news.

"Maybe not." Wanda Manning stood up as her receptionist came back into the room. "I believe it's in SeLi's best interests to stop this adoption. A biological father is one way. Perhaps I can find your answer."

Clay didn't like the gleam in her eye. But he'd read the professional certificates displayed on her wall. She wasn't a novice in this business.

"Where can you be reached?" she asked, thrusting a pad and pen at him.

Clay hesitated briefly, then reached for his wallet. "I have a business card with the phone number of my ranch. I'm staying here in San Francisco temporarily, but I'm due to auction some bulls before Christmas and I'll be spending the holiday down there. How long do you think it'll take?"

"I'm not sure," she murmured. "Maybe two or three weeks."

"Then this card should do it. I have an answering machine here, but I wouldn't want a message to fall into the wrong hands." He was thinking of Vanessa. "If you call and I'm not there, leave a number."

"No need to mention confidentiality. I understand." She took his card, then looked at him curiously. He was thumbing rapidly through the photo windows in his wallet. "Is something wrong, Mr. McLeod? Have you lost something?"

"What?" Clay looked up.

"I said, have you lost something?"

"A couple of family pictures," he muttered. Seeing her interest, he returned the wallet to his back pocket. "It's nothing," he said. "I assume this concludes our visit." Clay stepped into her office and took his hat from a brass rack. He came out and offered his hand. The fingers clasping his in return were bony and cold. It was all Clay could do to keep from snatching his card back and hightailing it out of there.

He didn't. He withdrew his hand and walked to the door.

"A pleasure doing business with you, Mr. McLeod."

Even her voice grated on his nerves. And the discomfort, the sense of being soiled, remained with him after he'd placed the solid barrier of the door between them.

As he clattered down the winding staircase of the old building, the noise of his footsteps helped rid him of the unclean feeling—although if Starr Lederman was any better than the woman upstairs, he wouldn't have two empty frames in his picture slots. One a school photo of Morgan, the other a candid shot of himself that Vanessa had taken last Christmas.

Starr had lied when she'd said nothing was missing from his wallet. Why? It was time he found out more about her. What if she was a blind? A lovely decoy for somebody who might be blackmailing his brother?

Clay tried, but he couldn't recall exactly what she'd said at their first encounter. Something about environmentalists or wildlife advocates. She worked in Fish and Game, and there was definitely something fishy going on.

He stopped on the first floor to dig out his keys. Outside the rain was no longer just a drizzle. It was a downpour. Traffic crawled. So what would the lady in question do, he wondered, if he grabbed a sandwich at the deli he'd seen nearby and just dropped in on her at lunchtime?

The harder it rained, the more appeal the idea held.

The deli was crowded. Clay placed his order, took the number they gave him and wandered through the packed tables into an attached flower shop that was all decked out for the holidays. The bright red poinsettias had originally attracted him, but he paused to touch the petals of a peach-colored rose that seemed out of place among the cedar and pine. Its petals looked lush and soft—like Starr Lederman's skin.

Flushing, he stepped back and glanced around to see if anyone noticed his odd reaction. Then, sidestepping the display, he turned the corner and promptly stumbled over an entire bucket of those same flesh-colored blooms. Clay stared at them for what seemed an endless moment—until he realized someone had announced his number over a loudspeaker.

It felt like a reprieve. Clay found it much easier to deal with a pastrami-and-provolone than these uncharacteristic emotions involving Starr Lederman that sucker-punched him at inopportune times.

Which was why it made not a lick of sense when, after paying for his sandwich, he wound up buying two of the roses.

A cheerful clerk wrapped them in waxy paper with stalks of some wispy white stuff and a sprig of Christmas greenery. All this for a woman he didn't even like.

As Clay inched through noon-hour traffic headed for Starr's building, he gave up questioning his impulsive action and just accepted it. He'd already parked, climbed out and was wondering idly why anyone chose to live in the city when he saw her dashing through the rain toward a waiting cab. She wasn't alone. Her fingers were linked with those of some skinny guy with a receding hairline and horn-rimmed glasses.

Clay suffered a swift feeling of betrayal. Anger nipped at its heels.

Calling himself all kinds of a fool for standing in the rain holding a wet bouquet like some idiot teenager, Clay tossed the flowers and the sack with his sandwich into a nearby trash receptacle. Then he yanked open the door and climbed back in, staring furiously out the windshield.

Like hell she was eating lunch at her desk today.

He watched the couple's taxi pull out onto a rain-slick street. Hands unsteady, he jammed the key into the ignition, started the engine and pulled out of the parking lot behind them.

Lie to him, would she?

Did Harrison know how she spent her lunch hours? Somehow Clay doubted he did.

Well, wouldn't little Miss Lying-through-her-teeth Lederman be shocked when he broke up her noon-hour quickie?

CHAPTER FIVE

STARR PAID the cabdriver and dashed after Dr. Stanley Ellsworth between parked cars and through the rain into a trendy new restaurant. She glanced at the ice blue Christmas trees with their crystal cherubs as she shed her dripping coat and smoothed her wet hair. It was time to engage in another round of verbal sparring with her colleague.

"Stanley, I need six serum-test kits and three extra packs of vials. You said Mr. Jensen explained I was going on special assignment—so why give me a hard time?"

Her companion removed his glasses and wiped them clean of rain spots. "Two!" Instead of answering Starr, he wiggled two fingers at a harried hostess, who nodded and beckoned them to a second room. Starr stopped to hang her coat on a heavily laden rack.

Stanley waited impatiently beside the booth. After she slid in, he took a seat opposite and picked up the argument where they'd left off. "The media base you've requested is strictly for mammals, Starr. Your area is the harbor." His lips turned down in something of a pout. Starr opened her menu. "I deserve to be let in on the secret, don't you think?"

Frankly Starr had never dreamed that someone of

Stanley's professional stature would act like a spoiled child.

His brown eyes, made larger by the thick glasses, blinked owlishly at her until he gave up and opened his menu. "Yikes! You didn't tell me this charming little eatery would cost me a week's salary. I'm not in the same league as your senator friend—who, by the way, called twice before you got in today."

"Senator McLeod called? Why didn't you tell me?"

He shrugged. "You were so late arriving at the lab I forgot."

"I cleared being late with Mr. Jensen."

"Did I say you hadn't? My, we're touchy. Is that because you missed Mr. Bigwig's call? Or because I griped about the prices?"

"You're the one throwing a fit, Stanley. Over giving me the gel-plates. Will it make you happier if I buy lunch?"

"Maybe. I still want to know what you're doing that's so hush-hush."

Starr closed her menu and put it aside. "The senator didn't say anything was wrong, did he? I mean..." She lowered her voice and darted a nervous glance around the room. But she didn't expect to see anyone she knew, so her gaze skipped over a dark-haired man seated alone in a nearby booth. Suddenly her gaze darted back, and Starr found herself locked in a glaring duel with Barclay McLeod. She sucked in a breath.

Stanley turned to see who or what had caught Starr's attention. His search got only as far as a half-filled old-fashioned glass lifted toward them in mock salute. "Who's that?" he asked.

"Who do you mean?" Starr buried her nose in the menu and feigned nonchalance.

"The fellow in the corner booth. I'm quite certain I've never seen him before." Stanley adjusted his glasses. "Disagreeable character, if you ask me. One of those macho cowboy types that women fall all over." He stiffened and hastily corrected himself. "Except you, Starr. You're more levelheaded."

Starr angled another glance at the corner. Guiltily she remembered saying she'd be eating at her desk. For one wild moment Starr considered dashing over to explain about the sheep and the gel-plates. But of course she couldn't. She'd given her word not to.

Fortunately a waitress zipped over to fill their coffee cups and to take their order. Her timely arrival kept Starr from making a fool of herself. She caught Stanley's eye. "Order light. I need to get back to work." Starr ordered a cup of soup and a turkey sandwich while Stanley continued to peruse the menu. "Oh, and put both orders on my check," she added.

The waitress nodded, then turned to Stanley. Before he made his request, Starr sneaked another peek at the corner. Clay was watching her the way a cobra eyes a mouse.

"I, for one, do not plan on rushing," Stanley informed Starr. "You dragged me away from work, Now I intend to enjoy every morsel. Especially since you're paying." He calmly ordered a three-course meal.

The waitress left and Stanley gathered up Starr's drumming fingers. "Does the odd way you're acting have anything to do with the full moon, love?"

"Full moon?" Starr shook her hand loose and with a nervous laugh said, "Stanley, I swear..."

Seemingly satisfied at gaining her attention, Dr. Ellsworth sat back and hefted his coffee cup. All at once he squinted over the edge and frowned. "That fellow, Starr—he's watching you. You must know him."

"I don't," she lied smoothly. It wasn't her fault Clay McLeod had decided to spend the day playing I spy.

"Maybe you two met at one of your mother's parties," Stanley muttered. "He looks like the kind of weirdos Patrice has hanging around."

"He doesn't look weird!" Starr regretted her outburst immediately. For Pete's sake, now she was defending him. Thank goodness a waitress had stopped at his table. Starr didn't dare let Stanley catch her looking that way again.

Except that the pretty blond waitress lingered too long, talking and laughing with him. Starr's mood turned dark as the weather.

Tossing her head, she crossed her legs and pumped her foot. Why did she care who Barclay McLeod chose to flirt with? Let the man fan his peacock tail at ditzy blondes. She, for one, had more important things to do—like talking Stanley out of those gel-plates so that she could save a herd of sheep.

CLAY JOKED WITH the friendly waitress to take his mind off the disturbing woman seated across the room. He declined coffee and ordered scotch and water while waiting for his steak. Normally he didn't touch liquor this early in the day, but Starr Lederman made him crazy.

He should have gone back to the apartment the minute it became apparent Starr and the boyfriend weren't destined for a motel. Vanessa had no doubt fixed lunch. Not that he owed his sister-in-law any explanations for his absence; he didn't. The guilt nagged more because Clay knew she worried. How many evenings had she watched out the window for a husband who never showed? Waited by the phone for calls that never came?

Clay had seen the number of times she choked back tears.

He could hear Starr laughing. It didn't look as if *she* worried about anything. Was that what Harrison found so appealing about her? Since his brother was such a *busy* man. Ha!

Clay's gaze skipped past the chatty waitress to the table across the room—where he could see Starr's rose-tipped fingers entwined with her partner's. As she pulled playfully free, Clay's stomach felt as if it'd been drop-kicked downfield.

Hell, he knew what qualities appealed to his brother. The same qualities that appealed to him. The woman was warm, funny, touchable. Dammit, if Clay didn't watch his step, she'd snare him, too.

Somebody, he thought, should warn that poor devil she was with to hold on to his wallet.

Clay drained his glass and set it down with a thump. He didn't owe a stranger advice. What he needed was to go call Vanessa, set her mind at ease. Taking leave of the waitress, Clay patted his hip pocket to assure himself his own wallet was still there.

He was very glad to have it back. The wallet had been a gift from Morgan last Christmas. It was the first present the kid had picked out all by himself. Sadness for his brother's son gripped him for a moment. Morgan was an intense boy who felt everything deeply; he'd be upset if he knew his school picture had been stolen.

Clay frowned as he punched out the numbers. If only he had some idea why Starr would heist pictures. He thought about the ones she'd left. A worn black-

and-white of his parents on their twenty-fifth wedding anniversary. A small wedding photo of Harrison and Vanessa—but of course she'd leave *that*.

He had other pictures of Morgan, but he liked the missing picture best. In it, the boy's blond hair had been mussed, and a rare grin showed a missing tooth. Van wanted him to wear suits and look like a little man. She had refused to buy the school packet of photographs, so Clay had slipped him the money.

Harrison should have handled that incident, not him. But Harris was never around. He hadn't even made it to the ranch last Christmas. Claimed he was tied up with important state business. Yeah, right.

Telling Vanessa goodbye, Clay went back to his seat. Damn, he didn't like thinking his brother had lied. Clay glowered at Starr. Now-untamed curls framed a face kissed by a smattering of freckles. He didn't let himself remember another place she had freckles; instead, he made himself concentrate on her eyes. Strangely iridescent irises shimmered around smoky centers and somehow intensified her look of innocence. Did knowing she *wasn't* innocent make her more exciting?

Watching her now, Clay was forced to admit he found her exciting for other reasons. She was beautiful, yet seemingly indifferent to the fact. He ran a hand around a suddenly restrictive collar. Why should indifference in a woman make her alluring?

Clay hadn't the foggiest notion, but it did.

Men, now, weren't so subtle. At least *he* wasn't. So why didn't he go ask lover boy if he knew he was just one man in a long line of suckers?

Clay slid out of the booth again and wove his way through the tables.

Having made up her mind to ignore the younger McLeod, Starr sat with her back to the room. "What do you suppose is taking them so long to fix a simple soup and sandwich?" she muttered. "I have a ton of reports to file. If my food doesn't come soon, I'm leaving."

Stanley unfolded his napkin and polished his silverware.

"Are you going to get me those serum-test kits?" Starr demanded as if they hadn't talked about several subjects since that one.

"You missed the whole point, Starr. My reluctance has to do with the odd way you're acting." Stanley laughed. "I mean, who'd trust you with a secret? Look at you. A bundle of nerves. What are you building with your silverware? A pen for your bighorn sheep?"

Starr dropped the knife she was threading through the tines of a fork, which formed a triangle with her spoon. "Who said anything about sheep?"

"I have your equipment list, Starr. Dart gun, big-game marking tags coded for San Jacinto. It hardly takes a genius to add things up." He looked sullen. "If this is about getting your doctorate, why the big ruse?"

Clay skulked behind a waitress who came to deliver Starr's lunch. He found the tidbit about San Jacinto very enlightening, and lingered in hopes of hearing more.

Starr accepted her order. Not the cup of soup she'd asked for, but a bowl. She weighed the value of sending it back to be corrected as Stanley pondered which dressing to use on his salad. Deciding not to make a fuss, she said, "It has nothing to do with my doctorate, Stanley. I thought Mr. Jensen explained."

"Bunk and rubbish!" With a vicious stab, Stanley spiked lettuce, tomato and a large mushroom all at once.

Fascinated, Starr watched him lift the fork toward his mouth. She held her breath until it met its goal. Closing her eyes, she counted to ten.

Clay continued to lag within earshot.

Stanley patted his lips with his napkin. "I made some inquiries and couldn't find anyone at U Berkeley who's heard of this project." He waved his fork under her nose. "If you got someone to pull strings so you can start compiling data for your thesis, you're nuts."

Starr's jaw was set in a stubborn line. "I doubt you've spoken to every single person at U Berkeley, Stanley," she drawled sarcastically. "Believe me, I know what I'm doing." The words were barely out of her mouth when a dark blur materialized in her peripheral vision. She dropped her spoon, and soup flew everywhere as Clay McLeod slid into the booth beside her.

"What's this I hear?" he asked with deceptive smoothness. "You're planning a jaunt to my neck of the woods? Funny, you didn't mention it this morning."

Someone who didn't know him might think his interest casual. Starr was close enough to feel the underlying hum of his anger. She should protest—but she felt confused, her thoughts disordered. Arguments, answers, clever comebacks—she couldn't produce even one. This man had a way of reducing her to a mindless amoebic mass. Not only that, Harrison would expect her to throw him offtrack. To erect roadblocks. Denial, however, stuck in Starr's throat, making breathing next to impossible.

"I thought you said you didn't know this man," Stanley accused as he speared a huge radish rosette.

Starr's breath escaped like steam from boiling water. "He's no friend, believe me," she managed at last. "Ignore him, Stanley. Maybe he'll take the hint and leave." She deliberately picked up her sandwich and took a bite.

Clay smiled benignly, stuck out a broad, tanned hand and clasped the doctor's smooth, pale one in a bone-crushing grip.

Stanley's eyes bugged behind his glasses. Then both men turned to look at Starr. Stanley's gaze was hurt and challenging; Clay's slumberous and faintly mocking.

"*This*—" Clay arched a brow "—is Stanley Stud?" His amused voice caused diners all around to stop eating and stare.

Stanley issued an ill-concealed oath.

Starr felt truly skewered on a barb of her own making—or rather, her daughter's making. Too late she realized she shouldn't have lied to Stanley.

His glare swung from the intruder to Starr and back again. Angrily he threw his napkin across his salad plate. But his tie got tangled in the folds and ended up landing in the Russian dressing, too.

Starr's eyes widened as she watched an oily red stain seep through the fine linen napkin into the elegant silk of Stanley's tie. Her colleague was nothing if not fastidious about his attire. She winced.

Stanley gingerly untied the offending article and let it drop. "I'd say you know him, all right," he growled. "It's not enough that you let that wretched, uncivilized little wharf hoodlum insult me to my face.

Now you allow her insolence to be passed on to your...friends."

"SeLi is not a hoodlum." Furious, Starr struggled to stand, but Clay's large body didn't allow it. "Stanley, wait," she said when he started to slide from the booth.

"Let him go," Clay advised. "I'll give you a lift back to the office."

A waitress arrived just then with Stanley's main course.

"Stanley, this is silly," Starr hissed. "SeLi knows exactly how to jerk your chain. If you didn't react, she'd quit doing it. Come on, finish your lunch. The spinach fettuccini here is to die for."

"Oh, here you are!" Another waitress, the bubbly one Starr had seen fawning over Clay, rushed up and handed him his steak plate. Stanley was more or less hemmed in. "How nice," the young woman cooed, her eyes only for Clay. "You found someone you knew. And to think you're only visiting San Francisco. It's a small world, I always say."

The woman's Pollyanna sweetness grated on Starr's nerves, as did the way she gushed over Clay. Oh, he made a show of nonchalance, but Starr knew he loved every minute. "Sit, Stanley," Starr snapped. "You're making a scene."

"Me?" he sputtered.

Clay calmly cut into his very rare steak and carried a piece to his mouth.

Stanley turned a sort of puce green. "How can you even watch this...this cannibal eat?"

"Don't rush off on my account," Clay said around a winsome smile. "Finish your tie, er, your lunch." His grin spread.

Stanley pulled back, looking miffed. "I can't believe you're friends with someone so uncouth, Starr."

Clay gestured with his fork. "Oh, we're not friends. It's more of a fraternal affiliation, I'd say, given her close association with my brother."

"And who might your brother be?" Stanley tore his gaze from the meat and sneered. "Dracula?"

Clay's smile faded. "Harrison McLeod. *Senator* Harrison McLeod. The rules are simple while he's in office. What's his is mine, and what's mine I keep." His cool blue gaze raked Starr.

She seethed.

Clay sat back. Under the table, his thigh brushed hers.

She went hot, then cold, then hot again.

"That does it!" Stanley hailed his waitress and asked her to box his lunch. "Being lied to, as well as insulted, is more than I can take. If the *senator's brother* knows so much about your plans, let *him* get your gelplates."

Starr had to shut him up before he inadvertently let any more slip. Harrison would have a fit. "Stanley, people are watching."

"Let them watch. I'm calling a cab. Are you coming or not? Leave your *non*friend the tab—he can certainly afford the prices here. In fact, I believe I'll send him a bill for my tie."

Without waiting to see if Starr followed, Stanley pushed past the waitress and headed for the door.

"Will he be back?" the confused woman asked Clay.

He shrugged and deferred to Starr.

Her response was to request the check. As the waitress pulled a sheaf of bills from her apron pocket and thumbed through them, Starr did her best to ignore Clay.

"So that's your daughter's idea of a stud?" he said the moment the waitress left. "You should really pay more attention to her education, Mom."

Uncomfortably aware that every eye in the place was trained on them, Starr scooted out of the horseshoe-shaped booth, choosing the long way around. "You are—"

"Despicable?" he filled in, standing when she did.

"Did you follow me just to make my life miserable?"

His dark brows drew together with chilling speed. "I told you, but you don't seem to get it—I want you out of my brother's bed. Instead, it sounds as if the two of you are planning a rendezvous on my turf." His arm snaked out and he caught Starr's chin. "Tell me, Starr. How does Stanley fit in? Or does he simply make a good cover?"

Her lips parted and her cheeks burned. It was all she could do not to blurt out the truth, Harrison and his secrets be damned. She wanted to smack that know-it-all smirk right off his face—except that as she stared into his eyes, she found herself slipping again. Found herself wanting his kiss.

If she stood on tiptoe, their mouths would be mere inches apart....

Clay groaned. "This is insane," he muttered, his senses tumbling like a barrel going over Niagara Falls. "Let's get out of here. Now."

Laughter from the next table penetrated the fog that clouded Starr's reason. She blinked, then savagely bit her lip. How could she have let this happen? And in so public a place. "No." She wrenched herself back, only to discover that no bonds held her in check.

Clay flushed. "You feel the chemistry between us. Don't try to deny it. Forget my brother," he said, lowering his voice. "He has a *family,* dammit."

He sounded anguished. And that was why Starr wanted to say *something.* Wanted to make him understand—without revealing any of Harrison's secrets. "The senator and I... We..." Clutching her purse, she shook her head. After all, what could she really say?

With a distressed cry, Starr reached into her purse for some cash and threw it on the table. Mindful of the curious stares of other diners, she hurried from the room.

Clay sank back against the cushioned seat, and wondered how he always managed to provoke her when that hadn't been his intent. And it wasn't as if he hadn't given her every chance to explain, damn her.

Caught in a maelstrom of doubt, Clay stood and matched the cash she'd left, then added some more to compensate for the mess.

"Goodness," someone gushed behind him. It was Miss Congeniality, the waitress who'd handled his order. "Your friends weren't very hungry," she said. "Oh, I see the gentleman had an accident." She lifted a corner of Stanley's soggy tie.

"Yes. Do you have something you can clip the label out with? I feel responsible, and I'd like to buy him another tie."

"Well, aren't you the sweetest man? Sure, give me a minute."

Clay didn't feel very sweet as he waited for her to return with scissors. Her eyes invited more than the thanks he gave her, but Clay pretended not to see. His mind refused to rid itself of a certain red-haired temptress.

STARR TRIED to regain control of her senses during the solitary cab ride back to work. Stanley's taxi was just pulling away from the curb when hers arrived. If only she hadn't stayed to fight that losing battle with Clay McLeod, she might already have made her peace with Stanley. They'd been friends since college and had always worked well together.

For the first time, Starr wondered if Stanley felt more than friendship for her. If so, it wasn't because she'd offered any encouragement.

Not that she encouraged Barclay McLeod, either. Nor would she. Ever. She knew his type—a talented womanizer like her father. She loved her father, but she'd never tolerate that kind of husband for herself. Reportedly, Samuel Lederman dallied with every starlet who walked onto one of his sets. Yet, true to double standard, he didn't want his wife so much as talking to another man. Starr had watched her mother live with the rumors—and realities—of his infidelities.

Women, young and old, threw themselves at her father. The man she'd just left back at the restaurant exuded the same kind of sexy charisma, Starr thought grimly as she paid her fare.

"Too sexy for my own good," she murmured aloud placing blame where it belonged. She dashed into the building.

At first the date to start Harrison's project had seemed impossibly close; now SeLi's Christmas break didn't seem close enough. Better to be camping at Idyllwild beyond reach of both McLeods than to be here, stuck in the middle of their family squabble.

Leaving the elevator, Starr walked right on past Stanley's closed door. She'd had all she could take of sulky men for one day.

Starr rolled up her sleeves and set to work filing. As a rule, she didn't mind filing volumes of lab slips or filling out reports in triplicate. Today her mind drifted to other matters, and she grew bored.

Budget cuts—which gave some indication of the shape their state was in—were responsible for a shortage in support staff. If Starr truly wanted to get back into Stanley's good graces, all she needed to do was volunteer her clerical services for a few hours.

By midafternoon Starr decided it was the least she could do, considering it was her daughter who'd come up with the silly name. Friends were important; Clay McLeod was a virtual stranger.

But *was* she guilty of using Stanley to keep the wolves at bay, as Clay had insinuated? If so, she wasn't proud of herself. She tapped on Stanley's door and poked her head inside.

"Stanley, I'm sorry. I do value our friendship. Could you use some help filing lab slips?"

Stanley didn't wait for her to change her mind. Nothing she offered could've worked half as fast at alleviating his hurt feelings. By the end of the day he'd even handed over the gel-plates.

"I still think I deserve your honesty," he grumbled. "You know I'm a team player, Starr."

Starr nodded and glanced at the clock above his head. "Wow, I didn't realize it was so late. Thank goodness Darcy picked the kids up from school. I guess SeLi can play with the boys until I get home. Thanks for the plates, Stanley. I've gotta split."

"Yeah. Go on. I'll put the kits on your desk."

Starr didn't like keeping secrets. It helped ease her guilt a little to get out in the fresh, rainwashed air. She more than half expected to see Clay McLeod's rig at the door and was at a loss to explain her disappointment at its absence. "Darn," she muttered, climbing onto the bus. His inconsistency threw her into a tailspin.

By the time her bus made the requisite twenty-two stops, darkness had fallen. Though the rain had all but disappeared, a thick fog had settled over the city. Until now, Starr hadn't realized how draining the day had been.

With any luck, Darcy would have fed SeLi along with the twins. On Saturday maybe she'd reciprocate—take the kids ice-skating, and let Darcy sleep late.

"Hi, Miss Lederman." Blevins rushed out of his office to open the heavy door. "You're later than usual tonight."

"Yes. It's that darned bus. By the way, SeLi and I are going to be heading out of town during Christmas break." Starr shook water droplets from her wildly curling hair. "I may borrow my dad's motor home, and it takes up two parking spaces. I'm telling you this in case anyone complains—like the owner," she said sarcastically.

Blevins chuckled. "Not much rattles young Mr. McLeod. Although he may not like hearing that you're leaving. Asked a lot of questions about you the other night. Mrs. Blevins thinks he's smitten." The old man winked when he saw Starr blush. "She feels sorry for him," he confided, "being saddled with that snooty wife of his brother's and all,"

Starr snorted. "I suspect your concern is greatly misplaced, Blevins. I doubt Barclay McLeod does anything that isn't self-serving." Voicing the thought left her surprisingly depressed as she rode the elevator to her floor.

To top it off, her key stuck in the lock. By the time she got the door open, her mood had disintegrated further. But that was nothing compared to the way it dropped off the scale when she stumbled into her living room—and onto an unexpected scene of domestic tranquillity.

There, on her floor, in a room she had every reason to assume would be empty, sprawled Barclay McLeod. All six feet of him—amid a circle of noisy children. He wore blue jeans and a cable-knit sweater in muted earth tones. One elbow was planted on her deep-pile carpet, and one smooth-shaven cheek rested on his open palm. Feet bootless, hair appealingly mussed, he looked for all the world as if he belonged.

"Mom!" shouted SeLi excitedly. "Clay's teaching us how to play Monopoly!" She waved a fistful of play money. "He says I'm a real ty...tycoon."

Starr's gaze skipped over the assortment of children and locked on Clay's lazy smile.

Instantly she resented his easy familiarity with *her* child. She resented the way he looked so at home in her living room. She resented the pain that ripped through her heart. In all her childhood, she'd never once experienced the joy of such familial warmth. And deep down she resented Clay McLeod for showing her the very thing Wanda Manning harped about most. *This* was what SeLi missed by not having two parents.

It was all Starr could do to hold back a sudden rush of tears.

CHAPTER SIX

"EVERYTHING ALL RIGHT?" Clay asked, sitting up, a concerned expression on his face. "SeLi expected you home earlier."

Starr didn't want him to know how affected she was by his presence. "I—I'm fine. Traffic moves slowly in this weather."

Several pairs of eyes chastened Starr for her untimely interruption.

"You're screwing up our light, Mom," protested SeLi.

"Yeah," complained Kevin. Or was it Mike? Starr could never tell Darcy's twins apart, even when they were side by side. Between the twins sat a child she'd never seen before. A thin boy with flaxen hair, who stared apprehensively at her from pale blue eyes. Any moment she expected him to take flight like a frightened sparrow.

Starr removed her coat and hung it in the hall closet. "I wasn't expecting company. As I recall, Monopoly can take hours."

"I'm winning," SeLi bragged. "I have all the railroads, Park Place and loads of money."

"Beginner's luck," scoffed Kevin glumly, counting a small stack of money tucked under his edge of the board. "It's Morgan's game, and he doesn't have any property at all, and less money than me."

Starr shifted her gaze back to the thin blond boy. *So this is Harrison's son,* she thought. The boy seemed little more than an anemic shadow. No wonder his father was worried.

Aloud she asked one of the twins, "Where's your mother, Kevin? Why aren't you kids upstairs?"

The twin she'd been certain was Mike answered with a self-conscious giggle. "'Cause Dad got home early. He and mom are in the bedroom doin' whatever they always do when he comes back from a long trip."

The boy's mirror image chuckled and threw a punch his way, "Shh, Kevin. That's private stuff."

Starr blushed and glanced at the only other adult in the room. She expected him to make some typically male comment, but surprisingly he didn't even meet her eyes. It was the kids who snickered and Clay who put a stop to the laughter and changed the subject.

"Morgan finally met Mike and Kevin today. This seemed like a good way to break the ice, plus give Darcy and Joe time alone. We would've used the penthouse," he said, "but Vanessa is in bed with a migraine. When SeLi offered your place if I'd chaperon, it made sense."

His dark eyes asked for her approval. She remained silent, and he spoke again, "SeLi's a natural. I can't believe the kid's never played Monopoly before. She has a mind like a steel trap when it comes to figuring money." His gaze slid back to the girl. "She said her mother never finished school. Perhaps SeLi's talent comes from her father."

Tired as she was, Starr resented his chitchat. Though his last remark was stated flatly, his tone implied a question, and it was none of his business, anyway. While she searched for an appropriate end to the conversation, SeLi chimed in with, "Hey, Mom. Are you gonna stand there all night shootin' the breeze? You're bugging us."

The child flopped onto her stomach and rested her chin on one hand. It was obvious she was copying Clay. Even more so when the girl dismissed Starr with a wave of her bare feet and demanded, "Whose turn?"

Following SeLi's lead, the others settled back into their game. Even Morgan McLeod appeared to relax.

Clay lifted a shoulder and an eyebrow simultaneously.

"What about dinner?" Starr demanded tightly. "Did anyone think about food?"

"Yeah, sure." SeLi raised her head, momentarily distracted. "Clay's gonna get us all hamburgers and french fries when we finish here." She tossed her mother an impish grin. "He promised not to tell Wicked Wanda I was eating takeout again."

Starr almost choked. What did *he* know about her ongoing battle with SeLi's social worker? She pressed a hand to her temple. Maybe she was overreacting. Why would he care? After all, he'd set this up for Morgan—or so he claimed. The man gave her a bad case of nerves, that was all. Starr closed her eyes and extended the minimassage to both sides of her head.

"Do you have a headache, too?" Clay asked, sounding genuinely sympathetic.

Starr dropped her hands and retreated a few steps. "No."

Clay sat up and made a slow survey of her body. He paused longest on her face. "A hot shower does wonders for tension."

Sympathy was the last thing Starr wanted from him. She opened her mouth, intending to send the bunch of them packing.

"Look," Clay said, anticipating that she was about to toss them out. "The kids are really having a good time. Let them finish this game. Maybe by then, Darcy and Joe will have completed their, ah, whatever." Almost without volition his gaze strayed to Starr's lips and clung there a moment. "I'll take care of the food. Maybe we'll forget the hamburgers." He ignored a chorus of moans. "I make a mean spaghetti dinner."

Starr felt herself slide under the spell of his lopsided smile. She smiled back, even though every nerve in her body rejected his plan. He was dead right about her needing that shower. Although she doubted mere soap and water could wash away all her tension. Especially since he was responsible for a large part of it.

She sighed. "Finish your game. A shower would be nice. By then I'm sure Darcy and Joe will want the boys home for a family dinner."

"Agreed," Clay said. "Don't rush. Kevin just bought Marvin Gardens and put up a hotel. That may slow SeLi down. I've tried to tell her not to get too cocky, because in this game moguls come and go." He laughed.

As Starr escaped into the safe haven of her bedroom, she thought about the easy way he dealt with children. Whenever *she* had SeLi and the twins, she was constantly breaking up arguments. Barclay McLeod's charm obviously spanned all ages. Senior citizens like Blevins and his wife, the young waitress at the restaurant and now an assortment of kids. Starr was careful not to include herself in his fan club.

And she was careful to lock her bedroom door. Charming he might be, trustworthy—not. The way his eyes had assessed her a moment ago told her his mind wasn't only on Monopoly.

Starr made short work of shedding her clothes. She gave a heartfelt sigh as she stood beneath the soothing spray of the shower. Her mind, however, refused to be soothed.

So the coolly beautiful Vanessa McLeod suffered migraines. Well, Harrison's little brother needn't look to *her* for consolation.

Liar, liar, hummed the water beating down on her tired shoulders. She didn't want to feel anything for him except dislike. But in truth, every time she thought she had him pigeonholed, he did something unpredictable.

Wrapped in a fluffy towel, Starr stared into space and considered the problem he'd presented by suggesting they dine together. Cooking for someone seemed so…so *personal* to her. Maybe that was an old tape, though. Her mother had always ordered the cook to fix gourmet meals for Samuel Lederman whenever he roamed. Starr had never been able to eat those meals. It was all such a farce. She still hated polite pretense.

But darn it, the man who was making himself at home on her carpet had been the reason she'd missed both breakfast and lunch today. She wasn't about to let him ruin dinner, too, she decided, vigorously brushing her auburn curls until they crackled with static. She was ready for dinner. More than ready. How long would it take a budding tycoon to win her first game of Monopoly?

After pulling on comfortable slacks and a baggy sweater, Starr realized she did feel better. Good enough to face an unwanted guest. Besides, the sooner they decided what to eat and got it eaten, the sooner Clay would leave.

The moment Starr stepped into the living room, she was hit by a flying body. "Mom, Mom, I won! I won!" SeLi hugged her mother around the waist.

"Good for you, honey." Starr returned the warm squeeze.

"I just love games, Mom. Moe says he has lots more. He said he'd teach me to play every one. Isn't that bitchin'?" Her jet eyes danced excitedly.

"SeLi!" Starr clapped her hand over the child's mouth.

Kevin and Mike weren't fazed. They were busy putting away game pieces, and from their long faces, it was easy to see they didn't share SeLi's delight. Morgan had a dejected slump to his shoulders, which told Starr he hadn't expected to win. Something about his resignation touched her heart.

She looked for the boy's uncle and found him seated comfortably on the couch, his arms draped carelessly over the back cushions. He was absorbed in watching something on TV. A football game. Once again Starr was struck by this homey scene.

It was more than a little unsettling. She'd neatly labeled him arrogant, egotistical and most assuredly a playboy. Anything but the relaxed family man he now appeared to be. Shaken, Starr deftly disentangled the girl's arms. "Win or lose, SeLi, everyone cleans up," she said, pointing at the scattered play money. "When you guys get this stuff put away, we'll decide what to do about dinner."

Clay turned and studied her dispassionately. "We took care of it while you showered. If you hadn't locked the door, SeLi might have checked to see if our plans met with your approval. The way it stands, Joe and Darcy went out to pick up hamburgers. Joe said it was a small price to pay for an hour alone with his wife. Surely Witchy Wanda can't object to burgers, fries and milk shakes. That would be un-American," he teased.

"*Wicked* Wanda...and you don't know her," Starr said. "She'll stop at nothing to take SeLi..." Catching herself, Starr let the sentence drift off.

Clay recalled his morning visit with the social worker and suffered a momentary stab of guilt. But nearby sat the reason for that visit. Two children. One dark and brimming with vitality, the other fair and timid. Each desperately wanting, needing a father. Clay hardened his heart. If Harrison was to blame or, more to the point, if he was in trouble of some kind, who better than his brother to have both kids' interests at heart?

Joe and Darcy's timely arrival kept Clay from pressing Starr for answers. If his brother had erred, Clay didn't understand why he'd risk repeating his mistake. Except that when Clay looked more closely at Starr, with her creamy skin, her stunning hair, her beautiful eyes, he knew. The thought of Harris spending nights here, wrapped in her arms, left him wanting to shake them both.

CLAY'S MOOD seemed to shift once he'd helped Joe and Darcy carry their burden of food into the kitchen. Starr was puzzled by it and thought, if he was going to turn surly, she wished he'd take Morgan and leave. Or she did until she saw the boy's first tentative smile. Then she relented. Morgan wasn't to blame for his uncle's roller-coaster disposition.

The noise level rose as all four children squeezed into her small breakfast nook. Nor did it taper off after they had their food in hand, which prompted Darcy to shout, "Why don't we take ours to the dining room, Starr?" Without waiting for an answer, Darcy and Joe picked up the remaining burgers and shakes and spread them out on the dining table.

Starr stepped between her friends to pass out plates and napkins. She noticed Joe and Darcy holding hands beneath the table like young lovers and felt a momentary stab of envy. Almost as quickly, she shook it off. It was SeLi's fault—all this talk of wanting a father.

The adults had no sooner begun to eat than Joe started relating a funny story. The phone rang, forestalling his punch line. Starr would have excused herself to answer it, but sank back into her chair when she heard SeLi grab the kitchen extension.

"Mom, it's a man," she announced, poking her head around the door. "You wanna take it here?" The receiver dangled from one catsup-covered hand, a mashed hamburger from the other.

Starr grimaced. "You guys go ahead. It's probably a salesman with one of those deals I can't refuse." Studiously avoiding looking at Clay, she rewrapped her burger and stood just as Joe finished his joke.

Starr tried unsuccessfully to stifle her laughter as she picked up the phone and said hello. Joe's jokes were always silly, and she was always taken in.

"If I'm catching you at a bad time, Starr, I can call back. SeLi should have said you had company." The low masculine voice threw her for a minute.

"Senator?" she squeaked, her gaze unconsciously flying to his younger brother. Instantly she flushed, although there was no reason. Cupping a hand around the receiver, Starr lowered her voice.

Clay was watching her.

"Joe arrived home earlier than expected," Starr murmured. "He, Darcy and the boys are here for dinner. It's noisy. Let me take this on the extension in my room." She purposely left out mention of Morgan and Clay so as not to hurt the senator. Did he even know his family was still in town? she wondered.

"SeLi, hang this up, please. I'll take it in my room where it's quieter. A business call," she added for the benefit of the adults, who'd fallen silent.

Leaving the room, Starr could feel Clay's eyes burning into her back. She prayed Joe would start another of his funny yarns.

Clay's misunderstanding of her dealings with his brother—even if his brother had created that misunderstanding—was reason enough to take the call elsewhere. Not only that, the very nature of their business necessitated privacy. Starr sat on her bed and reached for the phone. "I'm back."

"I understand you're already assembling equipment." The senator began without preamble. He explained which lab would be running the tests, said he'd arranged for airplane couriers, then at the end exclaimed, "Oh, say, Starr. Judge Forbes called about something—an unrelated matter—and in the course of our conversation, I cleared SeLi's travel with him. It's quite all right."

"I wondered how that came about. I thought I told you I'd talk to Wanda."

"Sorry. I hope it didn't cause you any problems."

She recalled her bitter exchange with the social worker. "Nothing out of the ordinary," she muttered.

"Good. Good. Everything's running right on schedule, then." Harrison spoke with the assurance of a man long used to being in control. "Now about the weather—that's a different ball game. Unusually cold. I'm told it gets up to about thirty degrees in the mountains during the day and down to minus ten at night."

"We'll freeze, Harrison!" Starr burst out. "Minus ten?"

"You want to put off going in until spring, kid? I don't want anything happening to my favorite biochemist."

He laughed when he said it, but Starr frowned. If this situation was as serious as he'd led her to believe, they might be condemning a whole herd. Starr didn't think it was anything to joke about.

"I'll survive," she said firmly. "As you know, I'm a resourceful person." She *was* resourceful—but he wielded the power. That had been evident the night SeLi's mother died. Starr had managed to scrounge a bed and blankets for a frightened little girl, but it wasn't enough for social services. They wouldn't approve her efficiency apartment for a night, let alone longer. The minute the senator offered her this place and Wanda's supervisor got a look... well, attitudes changed.

The senator had helped her. Starr knew she was returning the favor by helping him now—on her own terms, to be sure—and by not insisting that he divulge the truth of their relationship. But how could she tell him that Vanessa and his son were cozied upstairs with his own brother? Starr had already decided that she couldn't when suddenly a long shadow fell across her bed. She almost dropped the phone, but hastened to grab it before it hit the floor.

She gasped at the sight of Clay McLeod in her doorway. He might have one thumb hooked casually over his low-riding belt, but there was no mistaking the icy resentment in his eyes.

"Uh, I've got to go now," she murmured into the receiver. "Yes. We'll touch base before I leave." Hesitating, she frowned and said more softly, "I will take care . . . Bye." A click and a hum signaled that the senator had hung up.

Starr's heart pounded unevenly. She tried to act nonchalant as she replaced the receiver. She sensed more than saw Clay push away from the door and move toward her. Her hand remained on the phone. How much had he overheard? What, if anything, had she said about the actual project?

In a moment he hovered over her.

"I was just coming back," she said, dredging up a smile. "Thank goodness for microwaves. That burger will be stone cold by now."

Clay bent and smoothed the back of his hand beneath her jaw. "So, you'll freeze without your lover to keep you warm, eh?" His controlled voice was dangerously soft. "Some business call, Starr. Monkey business?"

Starr felt trapped. What could she say, bound as she was by a promise of secrecy? "No, you don't understand." The protest sounded feeble even to her ears.

"Oh, I think I understand," he said. "By the way, in case you care, Darcy, Joe and the boys went home. They gave up waiting for you to remember your manners. They were good enough to see Morgan home. And SeLi went to take a bath." His eyes glittered.

"You should have left, too," Starr said. Knowing she was virtually alone with him made her feel a little like a mouse cornered by a cat.

"I was just thinking it was a good thing I stayed—to see if *I* can't warm you up." As his work-roughened hands settled softly on either side of her face, Starr did indeed begin to feel an infusion of heat. It started at her toes and worked its way up her body.

"No," she whispered, even though part of her yearned to say yes to another of his kisses.

"Yes," he countered, saying it for her, lips a scant inch from hers.

At exactly what point the test of wills sparked genuine passion between them, Starr would have been hard-pressed to say. But somehow, one or the other closed the distance, bringing their lips together and Starr squarely into his arms. His mouth came down hard, then softened at once to a downy whisper.

The room around Starr faded as reality became a sudden feverish exploration of lips and hands.

Clay sank down beside her on the bed and trailed kisses toward the deep *V* of her sweater. He groaned. Wanting to touch more of her skin, he tugged it up from the bottom.

She ignored the brush of cool air across her lower back and leaned into his welcoming heat. When his fingers released the catch of her bra and freed her breasts into his waiting hands, Star skated smoothly past a boundary she rarely let any man cross.

Seeking the same freedom to explore him, she reached under his cable-knit sweater and separated the pearl buttons that ran down the front of his shirt. Her pursuit of his skin was stopped by the wide, silver buckle of his belt.

His control slipping, Clay let himself be dragged to the brink by what he knew to be Starr's practiced onslaught. Falling backward with her across the wide bed, Clay stripped off his sweater—in preparation for any or all pleasures she had to offer.

Dizzied by the comfort of his broad chest and the feel of his damp tongue tracing her ear, Starr missed hearing SeLi call out that she'd finished her bath.

Clay heard. He tensed and rolled away, cursing his lack of foresight in not closing and locking the door.

Unceremoniously dumped on the center of the bed, Starr sat up and surveyed Clay without comprehension.

He scrambled to his knees and passed a calming hand over his eyes.

Starr followed, trailing a hand up his chest.

It took more than a small effort on Clay's part to get off the bed and leave her there. His hands shook visibly as his fingers fumbled with the snaps on his shirt. Dammit, he didn't *want* to want this woman. He only wanted her out of Harrison's life. Was that so difficult to accomplish?

Starr saw the cold mask that dropped over his eyes. It edged out her glow of desire. Full realization of what had happened hit her when the weight of her sweater made it slide down, brushing the sensitive tips of her nipples.

She wanted to rage. She wanted to cry. Doing neither, she climbed off the bed, pointed at the door and said without any inflection, "It's time for you to leave now."

Clay shrugged into his sweater. Oh, she was a cool one, all right, damn her sweet little hide. With a brittle laugh, he chucked her under that haughty chin and murmured, "Like I said, you're easily warmed—but not by my brother. Not anymore." Looking her in the eye, he missed the twin spots of color that blossomed on her cheeks. "Is that clear, Starr? This is the last time I'm going to tell you to leave him alone."

"But I...I..." His hateful derision sparked a quick denial, until in the next breath she remembered how much was at stake. With the entire state of California on the edge of bankruptcy and a herd of endangered sheep dying, what did it matter if one man had a terribly false impression of her? And especially this man, who was far from sainthood himself.

But saintly or not, Barclay McLeod made her want things no man ever made her want before. Why was that? Darn it—life wasn't fair. Her stomach heaved in anger, then sank in despair. And she might have taken him to task for his own infidelity had she not heard SeLi skipping down the hall.

Struggling to maintain a semblance of dignity, she stepped past him to her bedroom door.

Clay didn't know when to let up. "If Harrison invited you to spend Christmas at the ranch, consider yourself uninvited. I've spoiled *this* love nest for you, and I can damn well spoil another."

"Get out," Starr snarled, grasping the doorknob for support. "Out of my bedroom. Out of my apartment. Out of my life." She was beginning to shake, and she hated having him see her fall apart. "You don't know *anything.*"

He moved close and stroked her cheek, ready to deliver a parting shot just as SeLi bounced into the room, her smile aglow.

Frilly baby-doll pajamas seemed at odds with her impish grin. For a moment she balanced on her toes, then with a muttered "Oops," backed from the room.

"SeLi, stay." Starr's plea sounded almost desperate.

The girl poked her head back inside apprehensively.

"Mr. McLeod and I were discussing some, er, unfinished business. He was just leaving," she said brightly. "Let me lock up after him, then I'll come tuck you in and read you a story. Did you have a nice soak?"

"Sure thing, Mom." SeLi glanced uneasily from one adult to the other. "You guys had business like Joe and Darcy, huh?"

Starr gasped.

It was all Clay could do to hide a smile.

Starr gripped SeLi's shoulder tightly. "We certainly did not..." Growling in frustration and not finishing her sentence, she loosened her hold on the child and marched purposefully toward the front door. SeLi, wise beyond her years, didn't need something like this added to her education.

Lips compressed, Starr opened the door and gestured Clay out. She hated it when his arm accidentally brushed her, and hated it more that her body reacted predictably.

He whirled suddenly, stopped and dropped an impersonal kiss on Starr's forehead. Near her ear he murmured, "Out of the mouths of babes..."

She recoiled, but not before he felt the fine tremor his kiss had caused.

"G'night princess." Clay aimed a smile and a wave at SeLi over Starr's shoulder. Sliding an arm around

Starr, he tugged the doorknob from her limp grasp and closed the door with a solid bang.

They heard his jaunty whistle as he headed down the hall.

What Starr didn't know was that he stood staring at the elevator for a long while, waiting to regain his own balance.

SeLi sighed and feigned drama, bringing a wrist to forehead. "Like I said before, Mom, whatta hunk!"

"To bed," Starr snapped. "I can think of several more accurate adjectives to describe Barclay McLeod, most of which would get your mouth washed out with soap. Now scoot—the subject is closed."

"But Mom, I gotta go see if the Christmas star is out. Nana Patrice swears it's magic."

She looked so eager Starr didn't have the heart to refuse. She wanted life to be magic for SeLi. Together they ran to the window. Both were disappointed to see only fog.

In his suite of rooms in the penthouse above, Clay gazed from a window that overlooked the bay. He'd searched until he found a stale cigarette. It was a habit he'd kicked months ago but now felt a desperate need to renew, thanks to the woman downstairs.

After two drags of the tasteless tobacco, he angrily crushed it in a spotless ashtray.

Leaning against the cool glass, Clay watched the wispy whorls of fog obliterate his view. Occasional searchlights from the harbor cut through the mist, making ghostly, shapeless patterns on the wall above his bed. His mind locked on the pulsing circles of light.

Clay wanted—no, *needed* to stay furious with Starr Lederman. It sounded simple; why was it suddenly so hard?

CHAPTER SEVEN

FOR THE BETTER PART OF two weeks, Starr managed to dodge Clay. Monday—with Christmas break starting on Thursday—she picked SeLi up at school. In frantic haste they hit the malls, looking at Christmas decorations and shopping for Starr's parents and SeLi's friends on the wharf.

"I can't decide what to get Trader John," SeLi wailed. "He has a pipe and never has tobacco to put in it. But he loves to play cards and his deck has one missing. He found it in the trash, so he and Woody hafta pretend."

Starr's heart gave a little lurch. She'd always had so much—at least material things. "Get John the tobacco and Woody the cards. I thought we'd buy them each a warm jacket, too. Yesterday when we saw them, I noticed theirs were thin and frayed."

SeLi's eyes misted. She scrubbed at them. "Way cool, Mom. I bet they never had nothin' brand-new before. But things get stole, ya know."

Swallowing back her own emotion, Starr cleared her throat. "Yes, well, I saw some advertised where they'll embroider a name on the pocket for free. If we get one green and one blue, that should work, right?"

Tears slid down the child's cheeks. "R-right." She sniffed into her sleeve as she curled her fingers tightly around Starr's hand.

Starr smiled and gave her daughter an awkward hug around the packages they both carried. "Who's next on our list?" she asked brightly.

"Mike, Kevin, Moe, and can I get something for Clay?" The tears were fully banked now, and the dark eyes gazed imploringly at Starr.

"Oh, SeLi, I don't think…" Starr's voice ended in a little catch.

"Please, please, please." SeLi finished with a skip and a bounce before Starr could restate her objection.

"Honey, we don't know the McLeods well enough to buy them gifts. Moe might feel obligated to get you something in return." It was late and Starr was too warm. Plus, she was tired and hungry. "Let's put these in the car and grab a bite to eat at Good Earth while we look our lists over again."

"Good Earth? Where we went with Stanley Stud? Yuck."

"SeLi." Starr pressed her lips, then decided to let it go. "I thought you liked their soup. Anyway, it's almost time for Wanda's monthly visit. I have to mention that we've eaten something nutritious."

"Okay." SeLi kicked one toe against the other sneaker. "But I ain't gonna change my mind about gettin' Moe and Clay somethin' for Christmas."

Starr pursed her lips, for all the good it did.

Later, somewhat renewed, they shopped again. SeLi managed on the money she'd squirreled away to combine the twins' gifts into a single board game. That left her enough to buy Morgan and Clay each something small.

Starr resigned herself to the fact, saying over and over, 'Tis the season, until they rounded a corner in one department store and collided head-on with the two males under discussion.

"Sorry." Clay reached out a hand to steady Starr, but it was too late. She lost her grip on a bag, which fell to the tile floor with an ominous crack, followed by a sickening tinkle.

"Oh, no!" she said, bending quickly to reach for the Baccarat bell she'd bought to add to her mother's collection.

Both children's eyes widened in horror. Clay knelt, too, picking up the bag first and said, "God, I'm sorry. We were looking at those picture frames and . . . well, this is a blind corner. Not expensive, I hope." His dark brows dipped.

It was. Very expensive. Although Starr wasn't about to tell him. He would assume the money had come from his brother. She shook her head, trying to make light of the incident.

But SeLi blurted, "It cost a hunnerd and twenty dollars."

Clay leapt to his feet, the bag clinking in his hand. "One hundred and twenty dollars? What is it, a Ming vase?"

Flushed, Starr snatched it out of his hand. "It *is* a collector's bell. Maybe what we hear is the clapper. Good day, Mr. McLeod."

"Wait." He caught her arm. "Moe and I were just going to get chocolate sundaes. Will you and SeLi join us? We can check the extent of the damage."

Starr glanced away. Why did he have to have such a winsome smile? Damn. Maybe the wrong brother was in politics. All she wanted to do was escape. But the kids were dancing up and down, and frankly she was ready to give up shopping for the day. "All right," she agreed grudgingly. "Will Morgan's mother be joining us?"

"No. She's ill. Anyway, do you think I'd put her in such an awkward position?" Shifting his packages, he reached to take Starr's.

She pulled back sharply. "Thank you, but I believe you've done quite enough damage for one day. And I don't need to stay and be insulted."

"I'm sorry, Starr. Don't go. The kids will be disappointed."

Starr looked around for SeLi, only to see that she and Morgan had joined hands and were skipping happily toward the ice-cream parlor. She sighed.

Clay followed her gaze. "They get along well. They've bonded...like kin."

Glancing at the children, SeLi with her dark braids slapping the back pockets of her jeans and Morgan so fair, Starr had to laugh. "That's some imagination, McLeod. For those two to be related would take multicultural blending in a Cuisinart."

As Clay reached for the door Morgan had opened to allow them through the door to the parlor, he frowned down at the top of Starr's head. Was it true—or was it meant to throw him off? He had no chance to question her further, because the small place was packed. And later, Starr refused his offer to walk them to her car.

Driving home, Starr thought she'd scream if SeLi said one more word about the man they'd just left, who had apparently become her idol.

"Wasn't it big-o of Clay to say he'd get Nana Patrice a new bell?" SeLi said for at least the tenth time. "Tomorrow, after school, he's gonna bring Moe to our place to play Parcheesi. Is it like Monopoly? Do you think we can have them stay for dinner again, Mom?''

"No. Absolutely not.''

SeLi pouted. "Why not? We all gotta eat.''

"I don't want to discuss the McLeods. They have their lives and we have ours. Morgan's mother hasn't been well. I'm sure she'd like them home.''

"She doesn't. Moe said. Jeez... at this rate, I ain't never gonna end up with a dad.''

Starr almost lost her grip on the wheel. "SeLi, you have to get that idea out of your head. He's the last man I'd consider. Give it up. Besides, tomorrow night we have to wrap these gifts. Wednesday we'll deliver them. And we have to pack. Friday we leave. One of my father's staff is delivering the motor home to us. I thought we might have to fly to L.A. to pick it up, but he called to say he had business here. Guess you'll have to wait for your first airplane ride.''

"Clay's got his own plane. Bet he'd give me a ride.''

"Enough, SeLi.''

The girl crossed her arms and sulked. Then, she sat up and asked, "Do you think Nana Patrice lied about that ol' Christmas star? I ain't seen a single star all week.''

Glad to be off the subject of the McLeods, Starr smiled. "I was born in Southern California. Stars are more visible there in the winter.''

"Izzat where we're goin' on vacation?''

Starr thought about having to drive a bulky motor home over the twisting Grapevine, south through the L.A. interchange. "Through there and beyond," she murmured.

Seemingly satisfied, SeLi leaned back and smiled.

Starr yawned, enjoying the welcome respite. In her head, she rechecked all that needed doing. But if time seemed short for her, the bighorn sheep had even less. Which was an awful, sobering thought.

FREE WAS THE FIRST WORD that came to Starr's mind as she maneuvered the lumbering motor home across the Oakland Bay Bridge in the quiet morning fog and picked up highway 580 southbound.

The past week had been draining.

Every time she turned around she'd tripped over Clay McLeod. She'd even packed the motor home in the middle of the night to avoid him. Thanks to Stanley, Clay knew she'd planned a trip to the San Jacinto preserve. Thank goodness he didn't know the exact dates, and she didn't want him—or SeLi, for that matter—to see her stashing Christmas gifts in the vehicle.

Not that she anticipated trouble. But in case she didn't get results within the allotted week, she'd packed presents and Christmas-tree decorations.

Her mother, bless her, almost lost it when Starr wouldn't promise to be back for *the* Christmas Eve party. There was a certain dentist Patrice Lederman wanted her daughter to meet.

Starr smiled. She'd deliberately left seeing her mother until the last minute because she could quote the lecture verbatim.

"Starr, you're crazy! *Cra...zee!*" Patrice had said— as Starr, of course, had known she would. "Whatever possessed you to take a child and go off into the wilderness?"

Nor was that all. "A man, that's what you need. A man to take care of you and SeLi. Just the other night

I met a divorced dentist at my group therapy who'd be perfect for you. Let me fix you up.''

Her mother was always trying to fix her up. First it had been a young psychiatrist with more problems than his patients, followed by a fortyish attorney looking for wife number five. Next had been a fairly decent-looking metaphysicist. Only it turned out that he wore more crystals than Merlin and spent most of a very boring evening talking about how their auras intertwined.

Good grief. If a man was single and had sufficient money, Patrice considered him a suitable candidate for marriage to Starr and roped him in to attending one of her famous parties. Starr's smile faded. Sadly she wondered if her mother would ever grow up.

She cast a quick glance at SeLi, who for the first time had nothing to say. The girl's excitement had peaked last night. She'd nearly driven Starr to the brink of distraction with her endless questions. And when Starr put SeLi to work gathering cold-weather gear, SeLi was convinced she'd lied—that they were going to Alaska where she'd never see the Christmas star. Now the same child sat in the passenger seat with her nose glued to the window, not wanting to miss a single rooftop in the slowly waking city.

Starr exited the Piedmont interchange, and she breathed a sigh of relief as the highway widened and traffic thinned. "Is something wrong, SeLi?" she asked ten minutes later. "I've never known you to be quiet for this long."

Button black eyes met Starr's. SeLi spoke in hushed tones. "Are you sure you can drive a house, Mom? I didn't know they came with wheels. Sometimes it looks like we're hangin' right off the road."

Laughter bubbled from Starr's lips. SeLi was always so remarkably self-possessed Starr hadn't considered the possibility that she might find this new experience frightening.

"Relax, kid. My dad used this on location for years. I cut my teeth driving it when I was sixteen. I'm a little rusty, but we've got a long stretch of wide, smooth road ahead to practice on. Check the map and pick a good spot for lunch. Remember, you're my official navigator."

SeLi stared at the pictures on the cover of the state map. "Moe's been to Disneyland oodles of times," she said. "He doesn't like the Pirates' Cave or the Haunted House, 'cause he says they're scary."

Starr took her eyes off the road long enough to watch SeLi touch the colorful pictures. A trip to Disneyland was something she was keeping in reserve until the adoption was final. She didn't want Wanda accusing her of trying to buy SeLi's affection.

Sounding very adult, SeLi said, "Moe's afraid of his own shadow. Kevin calls him wimpy." She grimaced. "For sure he's nothin' like his uncle Clay."

Starr's palms grew damp on the steering wheel at the mention of Clay.

SeLi flopped back in the seat and squirmed until she found a comfortable spot. "Moe doesn't have a dad, neither," she said abruptly. "That's why Kevin said that—'cause Moe told us he cries about it at night." SeLi's brows rose. "I told Kevin I'd smack him if he teases Moe again. I ain't cried for ages, but I know how Moe feels."

"But Morgan does have a father," Starr said. Noting SeLi's shock, Starr wondered why she'd opened her mouth. Still, wasn't it best to tell SeLi the truth?

If Harrison was right and Clay and Vanessa eventually went back to the ranch, SeLi might never see Morgan McLeod again. Just now, however, SeLi wasn't willing to let the subject drop.

"Who's his dad?" she demanded.

"Senator McLeod, Seli. You know, the man I'm doing this project for? Morgan's parents aren't living together at the moment, but that doesn't change the fact that Morgan has a father. One who loves him."

SeLi sat unmoving for so long Starr had about decided she'd either accepted the explanation or dismissed the subject. All at once she said, "Ain't that dude too old to be Moe's dad? Moe's mom's no older'n you."

Starr cleared her throat. "Fathers come in all sizes, shapes, colors and ages, SeLi. There isn't just one kind. I'm sure the senator would be a good father if he wasn't so busy. I know for a fact that he misses Morgan."

But instead of picturing Harrison in a fatherly role, Starr's mind conjured up his younger brother. A haunting memory of Clay intruded—the way he'd looked teaching the children to play Monopoly. It sent her heart rate up a notch or two. She forced her mind onto other things.

Shortly thereafter, although the motor home was running well, the monotony of mile after mile of farmland created a dull ache behind Starr's eyes. She stopped for an early lunch and a chance to study the map showing the maze of Southern California freeways.

Starr used to divide her time between her mother's home in Sausalito and movie sets in Hollywood with Samuel Lederman. Back then, she'd been proficient at jockeying the network of super highways. Her eyes clouded; she'd always hated being bounced between her parents like a rubber ball.

Trying to hide her disquieting thoughts, Starr helped SeLi out of the motor home. A brisk wind caught her poplin rain jacket, and she rubbed the tension from her neck; already the air smelled cleaner.

"Look." She turned SeLi's head into the east wind and pointed out the snow-capped Tehachapi Mountains in the distance. Rising sharply from the valley floor, they resembled a row of vanilla ice-cream cones.

Starr shared her daughter's excitement until it dawned on her that the Tehachapis weren't as high as the San Bernardinos, where they were headed. Starr thrust aside the vague worries and embraced the warmth of the small roadside café. Soon mother and daughter delighted in the antics of a family of birds outside the window.

"Come on, SeLi," Starr said reluctantly a good hour later. "Time to go." She sighed and patted her full stomach. "We've eaten enough for four people. If we don't hit the road, I'll curl up right here and take a nap."

"Me, too." The child yawned. "What time is it? What do you think the guys are doin'?" she asked wistfully.

"Homesick already?" Starr chided, although she suffered another quick, sharp vision of Clay laughing with the children. "Some world traveler, huh? We've barely left our own backyard."

SeLi skipped up to the cashier, making light of her momentary longing for home by talking Starr into buying her a candy bar, which she promised to save for later.

Starr topped up the gas tank, and their afternoon passed in a blur of miles. SeLi made a valiant effort to carry on a conversation, but the gentle sway of the big vehicle soon lulled her to sleep. Starr's heart swelled each time she glanced over at her. She loved SeLi so much. One dusky hand curled sweetly against shining black braids. In sleep she was an angel.

Wanda Manning had made threats before, but the last one seemed different. More dangerous. Enough to leave icy tentacles around Starr's heart. Still six long months before the adoption was final. Six months of Wanda chipping away at their foundation.

Were her reasons for wanting to adopt the child sound? Starr kneaded the back of her neck and thought about how many times she had longed for a brother or sister. Now SeLi was obsessed with fathers. Starr's neck muscles tightened again. She had no plan to remedy *that* situation anytime in the near future. None whatsoever.

Although one man's kisses certainly melted her shoelaces.

Increasing traffic soon claimed Starr's full attention as she entered the spiderweb of the Los Angeles freeway system. The motor home lumbered down the right lane of highway 210. Starr swore aloud when she discovered that getting to the Pomona freeway necessitated moving three lanes left.

SeLi was awakened by the blare of impatient horns. White-faced, she watched Starr slip the massive vehicle between two irate drivers.

"Holy shi—" SeLi, eyes wide in her chalky face, clapped a hand over her erring mouth.

"Don't panic, kiddo," Starr said. "We'll soon be out of this mess and we'll take a short break." They did, and in spite of SeLi's cajoling, Starr kept the length of the refueling stop to a minimum. She didn't want to tackle a winter mountain road after dark.

As they left the main highway in Banning, the road narrowed and began a steady climb.

SeLi hovered on the edge of her seat with her nose flattened against the window. Though she was enthralled by the thick stands of pine and cedar, she also seemed terrified by the tight hairpin curves. One moment she'd be saying "Look at that!" and pointing out some spectacular sight. The next she'd pelted Starr with strident cries of "Look out, Mom!" as she watched rocky cliffs drop off sharply below.

"Oh, Mom, look. Snow!" The little girl cupped her hands around her eyes and leaned into the side window. The high beam on the motor home's headlights picked out broad white patches in a deep, granite crevasse.

Starr glanced over, then pulled her eyes back to the road in time to slow down for an oncoming pickup and dim her lights. "Mmm, yes, I do see. Sit back and be quiet please, SeLi. I can't concentrate on driving with you demanding that I look elsewhere every two seconds." Because she met and passed another large motor home just then, her tone rose more sharply than she'd intended.

SeLi fell back in a pout. "It's gettin' too dark to see the trees and stuff, anyhow. I wish I hadn't come on this dumb old trip."

Even though she felt for SeLi's frustration, Starr didn't dare take her eyes from the winding road. Besides, she was simply too tired to pander to SeLi's mood at the moment.

Darkness closed in swiftly. Icy stars shed little light. Starr wished she'd taken a motel in Banning for the night. Beyond each new curve, the terrain grew more wild and rugged. Plots of snow along the fence seemed deeper against the posts. Turning on the heater only made the windows steam. Starr grumbled as she rubbed a larger peek hole with a jacket sleeve wet from an earlier attempt.

When at last the road leveled a bit, they were in a mountain community called Alandale. Starr vowed to pull off at the first overnight campground that came into sight. Easier said than done. The first recreation area was closed for the season, the next full of permanent residents.

Starr dug out their jackets and huddled beneath hers while she listened to the park owner's discouraging comments.

"You can try Pearson's in Pine Cove, little lady," he drawled tugging at one earlobe. "This ain't exactly tourist season. Most places hereabouts are closed up tight."

Zeroing in on what he *wasn't* saying, Starr knew that he thought her an idiot to be out here alone with a small child. Still, she thanked him politely through chattering teeth and climbed back into the driver's seat, determined to find a space to rent for the night. As the engine roared to life, her breath left vapor trails hanging in the night.

"I'm cold," SeLi sobbed. "Let's just go home, can we, Mom?" Starr felt like Simon Legree.

Pine Cove offered nothing and Idyllwild was shut up so tight it might have been a ghost town. Starr turned into a byway tracked with frozen snow and dropped her head to the steering wheel for a moment.

"Blast," She stiffened her spine and reached for the briefcase where she'd stowed the address of Harrison's ranch in the next valley. She'd be darned if she would navigate back down to Banning in the dead of night.

"It won't hurt to borrow the McLeods' parking strip for one night," she muttered, gazing through her icy breath at a hastily scribbled map. Harrison had offered hookups for the motor home. At the moment, Starr was too tired to stand on principles. And it'd just be for one night.

She drove slowly for another thirty miles until she spotted the turnoff. From there the cumbersome rig bumped uncomfortably along a graveled access road. SeLi remained huddled against the passenger-side door. Only her blinking black eyes attested to her misery.

Snow now lay in great patches near the roadside. Starr was about to give up when the wavering headlights illuminated a wooden sign reading Cloud Haven. She released the breath she'd been unconsciously holding. Beyond the sign, nestled in a stand of ice-encrusted trees, Starr identified a darkened house. Exhausted, she didn't give it another glance; her only interest lay in the concrete pad located some two hundred yards across a moonlit clearing. After the big vehicle came to rest on smooth cement, she could have kissed the pole holding the hookups.

She strained to see any sign of life. Harrison had mentioned a foreman. "No big deal," she grunted, stepping into the frosty night air. "I'll find him in the morning and explain. Surely I'm capable of hooking up a few cables."

"Maybe not," she muttered, after numerous attempts to connect the cables slung under the low motor home to the electrical box on the pole. She gave up and rubbed her aching arms. The long hours behind the wheel had taken their toll. She shifted from one foot to the other and blew on icy fingers. It felt as if she'd been messing with the hookups for hours. In reality it had been only minutes. Apparently some kind of adapter was needed to mesh the motor home's hoses with the facilities at the ranch.

As if that wasn't bad enough, the knobs on the butane tanks refused to budge. Starr wanted to cry—and might have, if SeLi hadn't been sobbing enough for both of them.

She hugged the little girl close until her tears abated. "Things'll look better in the morning, honey. The best we can do now is break out that down-filled sleeping bag, climb into our warmest jammies and try to get some rest. Tomorrow we'll find a new place." Starr was swamped by guilt as SeLi's tears resumed.

Once the engine was turned off, the interior of the vehicle cooled quickly. Starr rummaged through their suitcases with fingers that felt like ice cubes. Even the light from her one flashlight was growing dim. She was angry with herself for not having a better backup plan.

SeLi's mood improved slightly when Starr suggested she eat the chocolate bar she'd bought earlier. Then after being helped into her woolly, footed sleepers, the little girl burrowed into the sleeping bag without loosening her braids. Ruefully Starr resigned herself to dealing with SeLi's sore head in the morning along with everything else.

"Sleep tight." She aimed a kiss in the vicinity of the girl's hidden forehead, then turned to take care of her own needs. Too bad there was only one down sleeping bag. Teeth chattering, Starr gathered blankets from a box and piled them in a heap on the mattress next to SeLi.

She delved into her suitcase and found the first humorous thing about the entire day. Adult footed sleepers. Starr muffled her laughter in the fuzzy fabric—hot pink and chartreuse stripes that glowed eerily in the pale moonlight. The glow-in-the-dark sleepers had been a gag gift at last year's office Christmas party. SeLi must have found them buried in her bottom drawer and tossed them in.

"It's so-o-o c-cold," she stuttered. "Maybe these things are a blessing in disguise." Hopping on one foot, she yanked them on over her socks and jeans. She snapped off the flashlight, then dove under the pile of blankets. And stirred only once, partially wakened by a droning vibration. As the noise receded, Starr curved more comfortably around SeLi's warmth.

Suddenly she was jolted completely awake by a loud banging that seemed to rock the motor home.

SeLi moaned, turned onto her back, then relaxed in sleep again.

Starr rubbed her eyes. The interior of the motor home was swathed in inky blackness, and the cold air stole her breath.

As the noise escalated, Starr searched blindly for her flashlight. But when found and clicked it on, her frightened gaze met only continuing blackness. The batteries, already weak, had apparently given out. Starr tossed the worthless thing aside.

The pounding seemed to be coming from the area of one door. That could only mean the foreman had discovered them. At least, she assumed that was what it meant, since burglars didn't, as a rule, knock.

For a few seconds the pounding stopped. Starr watched as a light beamed through a window and flashed around the cab. Using this trail of light, she made her way to the door. She opened it a crack, shivering in the frigid night air. A gust of wind jerked the door from her grasp and slammed it into the side.

"Hello?" she called uncertainly. Another gust of wind ripped her words away. Starr heard the shuffle of feet moving along the cement and strained to see who was approaching. Too soon she was forced to raise a hand to ward off a blinding light.

"What the hell?" a voice muttered. Starr froze at the familiar voice. Surely her ears were playing a cruel trick. God wouldn't punish her like this. Fighting to calm her racing heart, she blinked, still trying to see the face behind the dazzling light.

Abruptly the beam lowered to her feet, and the pupils of Starr's eyes constricted to counter the sudden plunge into nothingness. Again the light moved slowly up her body, and again she was sightless in its wake. Not, however, before she identified the man holding the annoying beam.

"You!" The one shocked word was all that tumbled from Starr's blue-tinged lips.

Deep laughter skipped away on the frosty air, and the light bobbed.

"You look like a phosphorescent Easter Rabbit in that getup," said Clay McLeod, making an unsuccessful attempt to stifle his laughter. "Somehow I would've thought Harrison's tastes ran more to a different kind of nightwear." Again he struggled to rein in his mirth.

"What are you doing here?" Starr demanded. She stared with envy at his denim, sheepskin-lined jacket.

He could keep the dark Stetson he'd pulled low enough to hide his laughing eyes.

She tried to melt behind the door.

"Isn't that my line?" he growled. "Unless something's changed, this is where I live."

"Clay? Clay?" A trilling voice pierced the black night. Starr glimpsed a pale blur hovering in what appeared to be an open door at the main house. "Did you find out who's camped on our land?"

"I've got everything under control, Vanessa," Clay shouted. "Get back in the house out of the cold before you catch your death."

Jealousy ripped through Starr, unwarranted though it was. Damn him for worrying about his brother's wife when he didn't seem to have any qualms about keeping *her* standing in subzero weather.

But what did she care? If he let her stay the night, tomorrow she'd be gone—even if she had to find a place in Banning and drive that mountain every day, she vowed with a return of spirit.

She stepped back into the motor home, determined to get out of the cold. Clay, however, had other ideas. His wide shoulders blocked her attempt to close the door.

"Please…" she began tiredly. But he climbed in and held up his hand to silence her and flashed his light around the paneled walls.

"Good Lord, woman, it's as cold as a well digger's knees in here."

"Really? I hardly noticed." Her sarcasm was lost on him.

"You're not in the city. Turn up the damned heat." He stepped closer, enveloping her in a ring of light.

"My God, your lips are blue and you're shaking like a leaf."

"I can't turn up the heat," she said defiantly. "I couldn't figure out how to hook up the electricity."

"Doesn't this fancy rig have butane?"

It killed her to say, "No. The tanks are frozen closed."

Clay grinned and touched her cheek. "Somehow I didn't think that was your normal nightly attire. But what the hell was Harrison thinking, not to give you a key to the house? After all, he had no way of knowing I'd be here. I only decided today."

Not thinking how it might sound, Starr blurted, "Did he even know you and Vanessa were still in San Francisco? I certainly didn't tell him."

Clay let his hand fall away. That night at her place when they'd shared—what?—kisses, she'd claimed he misunderstood her relationship with his brother. Lord, but he'd wanted it to be true. He really had.

After all, when two men coveted the same woman, it spelled trouble in capital letters. And if those two men were brothers, it spelled disaster.

What a fool he was to come chasing after her. But Blevins had insisted it was a simple vacation. "Go back to bed," he ordered gruffly "I'll hook up your electricity and we'll discuss this in the morning. I still have to secure my plane."

"Plane?" Starr echoed blankly. She was numb from cold and exhausted. No wonder he looked so fresh, he hadn't spent twelve hours on the road.

"I'll lock up after you leave," she said stiffly.

"Do that." He slammed the door on his way out.

Dazed, she fumbled with the lock, turned on the electric heater, then stumbled back to bed where she lay awake staring at the ceiling. Maybe she could slip away early—she found the promise of further confrontation with Barclay McLeod distressing.

And what reason dared she give him for being here? What could she say that wouldn't jeopardize Harrison's project?

Unless—the thought left her breathless—he really was spying for some advocacy group and had followed her. If so, was there a way to let him know that they were really on the same side? How could she, though, and not risk spreading needless panic and confusion?

Lord, what a mess she was in. "You're here to find out what's killing some bighorns, and that's all," she muttered, plumping her pillow. "Leave the politics to Harrison."

Comfortable at last with her decision, Starr closed her eyes. The reassuring clicks emitted by the now-running electric heater were as beautiful to her ears as the most exquisite music.

CHAPTER EIGHT

STARR AWOKE to the smell of coffee. As she lay there trying to connect mind to body, the aroma of burned toast overpowered the more pleasant odor.

"SeLi?" she called when she discovered the down bag lying empty.

All trace of last night's misery apparently erased, the girl skipped through the door to their sleeping quarters. Her heavy pajamas had been discarded, but she still wore crumpled jeans and the shirt she'd slept in. Recently unbraided hair fell in corkscrews down her back. She paused long enough to view her mother's striped pajamas with a smothered giggle. "Holy shi—! Where did you get that neon prison suit?"

Starr raised a warning eyebrow, and SeLi switched to wheedling. "Get up, Mom. Get up! Wait till you see outside." Bright eyes twinkled. "It's snowing! It's snowing!" She twirled and clapped her hands.

"What?" Starr leapt up and yanked aside the curtain over the bed. "Oh, no," she groaned. "That's awful." She wiped a hole in the condensation with a corner of the blanket. Not a blizzard, but most definitely a snowfall. The trees around the ranch house were dusted white. Even as she watched, large, fluffy flakes drifted lazily toward the ground and settled softly on the covering of white already there. "But last night the stars were out!"

She sank back on the bed just as SeLi returned with a steaming mug of coffee. "Gosh, Mom. Did you see the Christmas star?"

"What?" Starr closed her eyes, savoring the first mouthful.

"You know, the *Christmas* star. The one I been wantin' to see."

Starr shrugged. "Honey, I was pretty busy driving. Maybe you should forget that silly star."

"No." SeLi crossed her arms. "It's not silly."

Soothing her daughter with a hug, Starr let her mind forge ahead to the condition of the trails leading into the preserve.

A loud knock shook the coach. Starr slopped hot coffee down the front of her sleepers and her breath stalled as SeLi ran to open the door. Damn, she'd intended that both she and SeLi would be up and gone by now. It was Morgan McLeod who stood outside, though—not his darkly handsome, very annoying uncle.

The boy's pale face was nearly obscured beneath a snow-covered wool cap pulled low over his ears. A light blue snowsuit and thick mittens added pounds to his thin frame.

"Mom! It's Moe!" shouted SeLi excitedly. A blast of frigid wind swept a trail of wet snowflakes along the vinyl flooring.

"Uncle Clay wants you to come to the house, Ms. Lederman," Morgan said politely. "And can SeLi come out and play?" Two pairs of bright eyes looked expectantly at Starr.

She smoothed tangled curls over one ear and tempered her retort. After all, Morgan wasn't responsible for his uncle's arrogance. "I can't go anywhere until I've showered and dressed."

Noting their long faces, she added, "No reason for SeLi to wait. Provided you stay where I can see you from the window."

Their happy cries were Starr's reward. "Wait there, Morgan," she directed. "It's too warm for you to come inside the way you're dressed. I bought SeLi a snow-suit. It'll only take a minute." Actually it was with the Christmas gifts she didn't want SeLi to see yet.

"A snowsuit?" SeLi's dark eyes glowed. Smiling, Morgan plopped down dutifully on a snowy step.

"Stay close and don't let yourself get too cold," Starr cautioned a few minutes later when SeLi, covered except for her face, joined the boy outside.

"We won't," they chorused, playfully scattering the white powder with booted feet.

"I'll bet." Starr smiled as she shut the door. She envied them. It'd been ages since she'd played in the snow. But duty called, she decided as she washed her hair. Then there was Clay's summons. She pulled a wry face.

While in the shower, Starr remembered a set of brochures she'd picked up from a travel agent. She backed out of the tiny bath and stopped midflight on her way to find her purse. Clay McLeod's rangy body lolled comfortably on her couch. His legs, clad in jeans, stretched into the middle of the floor. One of her coffee mugs rested on his knee.

Starr's heart failed to beat. She wasn't certain how long he'd studied her towel-draped body with that lazy smile.

"Big improvement over the sleepers," he said, gesturing with his cup.

Starr ignored the pulse that suddenly hammered in her ears. "What are you doing here? I told Morgan to tell you I'd be over later."

Clay's smile faded instantly. He sat up straight, gripping the mug between his knees with both hands. Why did she have to look so damned appealing? It was hard not to notice that her skin shone like sculpted marble, since so much of it was showing.

Unfortunately the real reason for his visit spoiled the view. "I brought a message from your lover."

"My what?"

"Harrison called this morning and got Hank Rogers, my ranch foreman. Oh, he hinted around, asking about the weather and did we have any unexpected guests. Hank didn't know what the hell Harris was talking about. *I* know he was checking on his precious Starr."

"No. I...he...we...I intended to stay else-where," she said.

"Don't blame you a bit. A wife gets in the way. Don't worry, sugar. I didn't say a word about your atrocious nightwear when I called him back. I'm sure he's much more used to seeing you as you are now."

She sighed, refusing to let him provoke her further. "You've delivered the message you came to deliver. Now I want you to leave."

"All in good time. When I lit into Harrison, he fed me the same crap you obviously laid on that poor devil, Stanley—about some phony project. You really should keep your stories straight. The Blevinses think you and SeLi are on vacation."

"Stories str—" Starr broke off to grab the large towel she'd wrapped about her body. It had slipped when she sucked in her breath. She gathered it close and raised her chin. "I can't have a reasonable conversation with someone as narrow-minded as you. Now would you kindly have the decency to go? I'd like to dress.''

"Good idea," he snapped. "Get some clothes on. It's damned difficult to concentrate with you standing around looking like some centerfold." Clay rose and glared at her. His towering height seemed to shrink the already small space. "I'll just warm my coffee."

He brushed so close Starr could feel the heat of his body through her towel.

"Do that," she spat, determined not to flinch. "You've had a lot of practice making yourself at home." She couldn't help tossing a barb. "Won't *Vanessa* wonder what's keeping you?"

Clay paused, gritting his teeth. Oh, how she loved to taunt him with his brother's infidelity. Only this time she'd gone too far. He spun away from the stove, sending Starr into full retreat, which forced him to yell at her through the thin wall. "Maybe you'd like to know that I left Van on the phone with Harrison—discussing divorce."

"Divorce?" Starr stuck her head out the sliding pocket door. She held a bulky sweater over her breasts. "Wh-what about Morgan?" she asked, recalling Se-Li's story about the boy crying in the night for his father.

"What about Morgan? His world is topsy-turvy. Has been for a year. But they say kids are resilient. So maybe in the end his life will improve."

Starr thought about how she herself hadn't been at all resilient as a kid. "Easy for you to take the cold-hearted approach," she sneered.

Clay looked as if he was about to explode.

Starr couldn't think why. But of course, he must feel guilty.

"Just get dressed," he said, turning his back on her and curling both palms around the edge of the counter.

His anger was almost palpable. Starr felt better once she was safely covered—in tan cords and that bulky sweater. In control again, she stalked past him, jerked open the front door and peered around outside.

"What in damnation are you doing now?" he asked, addressing her slender back. Lord, but that woman fit a pair of cords nicely. And her getting dressed hadn't done a thing to slow his pulse.

"I'm checking on SeLi. She isn't used to this weather. In fact, this is the first time she's seen snow. I worry about frostbite."

Clay gave an offhand shrug. "The kids are okay. They went over to the house to warm up and play checkers. I decided they'd had enough snow for the first time out. Promised them we'd take a look at their snowman."

Starr slammed the door hard. One of the many things about Clay McLeod that annoyed her was his take-control attitude. He might assume responsibility for Morgan, but he had no right to make decisions for SeLi.

"Since you're leaving, please send SeLi home."

"What's the hurry? They're having a good time." Clay lowered his gaze and sipped from his cup. Had he really expected to shake Starr up with news of Harrison's divorce? She was probably gloating. But she was a fool if she thought Harrison would marry her in an election year.

Clay watched through his lashes as she crossed the room to fill her own mug. *Damn her!* He'd like to wring her beautiful neck. He choked on a swallow of coffee. Who was he trying to kid? If he didn't leave now, he'd do something stupid—like carry her back to the bedroom and make very thorough, very passionate love to her.

Slamming his mug down on the counter, Clay got to his feet and stalked toward the door. To hell with Harrison, his mistress and her trumped-up project. It gave him immense satisfaction to know he'd upset their little rendezvous.

Starr gazed openmouthed as he stormed out, slamming the door without even a word of farewell. "Of all the nerve," she fumed aloud. "Who does he think he is?"

She peered out a small window, and her heart wrenched a little as she watched his lithe form move through the new snow. When the door to the ranch house shut hard behind him, she flinched.

Forget him, she told herself. *Save your feeling bad for Morgan and his father.* But the pain lodged in her heart said something different. Tall, lean, moody Barclay McLeod awakened yearnings in her that no other man had ever stirred. It helped only marginally knowing that when all of this was over, he'd know how wrong he'd been about her.

But at the moment, Starr reminded herself briskly, she wasn't here to moon over a man. Her mission was to find out who or what was killing those sheep. In fact, this would be a good time to read the file she'd picked up from a friend in the Sierra Club.

Starr dug a manila folder from a pocket in her briefcase. She sat down and quickly became engrossed, even though the legalese was often difficult to wade through. After reading three documents, she

thought she'd pretty well figured out what the data
boiled down to: yet again, some smooth-talking federal politician—someone like Senator McLeod—had
talked about oil and how the situation was "critical to
national survival" to sell the state a bill of goods. Oh,
there were phrases like "limiting exploration to non-
destructive seismic tests," but Starr knew how often
companies and their people stepped over those ambiguous lines. It was her fear, as well as the fear of other
conservationists, that unless tighter controls were ex-
ercised, accelerated exploration might scatter or de-
stroy herds it had taken years to build. Sierra Club
members foresaw elimination of entire subspecies if
wilderness protection was breached.

Starr sat back and pondered. Dedicated to saving all
animals, she viewed these oil explorations as a threat to
the Wilderness Act. Realistically, though, the deed was
done. Senator McLeod hadn't single-handedly cracked
the moratorium, but he bore much of the responsibility for exploiting its ambiguous clause here in California.

She got up and began to pace. Should she back out
now? If she did, who would Harrison and his cronies
get to replace her? Someone. Their kind always did.
Maybe someone not as interested in the fate of the
sheep. Or was she conjuring up tigers in the night where
there were none? She continued to pace.

That was the way SeLi found her an hour later when
she burst through the door, her cheeks rosy from the
crisp air, her lips curved in a happy smile.

"Moe taught me how to play chess." As usual, SeLi
talked with her hands. "We had hot chocolate and
marshmallows in front of a fireplace bigger than two

of Nana Patrice's. And we built a giant snow dude in Moe's front yard. Did you see him, Mom? Did you?''

For a moment Starr stared blankly at her daughter. Then with ease, she made the transition back into motherhood.

''Why don't I come look now?'' she asked, knowing she needed a break. ''I'm glad you had a good time, Skeeter.'' Starr tweaked the girl's button nose, then dived into the closet for her boots.

''Know somethin', Mom? Moe's mother is beautiful. When we first got inside, Moe thought she'd been crying. She was better after Uncle Clay came back. They stayed in the kitchen a long time. Say, do you think Moe's mom might be real sick, like my mom was?'' The child's concern wasn't feigned.

Starr's back stiffened involuntarily. ''Barclay Mc-Leod is not your uncle,'' she snapped, not really meaning to. The minute she saw SeLi's face begin to crumple, she said more gently, ''I just mean he's *Morgan's* uncle. Don't you think he'll take care of everything?''

SeLi still didn't seem mollified. Starr wished she could retract her jealous outburst. SeLi had suffered during her mother's long illness, and sickness of any kind truly worried her. Starr hugged the girl and stroked her hair. ''I'm pretty sure Moe's mom isn't as sick as yours was.''

When the child sighed and nodded, Starr took a heavy jacket from the closet and shrugged into it. ''Hey, let's go check your snow dude, huh? Then I want to talk to Mr. Rogers, the ranch foreman, about borrowing a horse. How would you like to take a horseback ride?''

SeLi barely contained her excitement over the prospect of seeing a horse up close, but her patience lasted long enough for Starr to properly admire the snowman. It was somewhat lopsided, and they joked about the way it leaned. The fun didn't quite outweigh the fact that the sooner Starr found out what was killing the sheep, the sooner she'd be free of all the McLeods.

Hank Rogers was pleasant enough, but he was adamantly opposed to Starr trekking into the high country alone.

"I told Harrison and I'll tell you, young woman—only fools go up as high as the bighorns with the weather this unpredictable." Faded blue eyes studied her from a solemn, weatherbeaten face. "You don't look like a fool, miss."

Starr met his gaze with a frown. "Today I'm only planning to ride to the viewpoint. I ride well. I'll take good care of the horse. I'll do my own saddling and rubbing down. I'm also an experienced biochemist, Mr. Rogers. Believe me, I have great respect for Mother Nature's fickle ways."

The old foreman's snort might have been accompanied by a smile, but if so, it never reached his eyes. "I'd feel a sight better if Clay wuz to go with y'all," he drawled. "He's out checking on a cantankerous bull. Can't this wait?"

Starr's fingers tightened around SeLi's shoulders. She could feel the tension in the slender frame as the child eyed the black horse that nudged the man's shoulder. "Uh, Mr. Rogers, my authorization comes from Senator Harrison McLeod. This doesn't concern his brother." Starr bit her lip, afraid she'd revealed too much even at that. But the possibility of being accompanied by Clay into the white wilderness sent her into near panic.

The old man narrowed his sharp eyes as he jerked a battered cowboy hat over his furrowed brow. "Everything on this ranch concerns Clay McLeod, young woman. The sooner you accept that, the better."

Better for whom? wondered Starr, watching Rogers stalk away. "Is that a yes?" she called. When he nodded curtly, she smiled and tried to contain SeLi, who punched the air and yelled "All right!" at the top of her lungs.

"SeLi, stop hopping about before you scare the horse." Starr did her best to restrain the excited girl. "I know you're ready to be off, but saddling up takes time."

SeLi squealed with a mixture of fear and delight some time later, when Starr boosted her onto the saddle of the dancing black gelding and quickly climbed on in front of her. As the horse responded to a mere touch of the heel, SeLi buried her head in her mom's back, and let fly with a barrage of expletives.

"SeLi! When will you learn that new experiences aren't license to swear like a seaman?"

"I'm sorry, Mom. Sometimes it just slips out." But she didn't remain contrite for long. "Do you think Moe could come with us some time? He said he never gets to go near the horses 'cause his mom doesn't want him to stink like one." She squeezed Starr. "I think it's a nice smell. A lot better than the wharf."

Starr laughed, her breath mingling with the wispy vapors from the snorting, blowing horse. Why did she find it amusing that Vanessa McLeod disliked the smell? It was that faint, earthy aroma mixed with a musky hint of leather that Starr found so compelling about Clay McLeod. She wasn't attracted to men like the ones her mother paraded around, who smelled of lemon and spice. And those she worked with carried an ever-present odor of medicinal soap. Barclay McLeod smelled wonderfully male by comparison.

Starr jerked her thoughts from their errant meanderings.

As it turned out, the vista proved to be a brisk ride from the barn. Once there, it was as if nothing moved in the vast wilderness except the restless horse beneath her. Starr muttered under her breath about forgetting her binoculars. Deep down, however, she knew the chance of sighting a bighorn from here was practically nil. She'd need to go higher.

"You know, SeLi—" Starr's voice shattered the stillness as she turned the horse from the magnificent panorama "—neither you nor Moe will be able to ride with me when I'm working. I'm afraid it'd be too dangerous."

"I s'pose," SeLi replied, sounding reluctant. "I gotta do the homework Prissy Polly sent, anyway—if I don't wanna give Wicked Wanda new ammo."

"SeLi," Starr scolded. "use proper names."

"Yes'm," came the innocent reply.

Starr really didn't want to argue. She was only too glad to see the corral come into sight.

Dismounting stiffly, she worried that it was too late to look for another place to park the motor home. The sun had dropped unexpectedly behind a thick layer of clouds. Starr shoved icy fingers deep in her jacket pockets in an effort to warm them before unsaddling the big black.

"You go on to the motor home, Skeeter. You can get out fixings for grilled cheese sandwiches. We'll have

them with hot soup. How does that sound?'' Starr
stamped her boots to aid circulation in her partially
numbed feet. It was beginning to spit snow again, and
she wanted to settle the gelding.

"Sounds real bad," SeLi shouted over one shoulder
as she skipped off.

Starr laughed; to SeLi, bad really meant good. She
pulled the horse toward the shelter of the barn and began to uncinch the saddle.

The barn door crashed open. Starr jumped and
grabbed at the saddle as it slid down the black's
steaming flank.

"Where in hell have you been?" Clay growled from
the doorway. With piercing eyes, he assessed the condition of the horse and shortly thereafter Starr's wind-
reddened cheeks. "Well," he demanded, "I'm waiting."

"Bully for you!" she snapped, shaken by his sudden appearance. Unfortunately he'd been uppermost
in her thoughts all day.

With one powerful wrench, Clay hefted the saddle
she was struggling to hold and deposited it easily beside a row of similar gear. He tossed a rough cloth her
way. "Rub him down and feed him."

Seething, Starr began rubbing the horse with vigorous strokes. "I intended to do just that. You are not my
keeper, McLeod. I don't owe you any explanation.
Harrison told your foreman I could have a horse." She
bit her tongue to keep herself from adding, *So there*.
Suddenly she was rudely spun away from the flank
she'd been drying. Clay's long fingers clamped tight
around her upper arms. His blue eyes glittered dangerously and his lips were compressed so tightly they
were almost hidden in his day-old stubble of beard. He

pulled her toward him, until her face was within an inch of his. "Get one thing straight. Harris runs the affairs of state, but I run this ranch. Understood?"

Momentarily mute, she nodded. By all rights she should be furious with his high-handed manner. Instead, his unexpected nearness undid her. Heat pulsed between them. They both felt it, and both grew still.

The big horse shifted, straining to reach the measure of oats someone had put in his feeder. His hindquarters brushed Starr and shoved her into the stall. Afraid of falling, she groped blindly with her hands. What she connected with was Clay's flannel-covered chest. Two snaps popped on his shirt, revealing thick springy chest hair. As her fingers tangled in the crisp strands, her tongue seemed to cleave to the roof of her mouth.

"Did Raven step on you?" Clay's arms, suddenly gentle and protective, herded her farther into the stall to make way for the big horse.

Starr's soft curves followed the lines of his harder body. The air around them all but sizzled as Clay sank with her into the hay and initiated a kiss he couldn't quite seem to dominate.

He thrust. She parried in the duel for control—or submission.

Starr's cry of surprise softened soon enough to a moan, and she slaked her thirst for kissing him back.

At that moment Clay McLeod was iron and heat.

She was jelly. Hot, bubbling, melting jelly. Thick and sweet, she flowed over him. Clay wouldn't—couldn't—have called a halt even if he'd been so inclined. Which he wasn't. Having tumbled like a KO'd boxer, Clay was more than willing to stay down for the count. Provided they both got rid of some of these clothes.

Plenty warm, Starr didn't object when he delved beneath her jacket. The snap of a button from her blouse hitting the hay only joined the fireworks going off in her head. His kisses did that to her.

Clay sighed when at last his hands touched her soft flesh. No words passed between them as he paid homage to first one perfect breast, then the other.

Starr let herself be swept along on a tide of new feelings. She reveled in the first rasp of his tongue, and the second. Suddenly, though, amid the pleasure, the sound of childish voices beneath the window outside intruded.

"SeLi," Moe whispered loudly. "Whatcha doin? Mama sent me to find Uncle Clay."

"Shh," SeLi hissed. "I'm lookin' for that Christmas star I told you about. It's too dark, I guess. Your uncle and my mom have been in the barn a long time." She sounded only marginally concerned. "I'm s'pose to go get out bread and cheese, but this is real 'portant. I got me a wish that needs magic."

"I wish on stars all the time," he bragged. "Just find one and say, 'Star light, star bright, first star I see tonight. Wish I may, wish I might, get the wish I wish tonight.' "

"Gol-ly! I didn't know that. You think any old star will do? My Nana Patrice said it hadda be the Christmas star."

As the children's words penetrated, Starr began to pull away from Clay. Prickly straw had embedded itself in her naked back. Realizing what had poked her, she struggled to get up. *Lord! What if Morgan or SeLi walked in on us?*

"Starr," Clay murmured, his fingers seeking the zipper of her tan cords.

"No!" She batted at his hand and scooted away.

He nipped her earlobe and then soothed away the sting with the tip of his tongue. Mesmerized by her eyes, which glowed like fine jewels, he gazed down at her and said fiercely, "I won't share you with my brother, Starr. Not with any man."

"Shh, you oaf. Get off me." Starr shoved him hard and sent him rolling across the hay. Panting, she said in a hushed voice, "Where's my blouse? Morgan and SeLi are right outside."

Clay jackknifed into a sitting position. "Forget them. I want this settled between us now. You may go for a ménage à trois, but I'm a little old-fashioned. So you tell big brother to buzz off, or I will."

The strangled noise she made in her throat nowhere near matched the outrage she felt in every fiber of her body. "You arrogant— I'll ménage-à-trois you. What do you call what you, the senator and Vanessa have going?"

Clay laughed. "That accusation is so ludicrous it's funny."

"Yeah, right," she said as she slid into her jacket and zipped it up to her chin. "I'm leaving. I hope you plan on taking care of that horse."

"Don't try to turn the tables on me or change the subject, Starr. Come on. We're getting too old for this. Don't you prefer the luxury of a soft bed?"

As Starr watched him calmly stuff his shirt back into his jeans, she stifled hysterical laughter. Why was he taking his time? Why was he talking at all? Didn't he hear the kids at the door? As she left the stall, he raised his voice.

"I can't figure out the harebrained scheme you and my brother have cooked up. But let me say this—I expressly forbid you to ride into the high country alone. If you *are* here to do some kind of tests, tell whoever sent you to get a professional to do their dirty work."

Hand on the door, Starr drew herself up to her full five foot six. "I *am* a professional, you goof."

Clay walked over and framed her face with gentle hands. "Trust me, sugar, even you can change."

Starr pushed his hand away. "Listen to me. I—we—oh, what's the use? And don't call me sugar!" Frustrated, she jerked at the door, which opened to reveal Morgan, looking confused.

Clay tensed. His smile slipped.

Brushing past the boy, Starr didn't know what else she could say that wouldn't dig her hole deeper. She had to get away from here. Had to find another place to rent a horse.

"Wait!" Clay hollered when it seemed she wasn't going to stop. "If you really are here to do some work on the preserve, maybe I can help." He bent down, and with a few words, sent his nephew trudging back to the house. Seeing Starr's steps falter, he rushed to catch up.

Someone had once told Starr that the best defense was a good offense. "All right." She slowed her steps. "We had a report that a couple of rams died up on the preserve. I did my master's thesis on the bighorns. I'm here to run some routine tests. From time to time I'll need a reliable horse."

"Rams died? Of what?"

She should have known he wouldn't let it go. "That, Mr. McLeod, is what I'm here to find out."

He gripped her arms.

She stepped back. "I'm not here to be mauled by you. Tomorrow I'll find a new place to park."

"Hold on a minute."

"I can't. I need to go check on SeLi."

"What's my brother got to do with this job of yours?"

"Nothing." Starr crossed her fingers behind her back. "He just offered me the pad here, but I've changed my mind about using it." Turning, she started to leave.

"You won't find another pad with hookups in this area."

She kept silent and walked faster.

He turned and walked backward in front of her, blocking the wind. "The kids are good for each other," he said quietly. "The real reason I came out to find you this afternoon was to ask if SeLi could join Morgan tomorrow. We're trimming the Christmas tree. The day after, Vanessa has a tutor coming. SeLi mentioned she has some schoolwork. It would free up your days," he said, staying her with a hand.

She shook it off and studied him carefully. She wondered about his ulterior motive, never doubting he had one, and decided the sheep were more important. "Okay. What time do you want SeLi there in the morning?"

"I'll check with Vanessa and let you know."

"Send Morgan," she said. "Either that, or SeLi can run over and find out." Starr burrowed into her jacket as a furious blast of wind struck them head-on.

Grasping her elbow, he stepped in front of her again, but she twisted away.

"Don't touch me," she hissed.

He pressed his lips into a grim line. "If you're waiting for my apology, you'll have a long wait. Liars have that effect on me," he said. "And be assured, sugar, I *will* get to the bottom of this."

Now she'd really done it. Why had she opened her mouth? She ran up the steps shaking so hard she had difficulty opening the door. "I'm not your sugar" was all she managed to say.

Her nervousness wasn't lost on Clay. What in blue blazes was she up to? He vowed not to let her take him for a fool. Just before she slipped inside, he called out a final warning. "Don't try contacting my brother. I'll be keeping close tabs on you."

LATER, AFTER HE'D GROOMED Raven, Clay stood at his bedroom window and watched the lights go out in the motor home. He smoothed a hand over a jaw that needed shaving.

After the last light was out, he dropped down on the bed and pulled off his leather boots. Flexing his newly freed toes, he kicked one boot across the room and watched it slide down the wall. If only Vanessa had a bit of Starr's fire, her husband might not be looking elsewhere.

He lay back on the pillow, fully clothed, arms crossed behind his head, and wondered why he gave a damn about any of them. It was their miserable little triangle and it didn't concern him—or rather, it *shouldn't*.

Still, he puzzled over what he knew. A single woman who bucked all odds to adopt a dock child. His brother, involved in the adoption up to his ears, even though his own son lacked a father. How long before the Manning woman shed some light? he wondered.

With a groan he stroked his eyelids closed. What he saw behind them was Starr Lederman. Beautiful. Well educated. A background of money. Why would she settle for the part-time affections of a married man?

The questions were clear. The answers elusive.

Clay rose and shrugged out of his clothes. Sighing, he crawled naked between gratifyingly cold sheets. He had a ranch to run and bulls to get ready for market. That was his first priority. If he had any spare time, he'd nose around. Otherwise, the best he could do was keep a very close eye on the woman who seemed determined to drive him crazy.

CHAPTER NINE

SUNSHINE SOOTHED the soul, no matter how battered that soul might be, Starr thought as she welcomed the morning rays.

Though the Chinook wind she prayed for hadn't come to melt away the snow covering the ground, neither were there ominous storm clouds in the sky today. Except for deep patches of snow lying under the tall pines and the shrinking remains of the children's snowman, the day might have been trying to herald spring, instead of a not-too-distant visit from Santa Claus.

Stifling a yawn, Starr shrugged into a robe and made her way to the kitchenette. She was surprised to find SeLi and Morgan seated at the compact table putting together a jigsaw puzzle.

"My, you two are certainly early birds this morning." Her yawn refused to be suppressed.

Both children answered her greeting with a giggle. "Moe came with a message for you, Mom. I hope you aren't mad 'cause he stayed—but you were sawin' logs."

"No, no, of course I'm not mad, SeLi," Starr assured her with more benevolence than she felt. "You were both very good." Unfortunately, however, Morgan's very presence reminded Starr of what had gone on last evening between her and his uncle.

"Uncle Clay thinks the tutor will be here tomorrow at nine o'clock. Today, can SeLi help decorate our tree and make gingerbread cookies?"

"Oh, wow! Please, Mom. I never made cookies." SeLi's eyes shone.

Starr felt a pang of remorse. Making Christmas cookies was one of the things she wanted to do with her daughter. Things were so hectic it seemed she never had the time for extras.

"Mom? Don't you want me to make cookies?" A frown replaced her enthusiasm.

Starr put a hand to her head. "It's not that at all. I sort of thought we'd make and decorate sugar cookies when we got back home. My mother's cook used to let me help her when I was about your age. I'd hoped you and I could make it a yearly tradition."

SeLi's frown deepened. "Why didn't Nana Patrice and you make 'em?"

Starr shrugged. "My parents were never home for the holidays. Their crowd skied at St. Moritz—that's a ritzy place in Europe," she explained. "Anyway, my mother isn't very interested in cooking. Remember, I told you that when we invited her for Thanksgiving turkey."

"Yeah." SeLi nodded. To Morgan, she added, "At the last minute Nana called and canceled. 'Cause her tea leaves said for her not to leave the house. Can you beat that? After me and Mom worked so hard to stuff that darned bird, too."

Morgan looked solemn. "My dad does that a lot. Calls and cancels, I mean." His pale blue eyes swept to Starr, and then he lowered his lashes quickly.

Starr felt guilty for no reason. Surely Clay hadn't passed his outlandish accusations on to a child. Although, he might have—to deflect his own guilt. Still hurt, Starr began measuring coffee into the filter.

"So, whaddabout the cookies?" SeLi asked from behind her.

Starr sighed. "It's okay. I don't know that we'll be home in time to do Christmas cookies this year anyway."

"Neat-o." SeLi jumped up and hugged Starr. "Now you can go chase your old sheep and I don't have to stay here and be bored." She plopped back into the chair and tapped a piece of the puzzle into place before she spoke again. "Till Moe told me today, I didn't know a kid could go to school at home. I like to read and figure and stuff—I just hate goin' to school. 'Cause of kids like Buffy Jordan and that smart-mouthed Heather Watson."

Morgan agreed. Then he stiffened and shot Starr a veiled glance, as if waiting for her to scold SeLi.

Starr weighed her response as she plugged in the coffeepot. "The world is full of people like Buffy and Heather, kids. Like it or not, you'll have to learn to deal with them. You can study all the books you want at home, but it's people who make the world go 'round."

"Well, I think Moe's mom has the right idea," SeLi said after a moment's contemplation. "I say Moe's a lucky duck to be taught at home."

Thankfully the coffee dripper emitted its last hiccup, giving Starr a chance to rein in her unwarranted resentment of Vanessa McLeod. "If you're happy, Skeeter, then I'm grateful to Morgan's mother for including you." Secretly, though, Starr felt sad for Morgan, a painfully shy boy who'd obviously had to spend more time with tutors than with peers.

The boy squirmed a minute then blurted, "It was Uncle Clay's idea. He and my mom argued about it last night." Almost reluctantly the boy's half-defiant eyes met Starr's shocked ones. Judging by his manner, she thought he had something more on his mind.

"Do you work for my dad?" The small, narrow chin jutted. "I was s'pose to be in bed, but I heard Mom ask Uncle Clay if you did. I didn't hear Uncle Clay's answer." Morgan's lower lip trembled. "If you do, uh, do you get to see him much?"

The plea left Starr's heart in a vice. There was no doubt Morgan missed his father. The poor kid was confused by the circumstances keeping them apart. What would it hurt to ease his mind? It wasn't like he'd be talking to any advocacy groups.

"I don't *really* work for your father, Morgan." Starr hesitated. What else had Vanessa and Clay discussed? Could be they were talking a different type of work, she thought wryly. In that case, maybe Morgan had heard other, *worse* things about her relationship with his father. Uncle Clay was a master of misinformation.

Regardless, Starr couldn't bear to see Morgan hurting. Gently she said, "I'm helping your father on a special project. We don't work together, Morgan. Mostly over the phone."

The disappointment lurking in those sad blue eyes startled her. Starr leaned her head against a cupboard door as she shakily poured her coffee. If only there was some way she could ease his mind. Except that Clay wouldn't welcome her intrusion into his family's affairs. Although, to hear him tell it, there was no *affair* between Vanessa and him.

No. He'd much rather make her the scapegoat.

Well, maybe she could repair a bit of the damage—without attracting undue attention from Uncle Clay—and help Morgan, too. "Your dad's a very busy man, Morgan. Do you know how important his work is for everyone in California?"

The youngster gave a little shake of his head.

"He's been asked to run for the highest office in the state. It's a great honor. But it's not easy. It means he has to travel, meet as many voters as possible. Even with a tutor, it would be hard for you and your mother to keep up with his schedule."

Starr bit her lip. She should probably have left well enough alone. But darn it, half her life she'd been shuffled between parents—always feeling like she was a bother to both. If by assuring this poor child that Harrison did love him, maybe his Christmas wouldn't seem so empty.

Well, why not?

"Remember, Morgan, your dad loves you very much. Love doesn't change or go away because you two aren't together. I'll bet he's just as lonely for you as you are for him."

Morgan's lashes dropped again. A faint frown etched his brow. After a moment he began to help SeLi take the puzzle apart.

Over the rim of her cup, Starr noticed he sat more erect. Sighing again, she punched bread into the toaster. Was she right to meddle?

IT WASN'T LONG before she helped the children bundle up and watched them walk, or rather race, across the field to the ranch house. As she dressed, Starr vowed to put the problematic McLeod brothers from her mind.

Taking a second cup of coffee to the table, she sat and opened a topographical map of the area. Stanley had given it to her without her asking.

Starr smiled. Somewhere beneath the surface of the dogmatic scientist lurked a soft heart. Too bad SeLi couldn't see through Stanley enough to be nice. If SeLi worried about his toothbrush filling that third slot in their bathroom, she needn't. Starr would never see Stanley as more than a colleague and friend.

Setting thoughts of relationships aside, Starr submerged herself in studying the map and readying her charts, graphs and equipment. Then she familiarized herself with all the disorders known to kill bighorns. The next time she looked up it was noon. A quick check at the window showed Clay on a ladder, busy stringing Christmas lights along the eaves of the house. Morgan and SeLi danced along below. Asking a million questions, no doubt. Starr started to laugh, but a pang of regret gripped her, instead. Why? she wondered as she dropped the curtain and walked to the small refrigerator to pull out a slice of cheese. Because of the Christmas-card picture he and the kids presented out there putting up colored lights against a backdrop of pine trees, lazy cattle and snow? Or because of the sweep of dark hair that drooped appealingly over his brow? Or was it his soft cord shirt, the kind it was a pleasure to touch? He wore them open over snug, ivory undershirts.

Surely she wasn't *that* shallow.

No. Her discontent ran deeper. She'd never been comfortable with the fact that life, especially during the festive holiday season, could appear so normal on the surface, yet be seething with heartache below. Like it'd been for her folks, who trimmed the biggest tree in town and bought each other, and her, the most lavish presents imaginable because it was Christmas.

Oh, for goodness' sake. Starr shook back her hair and returned to her work. Maybe Morgan's uncle *liked* the trappings of Christmas. With the ranch miles from anywhere, it seemed unlikely he was trying to keep up with the Joneses. For a moment, she tapped her pencil idly on the chart. She could walk over there on the pretext of checking on SeLi.

Her heart thudded irregularly. *And say what?* Nothing that wouldn't be patently obvious. Quickly spreading out the map again, she grabbed a pad and began to record the landmarks along her proposed route.

Around two that afternoon SeLi burst through the door. She was spread from ear to ear with gingerbread cookie crumbs. Starr suffered another pang. She'd never seen SeLi so animated. So happy.

But after all, wasn't that part of her reason for accepting this job? To give SeLi a "change of venue" was the way Harrison had put it.

Absently munching on the warm cookie SeLi had thrust into her hand before dashing off again with Morgan, Starr almost choked when someone pounded on the door.

Afraid it was Clay come to harangue her some more, Starr dropped the telltale gingerbread man and dusted sugar from her lips. Then she went to answer the door.

It was him. She just wasn't prepared to see him on an errand of mercy.

"Hi," he greeted her with a lopsided grin. Heavenly blue eyes peered over two large boxes brimming with tangled strings of outdoor lights. "The kids felt so bad about you being stuck inside missing all the fun of decorating that I decided to see if you'd like me to run a few rows of lights around your motor home. Give you a little taste of festivity while you're working."

Starr failed to close her mouth before the impact of his words made the breath catch in her throat. "I, ah..."

He shifted. "You don't have to. It was only a thought."

"Oh, it's a great idea," she said. "I, ah... you took me by surprise, that's all." She hooked her hair back over an ear and stepped back. "Brrr. Feels like it's getting cold again. Would you like to come inside to straighten out the lights?"

"Yeah. I need to do it while the kids are with Vanessa having hot chocolate." He gave a wry grin. "They helped far too much with the others strings. Took me twice as long."

Starr's laugh was immediate. "Been there. Done that. You have my sympathy. Kids can wear you out."

"I don't really mind," he said as he walked inside, stripped off his outer shirt and set to work.

Starr admired the careful way his long, suntanned fingers unwound the strands of bulbs. Her mouth dryer than normal, she decided it would be wise to get some liquid refreshment of her own. Not hot chocolate though. "Unless you need help, I'll go brew some hot spiced cider. A friend of mine puts together a mix every Thanksgiving. It's delicious. When you finish, maybe you'll try a cup?"

"You bet. My dad's specialty at holiday time is hot spiced wine. He calls it *glogg*. Cures whatever ails you."

She grinned. "Odd name."

He chuckled. "I think that's the last thing you say when you slide away from the table. Actually it's Scandinavian. Hey, these weren't quite as tangled as I thought. You put that cider on to bubble. I'll have these hung before you know it."

Starr caught herself humming a Christmas tune as she savored the cinnamon scent that began to permeate the air. The knot in her stomach tightened, but at the same time a strange sense of well-being stole over her.

The weak sun disappeared in a last puff of gold an hour later. Mugs of steaming cider in hand, Starr and Clay stood beyond the concrete pad to view his handiwork.

"Darn. Look there. Three blue lights all in a row. I tried to avoid that." He sounded disgusted and started to hand her his cup as he bent to retrieve the ladder.

"Don't." She caught his wrist. "I like it that way. It doesn't look so commercial."

Her fingers sent a ribbon of heat skittering along his arm. Or could it have been her surprising statement? It didn't strike Clay as something a person with four signed Monets would say. He shrugged and cleared his throat. "I really put them up for SeLi. Kid said she'd never driven around looking at Christmas lights. Seems to have missed out on a lot of other things, too."

Starr felt as if there was some hidden meaning in that gruff delivery aimed at her. Suddenly her pleasure wasn't half so acute. Before she could come up with a way to ask, Clay handed her his empty cup, gathered his boxes and ladder and had turned to leave.

"Bye. And thanks," she called a bit belatedly, still troubled by the jagged barrier that had fallen between them.

Five minutes later Morgan showed up at her door with SeLi. He said the tutor was confirmed for the next day. Starr was relieved, especially now that she realized she couldn't have taken SeLi up the mountain. Nor could she have left her alone, and it was important to get an early start. She felt an urge to hurry, to go after the answers she needed. Because these oddball feelings for Clay McLeod refused to be quelled.

And was it any wonder? As they ate, Starr was forced to listen to SeLi rave about the floor-to-ceiling tree that graced Clay's den.

"Ya oughtta see it, Mom," the little girl explained around a drumstick. "It's got this big star at the top that blinks. Morgan says at night when the lights are off, it looks like the star of Bethlehem." She swallowed then waved the leg in the air. "Is that the same as the Christmas star?"

"You mean the one on the tree or the one we see pictured over the baby's manger?" Starr teased, catching the mood.

"The one over the crib, silly. I know the one on the tree's just pretend. I had so much fun today, Mom. I just gotta see Nana's star. I got a 'portant wish."

Even though SeLi's sentences were disconnected, Starr understood. Biting her lip, she looked away. Darn it, she was still miffed at her mother for feeding SeLi such nonsense. Although in truth, considering SeLi's experience of reality on the docks, a little fantasy couldn't hurt.

"Maybe the star will be out tonight, Skeeter. After we do the dishes, we'll go out and look." Mentally Starr reviewed her sketchy astronomy. Was it the North Star that was so bright? It wouldn't really matter to a little girl dying to make a wish.

SeLi wasn't a lot of help with the dishes. Starr finished drying them and put up lunches, while SeLi did little besides talk about the star. "Is this wish something you want for Christmas?" The notion had just hit Starr. "If so, shouldn't you drop a line to Santa?" For the first time, Starr wondered if she should pay closer attention to this important wish SeLi kept babbling about.

The child pursed her lips. "Moe says if I tell anyone my wish, it won't come true."

Starr rolled her eyes. *Good for Moe.* Now how could *she* find out?

"It's time," SeLi announced. "It's real dark. C'mon, Mom. Get your coat." She rummaged in the closet for her things.

"All right, all right." Starr gave in laughingly.

But in the space of time it had taken them to eat, the clouds had moved in and snugged up against the San Jacinto mountain range. Clay's cattle looked ghostly as they roamed through the pale mist.

Starr and SeLi stayed out only long enough to admire the lights Clay had strung on the house and motor home. Diffused as they were now by swirling frost, they were magical, or so SeLi declared.

"I hope so, Skeeter," Starr said grimly. "I sure hope so. I need a little magic to find out what's wrong with those sheep." She set her full backpack just inside the door for easy access in the morning.

Starr's mind was so filled with sheep that within moments of falling into bed she drifted off without one haunting vision of Barclay McLeod.

Dawn blossomed cold but clear. Starr dressed in layers that could be easily removed when the sun showed its face above the mountaintops. As she and

SeLi trudged toward the ranch house, Starr gave her daughter explicit instructions to stay with Morgan until she returned from the mountains that evening.

Outside the kitchen door she dropped a kiss on SeLi's nose and waited until the girl slipped inside.

Her own soft leather boots crunched across the frozen ground as Starr jauntily made her way to the barn. Once she looked back. The house lay quietly silhouetted against the dark stand of sugar pine.

Starr took a moment to pat each of the horses before she chose a sleek sorrel with a blaze. She based her choice on a gut feeling that the animal was surefooted enough for the high country. As she carried out her preparations, she remembered the last time she'd been in the barn. Intentionally she skirted the area where she and Clay had tumbled in the hay; just thinking about it quickened of her pulse. She pulled the cinch tight and tried to throw off the thought. She was ready to mount when Hank Rogers came in with a couple of the wranglers.

"Good choice, miss," he grunted. "The boss said to give you a sturdy horse. Redwing here is about the best you can throw a leg over." He reached out a gnarled hand and gave the saddle horn a jerk. "She likes a tight cinch, but looks as if you know your stuff." Following the raspy-voiced comment, Hank held the animal's head as she climbed on.

"Thanks for the advice, Mr. Rogers. I'm glad to see you're feeling better about my using the horses."

"None of my business. As long as the boss says. By the way, he asked me to get your route and what time you plan to be back."

Starr toyed with the idea of telling him nothing. But realistically it was a reasonable request. After all, she was using a McLeod horse and SeLi would be in their care most of the day. She hesitated only the length of time it took to sling a dart-gun scabbard over the saddle horn.

"I'm taking Deer Springs Trail to the ranger cabin, then I'm heading up through Dark Canyon Pass. My return will depend solely on what I find. I suppose the snow is still fairly deep in the pass." It was a statement, not a query.

"Hmph," Hank snorted, withdrawing his hand from the reins. "Snow will be pretty deep all the way. If you have any luck at all, it'll have driven the sheep down to around nine thousand feet for food and water. If not . . ." He shrugged.

Giving a quick nod of acknowledgment, Starr kicked the sorrel in the ribs and cantered off at a fast pace. She half tensed, expecting Clay to emerge from the house and stop her. She was at a loss to explain her disappointment when he didn't even show up to wish her well.

Before long a thin sun rose overhead, and the snow-covered passage shimmered as though strewn with crystal. Comfortable with being alone, Starr uncapped her binoculars and paused often to study the jagged promontory for any sign of bighorn. The majestic sheep remained elusively hidden.

She had worked her way well past the vacant ranger station before dismounting to eat lunch. By midday she'd grown impatient with the continued absence of sheep. Although the landscape was beautiful, the eerie silence mocked her failure. So did the certainty of knowing it would be impossible to fade from Clay's life if she didn't find those sheep soon.

Starr ate the last of her lunch for a snack midafternoon and once again settled herself firmly in the saddle. She stood in the stirrups, ruefully rubbing her backside. "Bet I won't sit much tomorrow." She groaned. "I'm out of condition, old girl. Not used to these long hours in the saddle." She patted the sweat-darkened neck of the snorting, blowing horse, who'd just picked her way around a rocky ledge and up a sharp incline.

Suddenly Starr reined in sharply and reached for her binoculars. She trained them on a mound of snow that didn't seem to fit the other contours. Bringing it into focus, she gnawed at her lower lip.

Protruding from the misshapen pile of snow was the gray-brown curl of a massive set of sheep horns. Her stomach knotted.

Quickly she tethered the mare, grabbed her rucksack and slid down the rocky slope until she reached the downed sheep. The ram, a superb specimen, had been dead awhile. Some miracle had saved the carcass from carrion-eaters.

Starr carefully scraped away old snow, removing her gloves long enough to log information on a pad. She found no outward reason for the ram's death. No broken bones, no sign of starvation and no bullet wounds or marks from carnivores. He carried no tag from the game department marking him a weak male. And this was not a time when males fought among themselves.

Starr pushed the hair from her eyes, feeling baffled. This animal had died in the prime of life for no apparent reason. After finishing her examination, she scrubbed her hands vigorously with scoops of fresh snow. Her fingers stung from the bite of the cold.

The next step was filling vials with blood samples. Judging by how long he'd been dead, she doubted that blood would reveal much. Once that was finished, she carefully re-covered the body with snow and stamped circles around it to ward off any scavengers. It was possible she'd need a second opinion later. Depressed at not finding an obvious cause of death, she stowed her gear.

She was so engrossed in the task she was surprised to see that the sun had slipped behind the mountains. She decided not to push on. The wind moaned hauntingly through the jagged rocks, and she shivered. The sound brought with it a longing for companionship. For no reason she remembered how warm she'd felt the other night—in Clay's arms.

And where will those thoughts get you? she asked herself.

"Come on, Redwing, let's call it a day." She sighed. Why, at a time like this, would she want Clay Mc-Leod? It would make more sense to want a fellow chemist to help find answers to this puzzle.

Fortunately a brisk wind stung her cheeks and gave her something else to think about. Behind the wind rolled a new bank of clouds. Storm clouds. By the time Starr reached the corral, the top of the mountain was obscured, and those same clouds had begun to spit snow.

She was grateful for the shelter of the barn and lost no time rubbing down the damp horse. Again she deliberately avoided the stall where she'd shared kisses with Clay. Once the horse was fed, she hurried outside.

A light, steady snow had begun to fall. Starr was thankful for whatever inner voice had prompted her to turn back. Head lowered against the wind, she nearly missed hearing SeLi call her from the open door of the ranch house.

Starr waved. She might as well go in to phone for a courier; she'd also leave a report for Harrison. He'd probably be as frustrated as she was.

Morgan appeared behind SeLi in the bright opening. As Starr stomped into the foyer, it took both giggling children to close the door against the strong wind.

Boots dripping, she hesitated in the red-tiled entryway, quietly surveying Clay's home. This was her first glimpse. She hadn't been prepared to find it so...so homey. "Get your coat," she told SeLi abruptly. "I need to make a couple of phone calls, but it'll only take me a minute."

Her gaze lingered on a fire that crackled cheerfully in a massive beehive fireplace in one corner of a wood-paneled living room. Nearby the children had left a game spread out. Pieces lay haphazardly on a hand-woven Indian rug that had obviously cost a small fortune.

Where did Clay McLeod get off giving her a hard time about her artwork?

The room beyond gleamed in the flickering firelight and the soft reflection of lights on the Christmas tree. Starr felt uneasy about the absence of adults. Where were Clay and Vanessa? In bed? No. Not according to Clay.

Morgan broke into Starr's musing. "Uncle Clay was gonna come find you. He was 'most ready to go when he got a phone call. He told SeLi and me he didn't want you gettin' lost."

SeLi ran up and hugged her mother around the waist, bestowing a quick grin of relief. "Better let him know you got back, Mom. He's in the den. Moe and me'll finish our game.''

Feeling a stab of guilt for her thoughts about Clay and Vanessa, Starr headed in the direction of the Christmas tree. As she entered the room, all she could see were shelves filled with books. Finally, the edge of an oak desk.

A lump rose to clog her throat. She stepped to where she could see better and glimpsed Clay's dark head bent over his desk. He didn't notice her. Starr might have turned and made good her escape if he hadn't glanced up just then.

For a moment he looked happy to see her. Then he frowned. She couldn't hear his conversation over the children's chatter. If his call was private, he needn't think she'd come to pry. But because she was staring at him, she chanced to read his lips. Plain as day she saw, *Thank you, Mrs. Manning, we'll be in touch.* She shook her head, denying what she thought she'd seen. Anyway, Wanda wasn't the only Manning around. What possible reason would Clay have to speak with SeLi's social worker? None. There had to be another explanation.

Releasing her breath slowly, Starr experienced a sense of dizziness. Her stomach seemed to drop. *Honestly, talk about paranoid!* Surely she'd only imagined that Clay smothered a guilty look as he put down the phone and came to meet her. But fingers of doubt had already crept up Starr's spine and into her heart.

Dazed, her mind sorted out every conceivable combination of words he might have uttered. She kept returning to what she'd seen. Working in a busy, noisy lab, Starr—like everyone there—had become adept at reading lips. Yes, she was certain of the words. She just wanted some plausible reason for them that didn't involve her or SeLi.

"Starr." Clay clasped her cold hands in his warm ones. Feeling her stiffen, he let go. "Did the kids tell you I was ready to send out the dog with the brandy?" His twinkling gaze traveled to the pulse beating at the base of her throat, and his smile softened.

Starr could do little but nod and wonder why suddenly her limbs felt weightless.

"Are the kids finished with their game?" Clay asked. *Damn, but I want to touch her,* he thought. *To hold her and drive that wary look from her eyes.* When the weather socked in, he'd been worried sick. In fact, he was getting ready to go find her when that Manning woman called. She didn't have any information. Clay suggested they forget it, but the fool woman wouldn't take no for an answer. Truth was, he no longer knew what he wanted. All he knew was that what he felt for Starr Lederman made him want to believe she was not involved in anything unsavory.

"Did you have a productive trip?" He touched Starr's cool cheek.

She jerked away. "No." Why did she have the feeling that this sudden concern of his was really an elaborate smokescreen?

Clay frowned. He placed a hand at her waist and led her toward the fire.

She stretched out her hands, but they failed to get warm.

"I'm glad you showed sense enough to turn back before this storm broke. Don't ever underestimate the danger." He said this in the same tone with which he asked her to take a seat on the couch.

Before Starr had time to resent his little lecture, he withdrew and crossed to the bar, where he poured two drinks.

On returning, Clay pressed a glass into her hands. "I'm going to call Harrison. Whatever the reason for this project of yours, let them delay it until the weather turns. Or they can send someone else. I don't want you taking chances on the mountain."

The liquor burned a fiery trail down Starr's throat, but it was really his high-handed manner that choked her.

Clay grabbed for her glass. "Take it easy. Breathe slowly. That's hundred-proof cognac you're downing like soda pop."

At last the burning stopped and Starr found her voice. "I'm doing the job I was trained to do."

"Not on my horses."

"Fine. I'll walk."

He spread his palms, then clenched his hands and looked away.

"I found a dead bighorn." Her voice quavered. "A beautiful ram, about as perfect as could be. No obvious reason for his death." Her eyes filled. "If I don't find out what's killing them before spring, we might lose the whole herd."

Moved by her emotion, Clay knelt and grasped her hands. "That's a tragedy, and I can see you want to help. But when it snows, the mountain is treacherous. If Harrison really cared about you, I should think he'd insist on keeping you safe."

Harrison again. Starr studied the amber liquid in her glass. What could she say to make him see that *Harrison* wasn't the man she'd fallen in love with? Unable to think clearly when Clay touched her, she pulled away and set her glass aside. "Would it be all right if I used your phone to call a courier?"

Clay swore mildly as he stood. "Call Harrison, you mean?" he said bitterly. "Courier—is that a code word?" He reached for the phone. "I'll talk to my brother."

Starr felt a little like a bird caught in a trap. The number she was to call with her report was a message machine, but it had been set up by Harrison's secretary. Even if she gave Clay the number, he'd recognize the woman's voice and assume the worst. Either way, Starr knew she was doomed—and there was nothing she could do about it. These blood samples had to be tested.

CHAPTER TEN

CLAY HAD BARELY punched out the sequence of numbers to his brother's San Francisco home when a shuddering cry filled the room.

Starr was shocked to see Vanessa McLeod hovering in the archway. Her eyes were clouded and confused. Tears ran down her pale cheeks.

It had been more than a year since Starr had seen the senator's wife. She sat in awe of the woman's flawless beauty. Her light blond hair framed her heart-shaped face like a soft halo. She wore a simple silk dress with just enough frills to make her too-thin frame look feminine. The woman's most alluring feature, however, were her pansy-soft violet eyes. Widely spaced above a perfect nose and cupid's-bow mouth, those eyes held a haunting vulnerability. Starr sincerely doubted that there had ever been a more fatal combination of beauty and fragility wrapped in one package.

It was no longer a mystery why both brothers vied for Vanessa's attention. Nor why this helpless-looking creature turned to her brother-in-law for strength and support. Clay was a very masculine man—if not a touch predatory. Definitely a man to take command.

For one fleeting moment, Starr wished she could be delicate and needy like Vanessa McLeod. Then, as quickly, her independent spirit asserted itself. Wasn't the power imbalance what she'd disliked most about her parents' marriage? Indeed, in the film industry in general, there'd been an overabundance of men who misused power to get what they wanted—and even more women who let them.

Clay covered the phone's mouthpiece. "Vanessa, what do you need? Is your headache worse, hon? Is it time for more medicine?"

Starr couldn't help noticing how his tone gentled compared to his brusque orders to her only moments ago.

Vanessa glared at Starr. "Why is *she* here?" she asked as she swayed against the wall.

Clay picked up the phone, stretching the cord, as he moved to reach his sister-in-law. Not only was the cord too short, but Harrison chose that moment to answer. Clay sent Starr a silent plea for help.

He needn't have, she was already on her feet. She led the stricken woman to the leather couch by the fire and urged her to sit.

"Harrison, so you are home?" Clay barked. "No...no, nothing's wrong here. Why would it be?"

Surprised by his obvious fib, Starr glanced at him curiously. This time the pause while he listened was longer. Then as he caught her watching him, a sardonic curl of his upper lip bared his teeth below his dark mustache.

"Yes, we're having a storm of sorts. No, your precious Starr is right here in the room with me—safe and sound." Sarcastically he added, "Vanessa's here, too, Harrison. In fact, she's not feeling well. Maybe you'd like a word with your soon-to-be ex-wife."

"No...no, I can't. Let her." Vanessa pointed at Starr. "Or you talk to him, Clay. I...he...we..." She shook her head in unconcealed distress.

Well, Barclay McLeod, you're a real bastard, Starr thought. It was evident that Vanessa suffered from the strain of being unfaithful, even if Clay was heartless enough to rub his brother's nose in it.

Angered by his insensitivity, Starr marched over and jerked the phone from Clay's hand. She turned away from him and Vanessa before speaking. "Harrison...Starr here. I need a courier ASAP. I took some blood samples today, but I don't know how good they'll be. The ram had been dead awhile."

She felt Clay hovering. "Secrecy is pretty difficult," she snapped at the man on the line when he asked what his brother knew. "I'm virtually living in their laps, Senator." Glancing up and into a brass-framed mirror, Starr caught Clay's scowl. She lowered her voice, murmuring, "Of course you don't need to pop down here. No, I won't take unnecessary risks." Lord, she didn't even want to *imagine* the family squabble if Harrison showed up.

The mirror showed Clay leading Vanessa from the room. He had one strong arm wrapped lovingly around the woman's slender waist. When he bent to whisper something in her ear, a sharp ache shot through Starr's chest. So intent was she on watching the couple she missed what Harrison had said.

"Starr, Starr, can you hear me?" The sharp note in his voice brought Starr crashing back to earth.

"Wh-what did you say?" Her fingers relaxed on the receiver the moment Clay and his partner moved out of sight.

"I said I should have listened to you, Starr. I've tried to tell Van that there's nothing going on between you and me, but she refuses to believe me. Guess I blew it."

Starr sighed. "A lot of that around here."

"Clay, huh? Well, it doesn't surprise me. He can't accept what a person tells him. He keeps chipping away. It's the main reason I didn't want him to know about the sheep. Is he giving you a hard time?"

Inside she cried, *You don't know the half of it. You should see him fawning over your wife.* Aloud she assured him, "He doesn't know everything. Not about the test well. Although it might simplify things if he did."

"No. Have you seen the paper? Two counties are on the verge of bankruptcy. A controversy right now would be ruinous. The ranchers could gum up the works."

"That's terrible!" Starr exclaimed. "I wish you were already governor."

"With a divorce facing me, I may lose my backers," he said gloomily.

"Don't worry," she said, feeling he needed a kind word. "The people of California are more liberal than most. I'm sure they won't worry about your marital status when they go to the polls."

She stopped, her eyes drawn by a shadow. The hair on the back of her neck rose. Flashes of heat skittered up her spine as she turned and read something akin to agony in Clay's eyes.

"I'll t-talk to you l-later, Senator," she stammered, then dropped the phone into its cradle. But she was too far away, and it struck the desk with a clatter.

"What's wrong, Clay?" Starr sucked in her bottom lip. "Is something wrong with Vanessa?" With fumbling fingers, she righted the phone.

"As if you'd give a damn, you conniving little witch."

"Me?" Starr raised her chin. She was tired of taking the blame for Vanessa's problems. "People who live in glass houses shouldn't cast stones."

"I could wring your pretty neck."

"I'm not the one who called to rub Harrison's nose in it. Now if you don't mind, I've had a tiring day. All I want is food and a hot shower. You and your brother can fight over the same bone. Leave me out of it, please."

Clay looked as though he was about to unleash another tirade when Starr beat him to the punch and asked the question that had been nagging at her. "Who was the Mrs. Manning you were on the telephone with when I walked in?"

Her words flashed between them on electrically charged air.

Clay tensed. Damn. She'd caught him off guard. All he could do was avert his eyes and shrug.

An icy hand gripped Starr's heart. "Wanda. It was Wanda Manning." Her lungs screamed for air. "Why?" The single word whispered through lips gone numb with fear.

Turning away from her, Clay massaged the back of his neck. "I don't owe you any explanations."

"I'm not asking for myself." She clutched his arm. "Tell me this isn't about SeLi."

She stood close enough for Clay to feel her breath on his cheek. And he could smell the faint scent of whatever perfume she'd put on this morning. Floral, he thought. His pulse tripped. He didn't want to be having this discussion. He wanted to spirit her away and lose himself in her softness. Someplace they'd never be found.

Instead, he shut his eyes and held his breath to break the hold she had on his senses. In the next room were three living, breathing reasons he should run like hell. His brother's wife, his son and *maybe* his illegitimate daughter. God, what a mess.

"I know Harrison set you up in that apartment," he said grimly. "You could clear this up, Starr. Is my brother being blackmailed or simply hiding his love child?"

Icy shock waves started at Starr's toes and worked their way up to her brain. All that registered was the part about Harrison setting her up in the apartment. Preposterous! Harrison hadn't set her up anywhere. Reacting, not thinking, she grabbed the first solid object her hand came in contact with. It was a ceramic statue of a bucking horse, which sat on Clay's desk.

"Wait." He held up a hand. "Don't throw that! It's worth a mint. An original by a West Coast artist. My mom's going to give it to my dad for Christmas."

The urgency in his voice stopped her. She blinked and felt the weight of the object she held raised above her head. Lord, what was she doing? She who hated scenes? Quickly she set it back and brushed her palms on her thighs. "You're right. It's much too nice to waste on a scuzzball like you."

She took a deep breath. "I was right all along. The first time I saw you I suspected you wanted to use me to discredit the senator. Now I see you want to use SeLi, too. Well, I won't let you hurt her!" God, how could she have felt anything warm, anything *romantic,* for this jerk?

At the moment Starr thought she hated Barclay McLeod. Thoroughly sick at heart, she turned and ran from the room.

Clay took a moment to return his dad's gift to the box that sat under his chair. It had come in the mail and he'd just opened it when the Manning woman called. As he set the package aside, he heard Starr talking earnestly to SeLi; that was followed by the slam of the front door. A slam hard enough to rattle the mullioned windows in his den.

Clay lifted the curtain and watched her cross the clearing with long, rapid strides, SeLi trotting to keep up. Damn, he'd botched things for sure. Even now, he didn't know the truth about SeLi Lederman.

Someone, Morgan probably, turned on the porch light. It outlined two sets of footprints on the new-fallen snow. Ah. Good. At least with this weather, he didn't have to worry about Starr pulling up stakes and running away.

"Clay!"

He heard the tremor in his sister-in-law's voice. Poor Van. What would become of her when the media started ripping her family to shreds? And they would. Starr Lederman was dead wrong if she thought the voters of California would ignore Harrison's indiscretions. Voters liked nothing better than the smell of scandal. And the juicier that scandal, the better.

Clay let the curtain drop. Should he bide his time until Mrs. Manning called again, or hope Starr would reconsider and come clean? If all else failed, he could call Judge Forbes. Except then he'd have to say how sorry he was about Joel. Clay remembered the judge's distress when he'd called to offer his condolences after he'd heard about the accident; he didn't want to open any old wounds. "I'd better wait it out," he muttered as he went to see what his sister-in-law needed.

THE COURIER'S PLANE had come and gone. Starr sat up long after she'd tucked SeLi into bed. Clay's words continued to fester. As she'd said before, Harrison was the nicer brother.

Plopping down in the tiny kitchen nook, Starr thumbed absently through SeLi's math workbook. A photograph fell out, followed by another. She picked up the first—a picture of Morgan McLeod. She smiled. He must have given it to her. Morgan and SeLi. Two more unlikely friends she'd never known. This photo wasn't current—a year or two old, she'd guess.

She scooped the second picture up from where it had landed facedown, and her breath caught in her throat. Staring at her from the glossy, color print was Clay. The lens extolled the careless denim look he wore so well. The look that made blue jeans high art. He wore gleaming cowboy boots. One rested on the brick hearth, giving the appearance of studied ease. Blue eyes beckoned, although a faintly mocking smile told Starr he was only tolerating the photography session. He needed his hair cut, she noticed.

Starr ran a finger over his broad chest. Some bodies spoke for themselves. The picture slipped through her shaking fingers. Why did SeLi have a picture of Clay? She wasn't still entertaining any dangerous fantasies about him as her father, was she? Starr certainly hoped not.

What was it Clay had said? Something stupid about blackmail, and... Starr closed her eyes. When she opened them again, it hit her like a meteor racing through a starry night. *Harrison's love child.* She gasped. Was he implying that SeLi was Senator McLeod's daughter?

"My God, no!" Jumping up, she carried the picture of Morgan over to the light. What did she actually know about SeLi's birth mother? Only that she'd been incredibly sick. And small, dark-haired, excruciatingly thin.

Starr switched off the light and stumbled to bed. She welcomed the comfort of darkness. Even huddled under a mound of blankets, she couldn't seem to get warm. She reminded herself that the senator had only gotten involved in the adoption because she needed someone to vouch for her. Or had he?

She thought back to her own involvement with that situation on the wharf. Her dad had been on his way to film in Japan, and he'd stopped to take her to dinner. Harrison was at the restaurant with a group of friends. At one point he asked Samuel to join their party for an after-dinner drink. Starr would've gone home, but her dad insisted on toasting her new job at Fish and Game.

She'd been flattered that after insisting she stay, the senator had asked her to look into a problem with people on the wharf getting sick. He insinuated the Department of Health wasn't moving fast enough.

It took some time for her to connect the illness to bad water. Not the drinking water, but wharf water—the fish they ate swam in it. The media usually blew things out of proportion, so she found it understandable that the senator and his team wanted the mess cleaned up without a lot of fanfare.

At the time she'd assumed the senator had taken such an interest because a ship from a politically touchy country was involved. Or because it was his district and so many people were getting sick.

Had she been naive? Was his interest, in fact, personal? She sat up and switched on the light. If SeLi was Harrison McLeod's child, why had he allowed her to live in squalor? Unless he hadn't known about her until then.

Starr's head ached. Suddenly a host of doubts assailed her. If the senator was so nice, so considerate, why had his lovely wife sought solace in the arms of his younger brother?

And Clay. Starr couldn't even bear to think about him. The complexity of his role in this mess was more than she dared tackle tonight.

Sometime in the wee hours, she drifted into a troubled sleep.

The smell of burned toast awakened her. Irrationally Starr wondered why SeLi always burned the toast.

"Mom?" The little girl stuck her head pensively into Starr's face. "Are you sick or somethin'? You normally get up way before me. Did you forget I'm going to work with the tutor this morning?" Dark eyes moved restlessly over Starr's inert form. Since the death of her mother, illness of any kind worried SeLi.

"Ugh!" Starr dragged herself from a tangle of blankets. "What time is it, Skeeter?" She yawned and squinted up at the curtained window. "Looks dark out. Isn't it still night?"

"It's morning." SeLi giggled. "It's almost eight o'clock. The sky looks yucky, but it's not snowing. What are you gonna do today?"

Starr reached for her robe. With a quick twist, she sashed it around her middle. "Coffee first. Then I'll decide. I'd like to do more exploring on the mountain today. Maybe you should come with me," she said hesitantly.

"Do I hafta? Morgan and me have fun."

Starr frowned. For two kids who were so different they got along surprisingly well. What did that mean? Siblings usually fought, didn't they?

"I guess you can stay."

"Yippee!" SeLi bounced up and down. "'Cept the sky looks awful. Uncle Clay worried about you yesterday, and the sun was out. He probably won't let you go today."

Starr paused with her hand on the coffeepot. She spun and faced the girl squarely. "SeLi, I've already told you—Barclay McLeod is not your uncle! He isn't any relation at all. Got that?"

"Jeez."

The hand pouring coffee shook. Starr watched the dark liquid slosh out and she snatched at a paper towel. "Another thing," she said. "My work here does not concern Mr. McLeod at all."

SeLi eyed her with surprise, then gave a careless shrug and pulled a box of cereal from the cupboard. Filling the bowl to the rim, she said casually, "I like Clay. I think he's super." As if that was an official proclamation, SeLi helped herself to a carton of milk. She poured it onto the cereal and slid into the tiny nook. Her bowl stopped inches from the photographs of Morgan and Clay. Her spoon clattered to the floor. The minute she retrieved it, dark, guilty eyes lifted to meet Starr's. "Are you mad about the pictures, Mom?"

"Should I be, honey?" Starr took a sip of coffee and waited while the girl squirmed. From experience she knew SeLi had more to get off her chest.

"Remember when I heisted Clay's billfold?" SeLi asked in a small voice. Without waiting for Starr's confirmation, she plunged ahead. "I didn't know he was Morgan's uncle. I didn't even know Morgan."

Starr nodded once for encouragement. She shoved the photos aside and indicated SeLi should eat her cereal before it got soggy. She was not prepared for the instant quickening of her heartbeat as the image of Clay McLeod smiled up at her.

"I didn't intend to steal nothin'—really. I just wanted to see if I could still lift a wallet," SeLi mumbled. "I was PO'd at Buffy Jordan. She was always braggin' on how good-lookin' her dad was and how smart her sister was. You said I could have pictures of your folks, but they're *old.*"

Starr hid a smile. "Don't let them hear you say that."

The girl pushed limp flakes around her bowl. "When I saw the pictures, I sorta dreamed up an idea to get back at Buffy. I figured to tell her my folks got divorced, and that Moe belonged to my dad's new wife— only I didn't call him Moe." Her gaze narrowed. "I never dreamed he'd show up at my school. I bet that stupid Buffy would've believed me, too." Her eyes snapped. "I mean, Clay's got black hair. He could be my dad, don'tcha think?"

An unreasonable fear gripped Starr's heart. She fought to keep her features blank. If SeLi was Harrison's daughter, she might well resemble Clay.

Carefully Starr scanned the picture, searching for some irrefutable evidence. There was none. SeLi had inherited the fine features and almond-shaped eyes of her mother. Clay McLeod had crow black hair, but the similarity ended there. Sighing audibly, Starr devoured Clay's features with the hunger born of hopeless infatuation.

SeLi spoke again.

"What?" Starr blinked. "Oh, yeah. You have to go get tutored. Uh, SeLi, were you saying Clay doesn't know you have these pictures?"

The girl nodded ever so slightly, and Starr's stomach bottomed out.

"Then leave them, please. He must have missed them by now. Honey, we'll clear this matter up as soon as I get back today. I swore to him that nothing was missing from his wallet when I returned it."

SeLi had the grace to look ashamed, and for once she didn't argue.

Starr laid the photos carefully on the small counter. "I'm going to the pass today. But I'll try to be back early so we can plan something fun. If Morgan's mother isn't feeling well, she can do without two rambunctious kids hanging around all day." Starr gently tugged on one of SeLi's braids.

"There's cold chicken in the fridge for lunch. Don't use the stove, okay? If you want hot chocolate, use the microwave. I'll definitely be back before dark. If we have time, we'll go look for a small Christmas tree. I brought decorations. We'll do that together, just the two of us."

"I'm glad you picked me to adopt." SeLi hugged Starr, then dashed off to brush her teeth. Starr was still leaning against the counter when the girl rushed back in, grabbed her workbook, and whirled out on a blast of icy wind. It was the type of wind that made you reach for a warmer jacket.

Shivering, Starr pulled back the curtain and watched SeLi's small figure until she disappeared inside the ranch house. Without wasting time, she dressed for the mountain.

If Starr wished for anything on her way to the barn, it was for better weather. Although perhaps she should just be thankful it wasn't snowing.

By the time she'd selected a horse—Redwing wasn't in her stall today—and ridden toward the bighorn preserve, the wind had mercifully shifted. Now it blew against her back.

CLAY MISSED Starr's departure because he overslept. He stumbled tiredly into the kitchen, surprised to find his normally late-rising sister-in-law having toast and coffee.

"Well, you're looking chipper this morning, Van," he said as he helped himself to black coffee.

"It might have something to do with the pep talk you gave me last night, Clay." She pushed limp curls off her pale forehead and eyed her brother-in-law carefully. "Hank Rogers stopped by about an hour ago. He said to tell you Harrison radioed that he'd be flying in sometime this morning." Her grip on the cup tightened. "You did say I could make him notice me again if I'd get myself together and get off some of these pills. Did you mean it, Clay?" Wide violet eyes watched him anxiously.

So big brother was on his way to the ranch. Clay schooled his features to reflect a coolness he didn't feel. Especially since he was sure Harrison was coming to see Starr.

He took a long swig of coffee. Rising swiftly, he dumped the remainder in the sink. "Go soak in some perfumed bathwater, Vanessa. And put on something that will remind Harris of red-tile roofs and sultry nights.''

Clay shrugged into his sheepskin-lined jacket and muttered something about going to see Hank Rogers. He had a hard time meeting the hope that shone in Vanessa's formerly dull eyes.

Slamming the door, Clay stalked silently toward the motor home. He hadn't seen Vanessa express this much interest in her husband or anything else in quite a few months. This time he'd damned well lay it on the line to Starr. She could keep her sexy body and devastating smile out of Harrison's line of vision this trip, or she would answer to him.

As he neared the motor home, he saw the front door close. It was likely that Starr had seen him coming and decided to hide out. Angered, he jerked open the door without knocking.

SeLi jumped. She was still dressed in her jacket and mittens. Catching sight of Clay, she looked edgy. ''Jeez, Uncle Clay, you scared the pee-wadin right out of me.''

''Bite your tongue, young lady.'' Clay scowled. ''Or I'll help your mother wash your mouth out with soap.'' Stepping inside, he closed the door behind him. ''And where is she, by the way?''

SeLi shrugged. ''Gone up the mountain, I guess. I just came back for my math workbook. Why'dya want her?''

Clay's heart leapt into his throat. She shouldn't have gone. Didn't she look at that sky? He felt the coffee-pot, trying to judge how long since she'd left. His roving gaze caught sight of two photographs lying on the counter. Reaching for them, he heard SeLi's swift intake of breath.

"Holy shi—" she muttered. Eyes downcast, she bit her lip. When Clay's censure didn't come, she raised her lashes and met his frown.

"Where did these come from, Skeeter?"

His quiet use of her nickname caught SeLi off guard. With a rush, her story tumbled out. Amid a flurry of tears, she begged his forgiveness. "I didn't mean to steal from your wallet. I just wanted to shut that awful Buffy up. It would've too," she boasted, "'cause you're better-lookin' than her dad or Heather's. Younger, too," she added smugly.

Clay laughed self-consciously. "You mean it *was* you who lifted my wallet?" Even now he was shocked. "I'm afraid I blamed Starr," he said with a shake of his head.

"Starr?" the child hooted. "She wouldn't know how. She's so honest she squeaks. 'Sides, pickin' pockets is an *art.* "

"Not one Starr lets you practice, I hope."

"Heck, no! She's doin' her best to reform me."

It was stated with such seriousness that Clay chuckled.

"It's real hard breakin' old habits." SeLi's piquant features suddenly tightened. "You won't tell Wicked Wanda, will you Uncle Clay? She'd zap me outa Starr's house quicker'n you could say Jack Robinson. Least that's what mom says. I'm sorry I snatched your wallet. I'm tryin' to be good."

The girl sounded so forlorn that Clay dropped to one knee and took her in his arms, cradling her against his rough jacket. "Believe me, SeLi, I'd never do anything to hurt you or Starr." His voice was thick with emotion.

SeLi threw her arms around Clay's neck and grinned at her distorted image in the mirrored tile that bordered a row of cupboards. "So you like her?" she asked coyly.

Clay might have confided his feelings for Starr if the sound of an aircraft hadn't cut his remarks short.

"Run on back to the house," he said. "The tutor will be wondering what happened to you. I have other fish to fry, short stuff." Gently he turned her toward the door. "Here, keep these if you like. I have more."

"Gee, thanks! That's great." Looking relieved, SeLi grabbed her workbook and the pictures and skipped off toward the ranch.

Overhead a small plane had begun its descent. Clay shut the door and looked up, shading his eyes. Mouth set in a grim line, he watched the single-engine plane touch down smoothly and come to a stop beside his own twin-engine Comanche.

Almost welcoming the sting of wind, Clay strode to the edge of the clearing. He did his best to quash a slow-burning anger as the tall, distinguished form of his brother dropped gracefully to the ground.

Grudgingly Clay admitted that Harrison was a handsome cuss. Over six feet tall, broad-shouldered and slim-hipped, he had the type of solid confidence women liked. And the touch of silver at his temples didn't hurt, either. Or their father's blue eyes, which were not only direct but passionate.

Harrison McLeod wore a suit and tie like he was born to it, yet still managed a casual, down-home air. All those things, plus a youthful charm, made him the perfect political figure. On the surface, anyway....

Clay watched his brother's approach through eyes narrowed against the wind. Instead of meeting Harrison's outstretched hand with his own, Clay weighed the evidence, considered his action and balanced the consequences, then doubled a fist and wiped the welcoming smile from Harrison's face with a jarring right jab.

His brother staggered and nearly fell. A leather briefcase slid from his slack left hand. The hand he'd extended toward Clay quickly cupped his rapidly swelling jaw.

"What the hell was that for?" Harrison growled when he was able to speak. "Have you completely lost your mind?" He took a step back and gingerly wiggled his jaw. Eyeing the younger man's angry, rigid stance, he asked tersely, "Where's Starr?"

He jerked sideways, trying to avoid the left hook Clay threw his way next. Too late. Blood spurted from his split lower lip. "Dammit, Clay. Enough, already! I bust my butt to get here ahead of the storm, and this is the greeting I get?"

Hank Rogers sauntered up from the direction of the barn. Harrison made a direct appeal to the leathery old foreman. "Hank, what in the devil has gotten into my brother?"

"Dunno." He shrugged. "You've been such a stranger, maybe he thinks you're trespassin'." At best it was a weak attempt at levity. Closing in on Clay, Hank clasped his tense forearm in an iron grip. "Maybe Clay kin tell us hisself. How 'bout it, boss man? Git up on the wrong side of the bed today?"

Clay glared at Hank. Slowly all his pent-up anger began to ebb. "No quarrel with you," Clay said, breathing hard. "If you're heading out to feed stock, will you stop by the house and tell Mrs. McLeod that her husband's here? Not that she'll believe it till she sees it." Clay's words were laced with sarcasm. "Me, I'm goin' to bring in that last Brangus bull."

Harrison bent to retrieve his briefcase. A muscle in his jaw twitched, displaying his own rising anger. He waited to speak until Hank was out of earshot. "Is that what this little show's all about, Clay? You don't want me intruding on your and Vanessa's love nest?"

"Stop—wait! For God's sake!" Harrison skidded sideways and dropped to one knee as Clay lunged at him again.

The senator straightened and scowled at his brother. "I can't help it. I love her, Clay. I probably always will." His tone was bleak. "But if you can make her happy... I won't stand in your way." Heaving a great shudder, he dusted off his pant leg and studied Clay with pain-filled eyes.

"You love *who?*" Clay demanded belligerently.

"Vanessa, of course, you fool. Who do you think? Isn't that what this display of muscle is all about?" One dark eyebrow rose. "I've never known you to drink in the morning, but I swear..." Harrison's words trailed into merest suggestion.

Clay's heart thudded against his breastbone. Its tempo escalated with new hope. Still afraid he had it wrong, he turned away from his brother's handsome face. "What about Starr?"

"What *about* Starr? Where is she?" Harrison frowned as he dug out a handkerchief and touched his bloodied lip. "I picked up her preliminary lab reports. The team at the university worked all night and still couldn't make heads or tails of them. Dammit, we're counting on that girl to get us some answers."

Clay's broad back was set toward Harrison like a brick wall. "Since when do you give a damn about sheep, big bro?"

"Since now. And why are you so nosy?"

Clay said nothing, forcing his brother to make another appeal.

"I hate it when you clam up. You did that as a kid, too. I know you're pissed off, Clay, but I'll be damned if I'm gonna spend all day guessing why."

"Starr." Clay spat her name through clenched teeth. A strangled tightness in his lungs threatened to suffocate him. His hands, the knuckles scratched from his brother's hard jaw, were balled at his sides. Avoiding Harrison's eyes, he snarled, "Just where does your mistress fit in—if you love Vanessa so much?" Spinning, Clay turned on his brother like a cornered animal. "Tell me, Harris," he said stiffly. "Is it just power and sex, or somewhere in that rotten heart do you care for her, too?"

Harrison McLeod stared, mouth open and slack. The jaw his brother had socked flexed as the words sank in. Then his face slowly turned beet red and he began to stutter. "Y-you think that I... Y-you think St-Starr...we... My God, Clay, how could you?"

Reaching out, Clay caught the front of Harrison's suit with one hand. His tie and vest bunched beneath a florid chin. "Well, for one thing, you *let* me think it. Are you telling me Starr Lederman is *not* your mistress?"

To his credit, Harrison remained calm. He met the murderous glare in Clay's eyes without flinching. "She isn't and never has been. And I'm plenty steamed you'd believe that of me, Clay. Although I guess I could've made it clearer...."

"Well, I'll be damned. But since it's come up, I'm not too happy you didn't trust me with Van, either."

Harrison tried to straighten his tie, then gave up and rubbed his cheek again. "You almost broke my jaw. Tell me, what I was supposed to think, with the two of you thick as peanut butter and honey?"

"I never did one thing that wasn't brotherly. But I saw you in that fancy restaurant with Starr... and kissing her in front of the condo."

"That was just a friendly peck. But you and Van..."

"We're family," Clay finished, looking affronted.

"I'll be. Seems like we've got things to iron out, Clay. Let's go someplace and talk this through before we see either of the ladies."

Clay grunted approval. He jerked his head toward the barn.

Much later, he sat amid the tack contemplating Harrison's explanation. Feeling decidedly freer—but also like a fool—he savored the sweet smell of hay. Breaking off a piece, he chewed it thoughtfully.

Harrison had gone up to the house to plead his case with Vanessa. He'd asked for an hour alone with his wife.

Clay, on the other hand, was suddenly beset by an urgent need to see Starr. To see her and apologize from the bottom of his heart for not believing her.

He wanted to talk to her *now*. Calling Hank on his mobile phone, Clay asked the foreman to have one of the hands round up the old bull. Then before he could change his mind, he saddled a big bay gelding and cantered toward the trailhead.

CHAPTER ELEVEN

STARR FORCED her attention to the task at hand. Not for the first time since leaving the corral did she long for the surefooted sorrel with the blaze face. For this trek, she'd chosen a pinto mare with fire in her eye, but trim lines. It was a mistake. The pinto shied at the slightest provocation, making it nearly impossible to scan the rocky crevasses. At least controlling this horse had the advantage of keeping Starr's mind off Clay McLeod.

A mile beyond the ranger's cabin, Starr edged her mount toward a fork in the trail leading to Tahquitz Peak. Her breath floated mistily on frosty air and clung in puffs about the mare's ears. The terrain was beautiful. Hypnotic. Snow lay in deep drifts along the trail's edge. Ice crystals caught flickering sun rays and caused the skittish horse to whicker and snort.

Another thousand feet, and the trail slicked over. Less than a mile more and a thick fog settled around them. By now, the pinto was jumping at shadows. Her unsteady hooves slipped on patches of ice.

Yet Starr continued to climb. Her interest was aroused by ever-increasing signs of sheep. She paused frequently to scan the rock-strewn hills with powerful binoculars and took scant notice of the intense cold seeping through her clothes.

Before long, spitting flakes of snow slapped at her cheeks. They melted as they came in contact with her skin. Warmed by the pinto's body heat, Starr ignored the murky sky and pushed on toward a rocky promontory where she thought she'd glimpsed movement.

Pines bent from years of winter winds huddled like gnomes in sheaths of white. So focused was she on the prospect of finding answers that Starr missed the storm warnings.

Rounding a sharp bend, she reined to a halt. At the pinto's feet lay the snowy carcass of a bighorn. The nervous mare danced circles around the fallen animal.

Quickly Starr dismounted. She swept a thin coat of ice from the frozen body and bit her lip worriedly. Like the ram she'd found yesterday, this ewe was a near-perfect specimen.

Starr sat back on her haunches, one hand gripping the reins as she studied the ewe. The moan of the wind was broken only by the sharp clang of her mare's hooves on the frozen trail.

Farther up the mountain, a slight movement caught her eye. Horrified, Starr watched the staggering progression of a smaller ewe down a snow-studded crest. Without warning, the animal stumbled and fell from the ledge

Starr held her breath, willing the sheep to rise. When there was no other movement, she sprang to her feet. Swiftly she tied the pinto's reins to a tree branch, grabbed her test kit from the saddlebag and headed for the downed sheep.

The distance had looked short, but the rugged terrain was deceiving. And the air was thinner at this higher elevation.

Her breathing was already labored. When Starr stepped on a slick rock, her feet slid out from under her and she landed hard on her backside. For just an instant it brought tears to her eyes. At last she got to her feet again and rubbed her hip ruefully. Afterward she paid closer attention to where she walked.

The ewe was still breathing, and Starr tried to help the animal up. The ewe died in her arms. Tears froze to Starr's cheeks as she held the animal for a moment. Then she dutifully drew blood, watching the inside of the vial bead with steam.

The swiftness with which this illness struck worried her. At this rate the whole herd could be lost before spring lambing.

It was in the midst of a hasty prayer that Starr caught the muffled sound of a swift stream. That surprised her, as she hadn't seen any sign of a river. She stood. There was abundant evidence that sheep had broken through ice and snow for feeding. Stooping to inspect a patch of green, she pulled off her gloves, scraped— and blundered across another carcass. A much smaller animal. A squirrel. Was this carrier of death a tick or a flea? she wondered.

Though Starr's hands had been outside her gloves only minutes, her fingers were numb. She stamped her feet restlessly and tucked her hands beneath her arms to warm them faster. The silence in this graveyard made her edgy. But there was so much to do—samples of the grass and twigs to take. Stagnant water if there was any.

It was well past noon when she finished. Starr supposed she should eat. It was just that finding so many dead animals was unsettling.

As she carried her samples back to the pinto, she saw the merrily bubbling stream. If it fed into a lake, that'd need testing, too. Swift water cleansed itself tumbling over its granite bed.

Starr carefully packed the samples in a saddlebag. She should head back now; maybe she'd catch the incoming courier. If she was lucky, blood gasses from the first samples might have already cleared up this mystery.

Her stomach growled as she reached for the pinto's reins. Maybe she should eat one of those sandwiches. At the very least, the horse deserved the apple she'd tucked in.

The peanut butter was awful—stick-to-the-gums dry. It was amazing how kids ate so much of the stuff. Thank goodness for that stream.

Starr followed it to the spot where it ran swiftest. Kneeling on a flat rock, she made a cup with her hands and plunged them into the icy water. Laughing, she leaned back and drank it down. And Clay said she couldn't take care of herself. No pioneer could have done better.

Before she took a second, long swig, her tongue recoiled from the taste. It was dreadful. Like a straight dose of artificial sweetener. Startled, she let the remainder of the water seep through her fingers. It puddled and froze on the fabric of her jeans.

The chemist in her tried to identify the fleeting taste, but she was unable to pinpoint it.

Ignoring the cold, she dipped a finger in the water and touched it to her tongue. Once more her taste buds rejected the cloying sweetness. Not sugar. Not honey. Nothing pleasant, even. Nevertheless it was a flavor she should recognize. Desperately she tried to pull something out of—what? An old textbook? A lecture? Finally she gave up and looked upstream to see if something had spilled.

Her fingers began to cramp from the cold, and she found it difficult to push them into gloves that had grown stiff.

A dull ache began to throb at the base of her skull. "Time for some real sugar," she told the pinto. "We don't want to suffer from hypoglycemia in this weather." She pursed her chilled lips, remembering the almost acrid yet sweet taste. Hopefully the candy bar she'd stashed would take away the lingering unpleasantness.

Ten feet or so from the pinto, Starr was shaken by a sudden dizziness. She fell to her knees as a pain shot through her head. The taste returned, overpowering in its intensity.

Then, just as quickly, the incident passed, and she was able to scramble up. That was when she noticed her footprints were rapidly being covered by a layer of new snow.

When had that happened? Above and below her, the mountain offered zero visibility. A brisk wind whipped icy snowflakes in circular whirls. Starr felt as if she was standing in the center of a snowy paperweight turned upside down. It made her giddy enough to stop and catch her breath. She had the candy bar in hand when the second pain ripped through her head and immobilized her. Closing her eyes, she staggered back. When she opened them again, the spotted horse was almost hidden by the blowing snow.

Starr dropped the candy and reached for the mare. She almost had her when the animal reared and broke the frozen branch the reins were looped around. With a clatter of hooves, she disappeared down the trail.

Starr puckered her lips to whistle, but was driven to her knees when the saccharine taste washed through her in another sickening wave.

All around her the wind began to moan. Snow spiraled and snaked from four directions at once. A shining aura pulsed in the distance.

SeLi's Christmas star? No. Starr sank against a large rock to study the light. Was this some phenomenon like the aurora borealis? The pain struck again, and she shut her eyes. An image of Barclay McLeod appeared behind her eyelids. Odd, she thought. Did the clarity of his smoldering blue gaze mean she was freezing to death?

A grim but hysterical laugh clawed its way through her lips. In a moment of lucidity, she got to her knees. Why was she sitting on a snowy mountain analyzing death?

For an instant Clay's face faded and a clearer picture loomed. SeLi... The child beckoned in the impish way Starr had come to know so well. Too bad the pinto had run away. It was warmer now. The mare should have stayed. Had the wind fallen off?

Starr crawled for a while. She tried to catch snowflakes on her tongue. Wow! There was SeLi's star. Almost close enough to touch. So pretty. So bright. Starr wanted it.

"SeLi. What do you want to tell me?" Starr pushed at the girl, but the image faded. A word appeared up out of nowhere. "Drixathyon." It tumbled end over end through Starr's aching head to form thickly on her lips.

She cradled her head, commanding the alternately pulsing and receding word to stop its incessant hammering inside her skull.

Laughter soared aloft on the heightened wind. Was it hers?

Suddenly stars exploded in her head like a burst of fireworks. "The taste—" Starr knew then what was killing the sheep.

She struggled to stand. Thought she had. But all at once discovered she was still on her hands and knees. God, she had to find the pinto and get down the mountain while there was still time. It was all so simple. Why hadn't she realized it before?

Drixathyon!

Starr didn't know she'd shouted until the word echoed back at her from the frozen ravine. Frowning, she forced her thoughts to be orderly. The first time she'd heard about the chemical, she'd been in her last year at Berkeley. The Sierra Club had objected to a new chemical that Calexco was using in offshore oil drilling. A chemical designed to reflect traces of high-density petroleum. The kicker was, sea life began showing up on shore—dead.

Bright pretty lights shimmered up ahead. Starr smiled. One of her favorite professors at Berkeley had had her class follow the case. Sierra Club members swore the chemical was lethal; Calexco said it was safe enough to feed a baby.

Wait. There, overhead, were three lights. *Three* Christmas stars?

Starr licked her lips and effected a sliding descent down a steep part of the trail. It was an old battle— environmentalists hampering a quest for oil, and oil conglomerates coldly uncaring about the future of the planet.

God, but her head felt like a bass drum. She huddled under a tree and willed the stars and the memories away. But the group's experiment came back clearly—they'd drunk the water and not one student had suffered ill effects. Calexco claimed victory. Her class moved on to other things.

Starr frowned, and it hurt. She had to tell someone. *Harrison.* Wait. There was more. On another day, a warm, no, hot day. Part of the class had rowed out to a newly abandoned drilling site. That water had also looked clear. Harmless. It had tasted sweet—like the water today. They'd gotten awful headaches and hallucinations.

Starr closed her eyes and rested her head against a boulder. Who'd gotten really sick? She couldn't remember. SeLi's face appeared again in the shifting haze. Then Clay's. "Help me," she pleaded. He held out a hand but she couldn't reach it. He left as her memory returned.

A retired chemist had theorized that if water and Drixathyon mixed, it altered the components and made it a hallucinogen. He thought the chemical might eventually dissipate. It could take weeks, he said. Or months. He wanted the chemical banned.

Millions of lights flickered around her head. Starr reached for them. SeLi got there first and swept them away. "No fair." Starr laughed. SeLi begged someone behind her for help. Clay. Barclay McLeod? Yes. He knew these mountains. He cared about the sheep. But he didn't like her.

Starr felt as giddy as a child. She giggled. "Shh. It's a secret." Someone didn't want her to tell.

Harrison. Harrison didn't want her to tell.

No. She must. The sheep were dying.

Starr called for Clay. Just a test. No echo this time, only stillness.

There was something else. Something important. The chemical *wasn't* banned. Calexco moved down the coast. Like so many things, the issue of Drixathyon died a natural death. Like the sheep.

Starr's head pounded furiously. She wanted to get up. She needed to get up. But she couldn't. It was so cold. Maybe those sheep froze. Smiling, Starr reached for a rainbow that hovered above her. It glittered in the wind, but kept evading her grasp. Starr gave up chasing it. She was thirsty. Strange. She'd had that nice drink from the stream....

Oh, God! She had to get back to the ranch. If she didn't, who would learn the truth? Would some other chemist know to test the water?

A worse thought hit her. If she didn't find the pinto soon, what would become of SeLi? Wanda Manning would win, after all.

"Oh, please no! Clay," she cried softly. His image floated. He didn't want her out in a storm. He would come. "Clay!" This time she screamed his name and heard it bounce away on the wind. Then she pitched forward, and her head struck a jagged rock.

The wind was cold, but the snow was soft. So soft....

CLAY HEARD her call. At least he thought he heard a shriek on the wind that sounded like his name. He listened closely for a repeat and heard nothing but the fury of an escalating blizzard.

Gripped by fear from the moment he'd hauled in the riderless pinto right after the storm broke, Clay worried that maybe he'd taken the wrong turn at the fork. Only a fool would navigate Tahquitz Pass in the face of this storm.

But he'd seen a dead ewe and footprints. Starr had come this way, he was sure. Had she gone back and turned at the fork and gotten lost?

Dear Lord, he couldn't see a foot in front of him. He forged grimly on, leading the pinto mare.

His horse stumbled—over something lying on the trail. The gelding reared, nearly unseating Clay. With all his strength, he subdued the animal. It took him longer to fight the spooked pinto into submission.

What was that on the trail? A jacket? My God! *It was Starr!*

Clay's heart slammed against his ribs, and the battering wind drove Starr's name deep into his throat, choking off his breath as he dismounted.

Near as he could tell, she wasn't breathing. Driven by panic, he lifted her and covered her blue lips with his own. It was faint, but he felt a tiny thread of warm breath. He breathed a sigh of relief.

He had neither blanket nor slicker with him. Clay cursed his lack of foresight. Knowing she was close to hypothermia, he slipped out of his fleece-lined jacket and carefully wrapped her in it. He ignored the wet snow that seeped through his own flannel shirt and cooled his skin.

It wasn't easy, but he held her and mounted the gelding, urging the horse down a trail he could no longer see. He'd tied the pinto's lead to his saddle horn, and her nervousness was affecting his own horse. Bad weather hampered their descent. Time was suddenly his enemy. Lord, but they could both freeze up here on this peak. What if he never got to tell her that he'd been wrong about her association with his brother?

"You've been a real fool, McLeod," he muttered. The wind hurled his words back in his face. The bay stumbled and the pinto whinnied in fright. All at once, off to Clay's right, loomed a welcome sight. The ranger's cabin. It looked like a solid fortress against the opaque backdrop.

He tethered the horses to a lean-to that held firewood and stumbled to the cabin with his precious burden.

The cabin door was firmly hasped. Swearing, Clay splintered the wood with one well-aimed kick of his boot. Wilderness cabins should be left unlocked for emergencies. He would deal with the damage later.

Carefully he placed Starr on one of the daybeds angled near an old stone fireplace. A quick glance revealed that the two-room structure, built to house two rangers for several months' duration, boasted many comforts of home.

Clay dismissed the galley kitchen. Food was not a priority. His gaze settled on a shelf of radio equipment. He felt Starr's weak pulse and decided to build a fire first. After that, he'd call the ranch.

When the fire had taken on life and the room was starting to warm, he hurried back to her side. She moaned once and shifted beneath the heavy load of blankets he'd heaped on her. Heartened by that one small sound, he softly stroked her cheek. There was a fairly large bump on her forehead. She must have been thrown, as he'd originally feared.

A short while later he felt it was safe to leave her long enough to make that call.

"Hank, Hank—it's Clay," he yelled into the microphone and strained to hear over the static. "Yes, I found her. We're out of the storm," he assured the old foreman. "Weather's making one hell of a mess out there. I think Patches threw Starr. She's mostly out, but slowly coming around." He listened again, holding the headset close to his ear.

"No. Don't even consider rescue in this storm. Ask Vanessa to look out for the little girl, will you? And Hank...for the moment, her mother's condition is between you and me." Clay threw a worried glance toward Starr's still form. "If she doesn't come to soon, I'll check her over and buzz you back so we can figure out what to do."

At Hank's affirmative response, Clay clicked off, sighing heavily. What if she had internal injuries? He knew it was futile to attempt an airlift in this weather. He felt powerless, and he hated the feeling.

Bending over her, he searched her pale face for signs of consciousness. Her cheeks were translucent. Clay didn't like the bluish tinge around her mouth, or the way her dark lashes lay against her cheeks without so much as a flicker.

In spite of the heat now spewing from the mound of crackling logs and the warmth of five wool blankets, her skin still felt icy to his touch.

Maybe the angry bruise on her forehead was to blame, but she seemed to be sleeping like Rip van Winkle. Several times he called her name sharply. No response.

Reluctantly Clay decided it was getting warm enough for a more detailed examination. With great care, he removed the blankets one by one. Next he slid her from her jacket. Following that, he peeled away the pink cardigan. When he wormed her out of the white turtleneck, the tight neck of the fabric brushed the goose egg near her hairline and made her moan.

Damn, he hated the thought of hurting her, but a broken rib might mean a punctured lung. Holding his breath, he felt carefully along her ribs. "No marks. No unusual indentations." He let out his breath. "Thank God."

Then, he loosened her belt. After a moment's hesitation, he unsnapped and unzipped her worn jeans. Lord, he hadn't realized they were soaking wet from the snow. Ripping off her boots, he quickly shucked her out of the clinging, cold denim. Her feet were like cubes of ice. He rubbed them but to no avail. As he went to wrap her securely in a blanket, his breath caught. A large, discolored bruise spread across her thigh and disappeared under the left leg of lace-edged underpants.

It bothered him to think she'd been thrown from one of his horses, but the bruise was consistent with that type of fall. Still, the injuries he could see didn't explain her total lack of response. Puzzled, Clay covered her once again with the pile of blankets. Tucking each one beneath the daybed's mattress. Forced to be content with the knowledge that her breathing remained steady, he dragged over a chair and began a silent vigil.

Minutes ticked into hours. Deep rumblings in his stomach told him it was past time to eat. Not interested for himself, he did leave briefly to take care of the animals' needs. There was no letup in the weather, so he broke the lock on an old equipment shed and moved the horses in out of the driving snow. After fighting his way back to the cabin, the only concession Clay made to his own needs was to remove his wet boots at the door.

Starr's pale features claimed his full attention. So intense was his absorption, he nearly missed her broken request for water. Several times she mumbled, "Water," before he understood and ran to fill a glass.

His hands shook as he lifted her head. He knew her asking for water was a good sign. A great weight dropped from his shoulders.

Her lashes fluttered open as he held the glass to her lips. The smoky centers of her eyes were huge black orbs that crowded out the color. She said nothing and didn't appear to know him. Although, after draining the glass, she seemed less agitated.

He buzzed the ranch, reported the minute change and returned to his anxious watch at her bedside. Soon, feeling the effects of the long day, Clay's head slid to the wing of the rocker. He let his thoughts drift. His scraped knuckles still stung from his fight with Harrison, but it was nothing compared to the agony of finding Starr's riderless pinto. It was sheer luck that he'd found Starr. Sheer, dumb luck.

Clay awoke with a start. He was disoriented and unable to comprehend the sharp pain shooting up his neck. Memory flooded back, and he bolted upright. The fire burned low. The cabin creaked and shook. Wind. Heavy gusts. The storm had not abated. If anything, it'd grown worse.

Starr's condition had obviously changed. Where before she lay passive, now she thrashed. He reached to straighten her blankets. Several layers had slipped, leaving her limbs exposed. Clay covered her and cursed whatever weakness had made him fall asleep.

"Brrr." It was chilly. Rising, he added kindling and a log to the dying embers. On his way back, Clay yawned and eyed the second daybed. Though every muscle in his body begged for deliverance, he refused to lie down. He wanted to keep an eye on Starr.

It was a good thing too. Her restlessness increased. By midnight, Clay was unable to keep blankets on her.

When his fingers made accidental contact with her leg, he was shocked by the iciness of her skin. Ever so gently, he buttoned the cardigan around her shoulders.

Unfortunately her jeans were stiff in some places and still too damp in others for her to wear them.

For untold moments Clay watched her shiver. Then, with a muffled oath, he shed his own shirt and jeans and climbed under the blankets to warm her with his body. Uncaring that she might damn him in the morning, Clay hooked an arm over her breasts and pulled the blankets up to her chin. Ranchers learned early that if body heat slipped away, progress was all downhill.

God, she felt cold. His skin recoiled from contact with her floundering legs. Gritting his teeth, he curled around her. Icy or not, it felt right to hold her in his arms.

She settled instantly. After a bit his arms relaxed and he snuggled down, savoring her sweet womanly scent. Swamped by feelings of tenderness, Clay rubbed his day's growth of beard against her soft curls. It would be wonderful to curl up like this with her every night and awaken beside her every morning. All he asked was an opportunity to tell her.

Little by little he felt her skin grow warm. And he smiled.

He thought of all the time they'd wasted on mutual suspicion when he could have been learning more about her. He wanted to know everything. She seemed dedicated to her work, and she took motherhood seriously. That much he knew. He'd been wrong about his brother being her lover, but now Clay wondered—did she have another?

A swift stab of jealousy struck without warning. He didn't want any more mistrust between them; as if he could ensure that by holding her close, he wrapped her even tighter in his arms.

Then he slept.

Starr awakened once in the middle of the night. Not a complete waking, but the twilight kind where the body shifts, then burrows deep into the warmth of the bedding again. Something nagged at her.

She opened one eye. Her head felt fuzzy, but her ears picked up the steady howl of the wind. She muttered thanks for a toasty bed.

Even then her chemist's brain registered something amiss. It was more than the persistent dull throb at the base of her skull. Her lips were uncommonly dry and her tongue shied away from an unpleasant sweetness.

Starr freed a hand to rub her forehead. At that very moment, her backside struck a warm, immovable object. Experimentally she reached behind to explore.

Her fingers brushed and identified a hair-roughened leg. She whipped over so fast it made her head spin.

On seeing a sleepy-eyed Barclay McLeod hogging the blankets, she covered her mouth with the flat of her hand and stifled a scream.

"Hey, quit stealing the covers," he grumbled, wrapping strong fingers around the top blanket to tug it back.

His soft breath warmed Starr's neck as the muscled arm that lay across her midriff tightened. Quite naturally, it seemed, his eyes closed and his tousled head drifted back to his pillow.

Stifling a second panicked scream, Starr studied the long, dark lashes that lay against his stubbled cheek. Was she crazy? Or dreaming?

Suddenly he shot straight out of bed and flung covers to the four winds. "Oh, my God, Starr! You're awake!"

Though she clearly heard every word, Starr wasn't at all sure it was true. Careful not to move, she darted a gaze about the unfamiliar room. Following that, she deliberately pinched her arm. The pain convinced her there had to be another explanation for her unlikely bedmate. She really *was* awake.

"I trust you can explain, McLeod." Considering that her mouth felt like cotton, Starr was grateful her voice didn't crack.

"The storm," he said, not knowing where to start. "Patches threw you. Don't you remember hitting your head?"

Starr's fingers flew unerringly to the bump on her forehead. "Vaguely," she muttered. But that didn't explain her waking in her underwear beside a man who quite possibly wore less.

"Hey, I'm sorry I let the fire die." He looked sorry, too, as he gazed at the dead ashes in the grate.

Why was he being so nice? Had something else happened that she didn't remember? She felt headachy. Drugged. Not the way she should have felt after lovemaking. More like the flu.

Closing her eyes, Starr asked, "Is this your bedroom? If so, where's SeLi sleeping tonight, might I ask?"

Damn her. All this time he'd paced the floor over her—and all she could do was act as if he'd assaulted her. Disgusted, Clay climbed out over her and went to rebuild the fire. She was relieved to notice he still wore his briefs.

"Call me vain," he growled, "but when I take a woman to bed, she doesn't usually confuse the experience with being thrown from a horse and nearly freezing to death in the worst blizzard of the year."

"Well, excuse me all to heck. The way I ache, I thought maybe you...that we, uh... Oh, never mind."

"You weren't in any condition to make love—or do anything else. In fact, you were unconscious half the time and raving out of your head the rest." He stalked back and glared at her before he sank down on the edge of the bed.

"Let's not fight, Starr." His voice softened. "I was on my way to find you—to apologize. Harrison flew in yesterday." Clay brushed at the dried blood on his knuckles. "We cleared up a lot of misunderstandings. Stuff we should've cleared up sooner. That dumb plan of his to make Vanessa jealous, among others. Oh— don't worry about SeLi. They'll take care of her until we get back down the mountain."

Clay traced the bump on her head and moved his finger gently down her cheek and along the underside of her jaw. "Can you ever forgive me?"

She could only stare at him. An apology from Barclay McLeod? Why were there so many gaps in her memory? Starr closed her eyes and felt her heart beat faster. This was what she wanted, wasn't it? To have everything set straight between them?

Slowly opening her eyes, she raised her trembling fingers to his lips.

Heat shot like lightning through Clay's limbs. Without saying a word, he drew her into a kiss.

Starr melted into his arms. She reveled in the tickle of his mustache and the scrape of his unshaven jaw. When his tongue parted her lips and explored her sensitive mouth, whatever vague concerns she'd had all disappeared. How many nights had she dreamed of doing exactly this? Now, every one of those dreams was coming true.

Clay's lean contours welcomed the subtle softness of Starr's curves as he slipped beneath the blankets and let their bodies entwine. He didn't rush. Instead, he savored the taste of her lips—and other parts of her silken skin.

Every nerve in her body answered Clay's tender explorations with a message of its own. His kisses, her kisses, left them both weak from wanting.

His skin was warm in spots. Hot in others. On fire where her hands circled the waistband of his briefs. When she grew hesitant a scant heartbeat away from his arousal, Clay quickly skimmed away the last barriers of clothing that separated them.

Her soft skin tasted sweet—so sweet. Clay feasted from her lips to the tips of her toes. More than once, and it still wasn't enough.

She pleasured him, as well, a scant heartbeat behind his lead. Though she was ready when he entered her, his first thrust brought such intense excitement she felt as if a hail of stars had descended on them. Smiling, she thought about the brilliant star she'd seen up on the mountain. The Christmas star. SeLi's star. Pale compared to what she and Clay had just experienced together. She sighed in contentment.

He kissed the undersides of her breasts and made lazy circles with his tongue. Clay had known from the first moment he set eyes on this woman that making love with her would be like this. Just as he'd known that once wouldn't be enough. Nor twice. Nor ten thousand times. He needed a lifetime of loving her. For the very first time Barclay McLeod wanted to say, and hear in return, the words that went with the incredible experience they'd just shared.

Starr's satisfied smile told him the feeling was mutual—for now. But did she—would she—want him around for the long haul?

He found it a sobering thought.

"Starr." Clay leaned up on one elbow and crooked a finger beneath her chin. "We have to talk."

Before he'd shattered the moment by speaking, Starr had been content to drift along on the outgoing tide of passion. The whys and hows of the two of them ending up in this bed making glorious love had somehow faded into insignificance. His suddenly serious tone catapulted her back to reality.

Shocked at how easily she'd fallen into his bed after a simple *I'm sorry,* Starr sat up and began grabbing articles of clothing that had been abandoned where they fell. "No, we don't," she said coolly.

Clay didn't like what he glimpsed in her eyes. Yet how could he not be solicitous considering her accident? Considering everything that had happened? "Are you all right? I mean, I didn't hurt you or anything?"

Concern was the last thing Starr expected from him. That, coupled with a feeling of panic and followed by letdown, prompted a trickle of tears.

Those tears proved to be Clay's undoing. He gathered her onto his lap as he might have done Morgan or SeLi and rocked her gently. "Shh," he crooned. "There'll be other days for us. You took a rough fall from the pinto. I should be shot for letting things get out of hand."

She drew back. "Patches didn't throw me. My God, I just remembered! I know what's killing the sheep!"

"You what? You know? That's good, isn't it?" But his heart sank. Clay couldn't help feeling taken aback that she'd so easily made the transition from lovemaking to work. He stared bleakly at her for long seconds before he moved.

Swinging his legs off the bed, he set her aside, stood and yanked on his briefs and stiff jeans. He was in the process of zipping them when a staccato spurt of loud bleeps made them both jump.

Across the room, a green light winked on the shortwave radio. Hopping on one foot as he donned his socks, Clay was out of breath when he hit the button that silenced the nerve-racking noise. "Yes?" he all but shouted into the microphone. The volume sent the needle flat against one side of the gauge. Clay knew he'd made a mistake when Harrison's well-modulated voice floated out, sounding amused.

"Not interrupting anything, am I, old son?"

"Nothing," Clay snapped, deliberately turning his back on Starr, who quickly pulled on her clothes, her cool eyes were now icy cold. "What in hell is there to do on a mountaintop in the middle of a damn snowstorm?" Yelling at Harris eased Clay's tension.

Harrison laughed. "Well, brother of mine, I know how Vanessa and I spent the long, cold night. You aren't exactly alone on that mountaintop, now are you?"

Clay heard Starr's swift intake of breath. Guilt prompted his sharp reply. "Did you call to brag about your love life, or have you got something important on your mind?"

Harrison's gleeful chuckle let Clay know that his retort was received and recognized as a useless evasive tactic.

"Actually I was checking to see how you two weathered the storm. Hank mentioned that Starr had some kind of accident. He didn't elaborate, but SeLi's been beside herself with worry since breakfast. I thought it'd be good to set her mind at ease."

Clay shot Starr a quick glance. She refused to meet his eyes, and that irked him. Because he wanted more from her than one night in bed.

"Come talk to Harrison," he ordered. "Before he gets it into his head that you weren't a willing partner in this...encounter."

She marched past him, chin angled high.

Clay saw and leaned closer. "You were," he reminded her pointedly, shoving the mike into her hand just before he clicked it back to his brother. "Don't even think about denying it."

She was forced to temper her response in case SeLi was within hearing range. "Senator, hello. Tell SeLi I'm fine. Patches didn't throw me. I had her tied to a branch. She broke it and ran off. Left me stranded."

Harrison murmured an appropriate consolation.

Clay eavesdropped openly. He stroked his sore knuckles along grim lips and let a flood of emotion sweep over him. He wanted her to talk to him with that same warmth in her voice. Wait—what was she telling Harrison about the sheep being poisoned?

"I know it sounds farfetched," she said. "Just ask your little black-market oilmen if they used Drixathyon." She touched the knot on her head. "We're not talking one dead ram here. Animals are dying right and left." She shuddered. "I think the chemical is in the stream." There was a pause. "Why do I think so? Because I drank the water and reacted. Hallucinations—big time."

Forcing her eyes away from Clay's bare chest, Starr made herself listen to the senator's vigorous denial.

"Starr, you can't accuse Calexco of..." For a moment his voice faded out, then came back stronger. "We need this oil strike, dammit. I can't have you jeopardizing it on some supposition. I *won't* let you."

"Senator, I can't believe you said that! We have federal laws protecting these animals."

"Now, now, calm down, Starr. Clay told Hank you suffered quite a bump on the head. It's possible this is all fantasy."

Her voice hardened. "Ask Calexco if it's fantasy. You have until this storm blows over, Senator." Eyes flinty, she abruptly pushed the mike back into Clay's hands and marched across the room to search for her boots.

Clay stared after her. At last he clicked on and questioned his brother. "What's any of this got to do with you, buddy?"

Briefly—very briefly—Harrison explained. But beyond mentioning the state's debt and the need for oil money, he refused to talk. Following an uneasy silence, the brothers signed off.

Eager to clarify the situation with Starr, Clay turned. In the interim, she'd gone into the bathroom and shut the door.

Well, he didn't want to argue with her, anyway. He'd misjudged Harrison once already and her, too. This time he wanted to get all the facts straight first. Starr *had* been in pretty bad shape when he found her. That bump on the head might have caused her to hallucinate. People did strange things when they were close to freezing, too. It probably *was* that, and she'd recognize as much when she calmed down.

Clay pulled on his boots, shrugged into his jacket and went out into the raging snowstorm to find grass for the horses. When he finished with that, he'd go back inside and they'd discuss the issue like two rational adults.

CHAPTER TWELVE

THE BATHROOM DOOR rattled when Clay left the cabin. At the sound, Starr glanced up and met her own eyes in the mirror. She gazed at the livid bruise on her forehead, then bent her head to rinse her face with the cool water. She cupped her hands to catch some for a drink, her mouth puckered. The instant the water touched her lips, more of her memory flooded back. As the tap water ran over her fingers and disappeared down the drain, her hands began to shake. The sheep drank from a tainted stream and died. By the grace of God, she hadn't.

Starr mulled over possibilities. The most logical was that Drixathyon only stunned. In the case of the sheep, maybe they'd actually frozen—making them appear to die of natural causes. If, in the earlier instance, the fish had lost their bearings and accidentally flopped onto the shore, they would have died being out of water.

My God! If not for Clay, the fate of the sheep would have befallen her. While she stood in the tiny bathroom, weighing all she owed him, Starr wondered whether a debt of such magnitude was repayable.

Outside Clay cursed the snowdrifts that made gathering winter grass tedious. Snow fell, thick and wet, as he carried what grass he'd found to the horses. Before long, his pant legs were soaked to the knees. But the work left his mind free to wander. He hoped that Hank had brought the last bull in off the range, and that the hands remembered to mix warm mash with the horses' feed.

Harrison mentioned that SeLi was worried about Starr. Maybe the kid wasn't as tough as she wanted everyone to think. Clay recalled the incident with the pictures. Did Starr know how badly SeLi wanted a father?

He'd do his best to make her a good one.

Then it hit him—he hadn't asked Harrison about his involvement in SeLi's adoption. *Damn!* Clay assumed he'd broken down all the barriers between himself and Starr. Now he wasn't sure. Two questions remained. Who was SeLi Lederman, and why was her file closed?

Yesterday during his very informative chat with Harrison, the only thing they'd really cleared up was that nothing—nothing at all had gone on between Harrison and Starr, or between Van and himself. Come to think of it, Harris had still acted damned funny. He'd called his own brother nosy, and now he refused to discuss his dealings with Calexco. Clay didn't like loose ends.

He left the shed and sucked in a bracing lungful of icy air before fighting his way across the deep drifts. When he finally pushed past the broken door, he was determined to press Starr for answers.

Startled by his sudden entrance, Starr glanced up from where she stood on tiptoe searching a kitchen cabinet. Moments ago she had promised herself that she could be sophisticated about what had happened between them. Now she desperately groped for something clever to say. "You look like the abominable snowman. Tell me," she teased, "what do snowmen eat? Mother Hubbard's cupboard is almost bare."

Clay put a shoulder to the warped door and closed out the blowing snow. Even then he was forced to tuck a chair beneath the handle to keep it shut. He gaped at Starr, but suddenly not one question remained in his head. When he found his voice, he called forth lightness, too. "I'm afraid the sight of auburn-haired witches turn abominable snowmen into puddles. Feeding them won't help."

She laughed in spite of herself. "Maybe that's good. I can't cook without a deli down the street. We've got no eggs, no milk, no bread. No... anything."

Clay shucked his wet jacket, pulled off his boots and shook himself in front of the fireplace like a wet pup.

"Out of the kitchen, city girl," he grumbled good-naturedly. "Everything in the country is either powdered or canned. Step aside and let this cowboy get a meal together." He spanned her waist and moved her over.

"You're soaked," Starr exclaimed, staring at his jeans which were dark to midthigh. Form fitting, they hugged his muscular legs and set her heart thrumming.

"What did you expect? Sunburn?" He'd seen her pulse speed, and suddenly the tension was back. "In case you hadn't noticed, we're marooned in a blizzard. You'd better learn to like C-rations, lady. It's your fault we're here."

The tension between them kindled.

Stepping forward, Clay grasped her arms. When she winced, he saw that he'd unintentionally caused her pain. He eased his hold and ran his hands lightly down to her elbows. "God, Starr." His husky voice broke. "When I think how easily I might have missed you... that I might have been too late..." His throat worked convulsively. His eyes reflected the torment he was feeling.

Staring deep into them, she whispered, "I never thanked you for saving my life. Clay—let's not fight."

She leaned into his embrace.

Clay's rough cheek rasped gently against her hair.

Starr's hands inched around his waist. Slowly the racing tempo of their heartbeats blended into one. She found it comforting to be held by him.

He broke away first. "I'm all wet," he protested. "And you must be starved. It's past time for lunch. I'll rustle up something if you'll find me dry pants in one of these closets. Maybe the ranger left something."

Stung by his hasty withdrawal, Starr pivoted away and accidentally struck his hand with her body.

He flinched.

She paused, skimming her eyes over the scraped skin on his knuckles. "Clay, you hurt yourself out there." She caught his hand and ran her thumb over his injury. "I saw bandages and stuff in the bathroom. Let me clean this before it gets infected."

"Save the Nightingale act. I didn't get this feeding horses." He pulled back brusquely. "I banged it on Harrison's teeth while defending your virtue."

"My vir— You two were in a brawl?" First she looked appalled. Then angry.

"It's over, Starr. Surely you see why I assumed the two of you were having an affair. But I can't believe either of you thought Van and I—"

"Really?" Starr's eyes blazed. "When you lived together?"

"I told you that apartment had two suites. Besides, *I* wasn't the one acting weird." Clay stepped past her and yanked open a cupboard. "Just find me some pants, will you?'' He wanted to have this out with her and clear the air once and for all, but everything considered, he worried that the feelings of mistrust might run too deep. Not only that, she still looked pale from her experience. No, he decided, it was too soon for the kind of no-holds-barred discussion he wanted.

Seeing the closed expression on his face, Starr crossed the room to the closet. She sneaked a quick peek at him and wondered what he was thinking.

Clay found a skillet and slammed it down on the small electric stove. He immediately regretted his behavior and opened various cans more quietly.

A few minutes later Starr was back with a variety of pants and shirts. The smell wafting from the skillet made her mouth water. ''I think the ranger who lived here must've been Paul Bunyan's twin.'' She reached around Clay to lift the skillet lid, then dropped it when the steam burned her fingers.

Lost in thought, Clay gave a start. Her face twisted in pain, and he rushed her to the sink to run cold water over her hand. ''Paul who?'' he muttered.

''Bunyan. These shirts and pants are the biggest I've ever seen. Even belted, I think the pants would fall off you.'' Starr pulled her hand away and showed him a pair of blue jeans big enough for both of them with room to spare. The shirt she draped around her shoulders hung like a granny gown.

''Well, maybe the shirt alone will be enough. If I put my jeans by the fire, they should dry by the time I have to go out and feed the horses again.'' Clay snatched the shirt from her and handed her the spatula.

''Dish this stuff up, will you? I'll be back in a flash.'' He disappeared into the small bathroom.

Using a pot holder this time, Starr removed the lid. "Yum." She peered hungrily at two stacks of golden pancakes and thick slabs of canned ham.

When Clay reappeared, Starr thanked providence that she'd already taken a seat at the table. Much too much of Clay's well-muscled thighs showed below the curved hem of the shirt. Need roared through her like a runaway freight train. She couldn't even meet his eyes.

Unaware of the effect he had on her, Clay took a chair opposite and reached for his plate. "Thanks for waiting," he murmured.

When she didn't say anything, he glanced up and caught the hunger in her eyes. It was a dangerous look for both of them. Clay battled his own desires that sent goose bumps along his bare legs. "Don't tell me you have lecherous designs on my body," he joked, passing her the syrup.

She flushed and all but drowned her pancakes.

"I was teasing, Starr." He smiled. "Isn't that what men get accused of any time they admire skimpily dressed women?"

"Don't, Clay."

Shrugging, he cut his ham. "Then you pick a subject," he invited amiably, "since mine is unacceptable."

"Do you know how long we'll be stuck here?" she demanded.

"Not long, I hope," he snapped back. "There's not much for the horses to eat. Or for us, either. I don't think Paul Bunyan planned on company for Christmas."

Starr dropped her fork. "We can't be here that long. This is SeLi's first real Christmas. Not only that, this mountain is littered with dead sheep. I'm in a race against time."

"Up here, winter storms are unpredictable. Starr, I heard what you said to Harrison about thinking some chemical killed the sheep. I also heard his response. Maybe you're barking up the wrong tree."

"I'm not. He's putting too much faith in Calexco. I don't trust them."

"But you trust Harrison?"

She slanted him a sharp look. "Depends."

"On what? We have all day—and all night. Suppose you tell me."

She touched the painful lump on her forehead. Her brain had that disjointed feeling again. She wanted to tell *someone*. But Clay hadn't believed her before. What made her think he'd believe her now?

Sighing, she offered a condensed version, beginning with her first contact with his brother. When she got to the part about the chemical, Clay pushed his plate aside, sat back and steepled his fingers. Once or twice his brow furrowed, but he didn't interrupt.

Abruptly Starr got up and carried their empty plates to the sink.

Clay fired off several questions as he rose to help.

She told him all she knew about Drixathyon, taking care not to implicate Harrison when she accused Calexco of willful misconduct in their drilling practices.

Clay jumped to that conclusion himself. "Why didn't you explain this to Harrison? He's so caught up in his campaign he probably can't see beyond the jobs it'll bring to the state."

Starr didn't think many men could sound as convincing as a court attorney dressed in little more than a khaki shirt. Clay McLeod did. She just wished she was half as sure as he. "Maybe," she murmured. "Can you swear to that? For a month you've thought he was guilty of... all kinds of things. Now you claim he's Mr. Ten Carat all the way."

"It's not that exactly."

"Then what?"

"People do imagine things when they're freezing. I'd like more proof that you weren't dreaming. Or... what if he's somehow being coerced?"

"Blackmail? You mentioned it before." She frowned. "But that's a contradiction if he's innocent..."

"Of course he is."

Starr plunged the plates into soapy water. "Why *of course?*"

Clay raked a hand through his hair. "It's too far-fetched. He's never done anything illegal or even questionable before—as far as I know."

"Technically I guess it's not illegal—some of the federal preserves have been opened for selective oil exploration." She shook her head. "These preserves were set aside to protect animals in danger of extinction. I'm not sure a state should be able to override that for reasons of greed." She waved a soapy hand.

"Greed?" Clay's stomach lurched. "Are you saying you think my brother's on the take?"

Common sense told Starr to shut her mouth. It was clear that Clay didn't want to believe her. "I wish he wasn't involved with Calexco," she said after a moment's hesitation. "Do they contribute to his campaign fund?"

Clay stopped pacing beside her. "Not as a company. But yes, I think both the president and chairman of Calexco's board support Harrison with donations. Is that a problem?"

Starr hedged. "I'm not sure." And she wasn't. Since she'd talked with Harrison on the radio, a not-so-nice possibility had been nagging at her. What if Calexco's executives were the men who insisted she be hired for this project? What if they'd covered up something she didn't know about that freighter in the bay last year? Could she be guilty of something illegal by association?

"What is it, Starr? If you can prove Harrison isn't on the up-and-up, spit it out."

"I can't afford to get involved in *any* scandal. Wanda Manning wants to block my adoption of SeLi."

Clay filled two coffee mugs to keep his hands steady. The time for getting answers had come. He set the mugs on the table and asked her to join him. "Isn't it unusual for a single person your age to adopt?" he asked casually. "Especially a nine-year-old?"

Starr tensed, so Clay tried to be more tactful. "I mean, even though California's testing unusual adoptions, it can't have been easy for you to get SeLi."

"I was winding down a job on the wharf the day SeLi's mother died. SeLi was terrified. At first I only planned to give her a bed on my couch until after the funeral. But child-protection services took her into custody. When I went by to see how she was doing, I found it a terribly depressing place. I knew then that I didn't want her to live her life in a series of foster homes." Starr ran her finger around the edge of the cup. "The rules for adoption are tough. My apartment only had one bedroom, which is a no-no. The committee wasn't pleased that I'd come from a broken home, either. I asked the senator to vouch for me.

He knows my folks. Knows that my grandfather left me a trust fund. He offered to lease me the condo for a year at a reduced rate—until I get the trust turned over to me. And he said he'd vouch for me at the hearing."

She stared into space. "That was a good thing. He and Judge Forbes were friends. The judge was on my side all the way. He waived the hearing and signed the forms to initiate the process."

Clay stopped her story. "Did Harrison intervene on your behalf—or SeLi's? I can't believe how alike those two are. Harrison conned everyone in our neighborhood by the time he was nine, too."

"Not this again." Starr glared at him over the rim of her mug. "Frankly I don't see a shred of resemblance. Maybe it's his silver sideburns," she said sarcastically. "Or does he dye them to make himself look distinguished?"

"Only his barber knows for sure." Clay laughed. "It's not so much that I think they *look* alike, Starr. It's more their mannerisms, I guess. And SeLi's always a step ahead of her playmates when it comes to figuring the angles."

"That's a fact." Starr sobered. "A learned response? I can't begin to imagine living by my wits the way she did." Starr set her mug down and ran a fingernail along a crack in the tabletop. "Do you remember when your wallet went missing?"

He nodded, ready to apologize for thinking she'd taken it. But she didn't give him a chance.

"SeLi picked your pocket, slick as you please. I knew the day I took it up to you. Just yesterday I found out she'd taken some of your photographs. I'm sorry about that."

"I know. She confessed to me. I stopped by to see you. She was in the kitchen collecting a workbook, and the photos were on the counter. I'm sorry I blamed you. I still can't figure out how she did it without my being aware." He frowned. "Although, if memory serves, I was preoccupied with you at the time."

Starr felt her cheeks heat. He'd had a powerful effect on her, too. Still did. She just didn't know what it was about SeLi that made him uneasy. She and SeLi came as a package, and if he had a problem with that, anything between them was over. "Tell me what business you had with Wanda Manning." *There. That should get things out in the open.*

Clay stood. He stretched the kinks out of his back and started to pace. "Harrison has always led a charmed life. Things come easy to him. Attorney at twenty-six. DA at thirty-five. State senator at forty-five. Young, pretty wife, and the first grandson on either side of the family. You get the picture. Plums fall into his lap, and he accepts them as his due. I have never, not in thirty-five years, seen him stick his neck out for anyone."

"Never?" Starr flew out of her chair. "You don't still think he . . . I . . . we're . . . Oh, for Pete's sake."

Clay smoothed a hand over his mustache. "I know better than that now." He shook his head. "Do you know why SeLi's adoption file is closed?"

Her eyes widened. "I didn't know it was. Who said?"

"Wanda Manning—when I went to see if Harrison's name was on the birth certificate." Clay felt a certain satisfaction in seeing her shocked expression.

"If you McLeods don't beat all." She pointed an accusing finger at Clay. "You suspect your fine, up-

standing older brother of having a love child hidden
away on the docks. Meanwhile, he's convinced you're
having an affair with his wife. What a family.''

Clay bristled, then shrugged.

"I know politics is a dirty business,'' she said, "but
you two guys have enough material for a third-rate
soap opera.''

Suddenly claustrophobic, Clay pulled back the curtain and sized up the weather. It was still snowing "Put
like that,'' he muttered, "it does sound sordid. Yet if
you'd ever met my parents, you wouldn't believe any
of it. They've been married for more than fifty years,
and they're still crazy about each other.'' Letting the
curtain fall, he crossed the room and placed another
log on the fire.

Starr didn't realize she'd been holding her breath
until she let it out. It was nice to hear that about his
parents.

Clay paused to inspect the clothes he'd hung near the
fire to dry.

Starr's gaze followed him and softened.

Casually he stepped into the stiff jeans, but when he
realized she was watching, he turned away to zip them.
Then he laughed. "Guess it's a little late for modesty
between us now.''

Starr jumped up nervously and went to refill their
mugs. But the day stretched long before them. If she
shied away from everything he said or did, they'd never
make it through this forced confinement.

Clay joined her at the counter. Apparently he had
the same idea. "Maybe if you could see where I was
coming from, Starr... Not every woman is as strong
as you. Vanessa was raised by her father—a very old-
fashioned Southern gentleman. Her upbringing is at

odds with the demands of her life. I think that's the cause of her migraines.''

He accepted the mug from Starr and took a sip. ''In the early years of her marriage to Harrison, he treated her like a hothouse flower. She thrived on it. Then he began dividing his time between home and Sacramento, and little by little things changed. I remember when Morgan was born. Van wanted a full-time nurse. Harrison said he needed to bond with his constituents—most of whom can't afford that kind of thing— so he refused. They argued about everything after that.''

Clay covered a yawn, then resumed. ''To make a long story short, Harrison turned the ranch and other assets over to me. He stuck Vanessa and Morgan in a big old house in San Francisco while he went off glad-handing all over the state. I'm not excusing Van, but isolation and motherhood took their toll. The busier Harrison got, the more time she spent at the ranch. Most nights I was at least home for dinner. I swear to you, Starr, I've never touched her in anything but a brotherly way.'' His flashing blue eyes dared Starr to say otherwise.

''I do believe you—now.''

''Good.'' He went to inspect his boots that sat by the crackling fire. ''At first Harris drove down on weekends. If I made a trip north, I took Vanessa and Morgan with me. Last year I noticed Van had begun to smother Morgan.'' Clay sat and pulled on one boot. ''I tried talking to Harrison. In hindsight I can see I may have added fuel to the fire. My brother's indifference drove me nuts. Finally, last Christmas, I said to hell with him and did what I could for the boy. I never dreamed Harrison thought…" Clay swore and yanked on his other boot. "You know the rest of the story."

She frowned. "There's more?"

"The day you met Harrison at the restaurant, I'd just decided to find out what was going on. Why he never called. Why he seemed too busy for his wife and son. Maybe you don't realize how much he's changed. Anyway, once I got a look at you, I figured I'd found the problem. Except we've cleared that up, and I still think he's acting odd—like he's hiding something. God, Starr. I want to be wrong about his name being on that birth certificate. I really do."

Jumping to his feet, Clay shrugged into his jacket and headed for the door. "None of this makes sense. But right now, I need to locate food for the horses again. Maybe we can get out of here tomorrow. Why don't you take a nap while I'm gone? You didn't get much rest last night."

Before Starr could blink, the broken door vibrated on its hinges. Phew, he'd been carting around some burden. But the stuff about Harrison fathering SeLi and the blackmail… Of course, Clay knew his brother better than she did.

Starr yawned.

A nap did sound inviting. But if she slept now, would she be awake all night? Her breath caught. Would Clay expect her to share his bed again?

Did she want to?

Restless, she circled the room. Clay McLeod made her feel … well, to put it another way, he was the one she'd wished for on SeLi's Christmas star. Yes, in spite of everything, he'd worked his way into her heart.

The sixty-four-dollar question—was she in his?

"Darn, darn, darn!" Starr kicked a leg of the heavy old rocker. All thought of sleep gone, she limped across the room to look over a supply of books the rangers kept. Technical manuals to do with forest preservation. A bunch of science-fiction novels. Several spy stories. She wasn't in the mood. Well, her only other choice was a three-hundred-page book called *Whistlepunks and Geoducks*. A collection of oral histories of fishermen, wheat farmers, loggers and saloon-keepers from the Pacific Northwest. The author's previous book was called *River Pigs and Cayuses*. It sounded as if the man had a sense of humor. She could use a laugh or two about now.

Only she couldn't keep her mind on the stories. Instead, her thoughts drifted to Clay McLeod—and what living with him would be like.

CHAPTER THIRTEEN

CLAY KNEW he'd had to get out of the cabin. Every time Starr ran her tongue over those kissable lips, he'd wanted to forget small talk and take her back to bed. Physical labor—that was what he needed.

After spending half an hour digging out greenery for the horses, he cut and stacked enough firewood to last a decade. But the more he cut, the more visions of Starr crowded in. Swearing, he paused briefly to wipe sweat from his brow. Again his ax bit deep into a snow-encrusted log. Chips flew. The horses shied nervously. He glanced out the shed door and saw the sky had grown murkier and the flakes had turned into stinging sleet. His watch said four o'clock.

Damn. He'd suggested she go to bed. That was stupid. It wasn't even suppertime. How in blazes could he sit around for hours watching her curled under a blanket he knew would bear her scent? Clay laughed. If he stayed out here much longer, this woodpile would make it into *The Guinness Book of World Records*.

STARR TOSSED her book aside and plumped the pillow into a corner of the daybed. Either Clay's earthy aftershave lingered on this pillow case, or she had a vivid imagination.

The fire cast a warm circle of light. Staring into the dancing flames, she couldn't help wondering why no one had mentioned to her that SeLi's records were sealed.

Would she be able to get her daughter a passport?

Not that she had plans to travel anytime soon. She didn't think her dad would invite them to visit him in Japan; she'd seen on the cover of one of the tabloids that he had a new girlfriend. A Japanese actress. At least now he was single, and this one was actually old enough to be her mother.

Starr's eyelids drooped. She should remind SeLi to add a clause to her wish list for a dad—that he not have a wandering eye. Starr stretched out on the bed. Maybe a woman forgot such things when she fell in love. *Love.* The word evoked warmth, like the fire. *To love and be loved.* That was what she wanted in marriage. Was that so difficult, so much to ask? Clay seemed loyal to his family. Would he also be loyal to a wife?

Sleep overtook her in the middle of that thought. Soon Clay McLeod had worked himself into her dreams, too.

Clay found her asleep, snug as a bug when he staggered into the cabin under a massive load of firewood. The sweetness shimmering from her hit him like a stab to the chest. Walking softly, he deposited the logs, then sat for a moment in the straight-backed chair opposite the daybed. He studied her as he idly brushed wood chips from his jacket.

She possessed a natural beauty and a warm sense of humor. She was caring and loyal. A man could share secrets with this woman.

Clay felt a sharp wrench in his heart. He was in love, and he hadn't recognized the symptoms. Amazing. But maybe not. He'd been in lust before, but at thirty-five, he'd pretty much given up on love.

The bleep of the radio broke into his reflections. He ran to answer it before the noise woke Starr. After her ordeal yesterday, she needed the rest.

Harrison's voice boomed into the cabin. "Base station to ranger cabin three." Twice, Harrison barked the phrase.

"I read you, Harris." Clay let his annoyance show. "What's up?"

"Let me talk to Starr," his brother ordered. Static took over the airwaves before Clay could answer.

He fiddled with the dials, unsure whether to tell Harrison she was sleeping. His brother had a cutting sense of humor, and suddenly Starr wasn't someone Clay wanted to joke about.

"Good afternoon to you, too," Clay said coolly. "Starr's asleep," he admitted after seeing no way out of it. "May I relay a message?"

"I'm not asleep," she said with a yawn at his elbow. "Not anymore."

Clay wheeled around. His arm brushed her breast. If her softness hadn't stoked fires he'd thought successfully banked, the sight of her tousled from sleep would have.

"Get her up." Harrison demanded, unaware that the two were standing there, by the radio, staring into each other's eyes.

Fumbling, Starr took the microphone from Clay's hand. Her voice bore the sounds of recent sleep. "I'm here, Senator. Who could sleep through the racket you made?"

"You're barking up the wrong tree," he said without preamble. "We want you to pull out. We'll send somebody back in the spring to see if the cold weather has stamped out this virus or whatever. You're off the hook, kid. In fact, why don't you and SeLi join us for Christmas?''

Starr chewed on her lower lip. "You mean Calexco denied using the chemical?"

"I mean it's no longer your concern. Relax, Starr. It has nothing to do with Calexo's test well—which, by the way, showed excellent preliminary results."

Starr heard a hint of nervousness in his tone. Clay heard it, too and frowned.

"Senator," she said, "I work for Fish and Game. Those sheep are very much my concern. I know there's Drixathyon in that stream. You have more clout than I do, Senator, but if you don't apply pressure on Calexco, I will."

Harrison snorted. "Clout. I'll tell you about clout. *Money* is clout. People need it. Our state needs it. Who do you think has money? Companies like Calexco."

"The price is too high. Tell them to go to hell," Clay cut in.

Harrison was silent for so long both Starr and Clay thought they'd lost transmission. Finally his voice was back, cool and a bit stilted. "It's not all that easy, Clay. You don't understand."

"You're damn right I don't. Spell it out for me, bro. Do they own you, or is it a simple matter of returning a few contributions?"

"For God's sake, Clay. I don't like being called on the carpet. We aren't talking about the mob here. They're businessmen, like you and me—friends. A few of us go way back. Besides," he grumbled, calming a bit, "I believe it's some new virus. I know these men. They have no reason to lie."

"No reason?" Starr gaped at Clay. "They have the biggest reason of all. It's called greed, Senator."

"I didn't realize you were a flaming socialist, Starr," Harrison snapped. "Dammit, we need those jobs, and—"

Fortunately to her way of thinking static broke up the transmission again and whatever he said after that faded completely. Starr was so angry she could have spit. Unable to speak, she shoved the mike back into Clay's hands and moved away.

Clay stroked his mustache for several seconds before he depressed the talk switch again. "Hey, bro. No need for tempers to get out of hand."

Harrison's laugh sounded garbled. "Pot calling the kettle black, Clay? This from the guy who rattled my teeth yesterday? I hope your hand is as discolored as my jaw."

"If it means anything, I'm not proud of the way I acted. But our fight wasn't about life and death. Take another crack at your friends at Calexco, okay? If Starr's right about this, you guys might all be in hot water."

The laugh that came through the speaker was brittle. "You wound me, little brother. Have you forgotten 'tis the season to be jolly? This morning Van invited Mom and Dad and her dad here for Christmas."

"And they're all coming? Hey, great. Now I won't have to ship that damned statue of mom's."

Across the room Starr listened to the banter between brothers and a sinkhole opened in her stomach. She nearly missed Harrison's next comment.

"By the way, Clay, not to change the subject, but Vanessa took a call for you from a very disagreeable woman this afternoon. She refused to state her business and hung up when Van said we didn't know when you'd be back. Are you telling me all of *your* activities are aboveboard?"

Wanda Manning. Damn! Clay gave a guilty start. Why had he been foolish enough to get involved with that woman? Harrison didn't sound like a man embroiled in blackmail. Well, when he got back to the ranch, he'd just have to call and tell her to get lost. To Harrison, Clay said, "If you didn't get a name, I can't very well defend myself, now can I? Uh-oh, transmission's breaking up again. Before I lose you completely, tell me about the weather."

Harrison seemed willing to change the subject. "If we can believe the weather bureau, your idyllic mountain vacation is almost over. They're predicting a mass of warm air blowing in from Baja and snow should melt in lower elevations tonight. It'll hit you by morning."

"Vacation?" snorted Clay. "This is hardly Club Med."

Harrison laughed. Clay saw Starr signaling him, so he clicked off for a moment.

She came back and took the mike again. "How is SeLi?" she asked a bit wistfully. "Is she where I could talk to her?"

"I don't quite know how to tell you, Starr, but I don't think she even misses you." Harrison laughed, sounding his old self. "I'm out in Hank's office. SeLi and Morgan are up at the house writing letters to Santa. I tell you, Starr, those two are acting just like brother and sister. She's been good for Morgan."

Starr was positive the color left her face. But maybe not, as Clay took the mike without giving her an I-told-you-so look. She clenched her fists. SeLi and Morgan were nothing alike. They weren't!

"We'll sign off now," Clay said. "Call if you hear of any change in the weather."

"Roger. Say, if that woman calls back, what shall I tell her?"

"I'm sure it's nothing," Clay said. He didn't want Harrison brooding over it and perhaps remembering Wanda's voice. "If we get a Chinook, maybe Starr and I'll poke around some more out where I found her. I started thinking. What if it's fumes of some kind? Maybe Calexco's flunkies didn't cap their test well properly."

Harrison didn't reply. Clay tried to make contact several times and finally gave up. "Guess we lost him. Must be the storm. I'll buzz him back tomorrow."

Starr sighed wearily. "It's not fumes." She slumped into one of the two kitchen chairs, dropped her head and began to rub her temples. "I'm not sure what chemical action takes place. Somehow, when Drixathyon is mixed with water its properties change." She shook her head and sat upright. "Did you get the feeling that bunch at Calexco thinks wildlife is dispensable? I don't understand people like that."

Clay's heart twisted. She was such a compassionate person. Animals. Kids. She'd been giving as a lover, too. Only too aware he shouldn't touch her when he was in this frame of mind, Clay walked up behind her and began to slowly massage her neck and shoulders.

"Would you tell me again everything you know about this Drixathyon?" Tilting her head back, he smiled down into her eyes.

Although her headache was subsiding under Clay's hands, a different type of tension had built. She reminded herself she didn't want him picking her theories apart.

But even after she told Clay she didn't want to go back over old ground, she hadn't counted on his persistence—or his magical fingers.

Her head lolled back and she groaned.

"Please." He kneaded her shoulders and smiled that engaging smile again.

Maybe it wouldn't hurt if they batted it around. After all, he might pick up on something she'd missed. Bit by bit, Starr went over what had happened from the time she left the ranch.

Clay's fingers tightened when she told him how she felt after drinking from the stream.

"That's basically all there is to tell," she said, pulling away. She stood up and crossed to the kitchen to brew a new pot of coffee.

"Not much solid evidence to go on." Clay carried their cups to the sink and rinsed them.

"Enough for me. I'm sure it's Drixathyon. I just don't know how it got in the stream. I hadn't realized they used it in drilling on land. To be truthful, I didn't dream I'd ever run across it again. If I knew more, I might have saved those last two ewes," she said sadly.

Clay slid his hand beneath her chin and turned her face to his. "Don't blame yourself. You did everything possible given the weather. If it clears tomorrow, as Harrison said, we'll go find that stream and take a look around."

"I will. You should go back to the ranch. This is my job, not yours, Clay."

"Nonsense." He ran his thumb over her bottom lip. "That stream originates underground. Maybe the drillers accidentally blundered into it. Do you have any idea what we'd be looking for? Pellets? Granules?"

Starr gazed at him helplessly. "On the offshore rigs it was liquid. They pumped mud or sludge through the Drixathyon. The way I understood, it changed color if the properties in crude oil were present. On land, I honestly don't know how it would work. And I've turned it over in my head so many times I feel like my brain's going to self-destruct."

Clay led her to the kitchen table, pushed her lightly down into a chair and returned a moment later with a steaming cup of coffee. He ruffled her auburn curls. "Why don't you relax? I'll see what Paul-baby has stashed for supper. There's nothing we can do until it stops snowing. Might as well make ourselves at home until it does."

Starr didn't return his smile. "Clay, if you're suggesting we play house..."

"I wasn't. But I'd certainly entertain the idea." He bent and brushed a soft kiss on her forehead.

She pulled back. Even the rough texture of his shirt-sleeve where it touched her cheek was much too appealing.

However, Clay read the truth in her eyes—that she was just as affected by the kiss as he. Gently he pulled her from the chair and settled a real kiss on her lips.

Their two bodies fused perfectly. On a sigh, she rose up to kiss him back.

Groaning, Clay took the kiss deeper. All at once a gust of wind rattled the door. It blew open and the chair that had been tilted beneath the knob fell to the floor with a crash

They sprang apart.

Starr licked her lips. "Clay, we can't do this," she said.

"If we don't, it's going to be a long night," he muttered, dashing over to right the chair and close the door.

When he came back, expecting to take up where he'd left off, she reached up to touch his face. "Listen to me, Clay. I didn't have anything in the way of birth control. We took a chance this morning."

"I see." He cupped her hand. "Everything happened so fast I didn't think." Truth was, he wouldn't mind if she *was* pregnant. He wanted her to be the mother of his children. Obviously she didn't feel the same way.

"Maybe we should eat," he said gruffly. Leaving her hand hovering in midair, he turned and stalked to the stove. He savagely ripped the top off a box of macaroni and cheese that he'd set out earlier, filled a pan with water and slapped it on a burner. "Rifle through those cupboards under the shortwave and see if you can come up with a deck of cards or something," he growled without looking at her. "We're gonna need something to occupy our time." He grabbed a packet of skim-milk powder. "Should never have started this," he muttered. *Should have waited,* he meant, until circumstances were better.

She gazed at him steadily. So there it was, plain as day. He regretted their lovemaking. *Sex,* she corrected. If he didn't care for her the way she cared for him, it reduced what they'd shared to a one-night stand. Meaningless sex. *One-morning stand,* she thought hysterically.

If Clay had the faintest idea what was going through Starr's mind, he might not have been so desperate to focus on the recipe for macaroni and cheese. What kept getting in the way of his reading the fine print was the knowledge that if she didn't find something to keep them entertained—and his mind off making love to her—Clay thought he'd have to spend the night in the shed with the horses.

Maybe he should do that, anyway, guilty as he felt. This was the first time in his life that he hadn't taken responsibility for protecting his partner. To make matters worse, the issue between Starr and him was a whole lot more complicated than sex. And dammit, they still had some unfinished business to clear up before he could, in good conscience, declare his love.

Just then the water boiled over, sizzled and spat against the hot burner. Clay leapt back and swore. Earlier, when he'd been chopping wood, he'd planned out how he'd court her. She deserved candlelight, wine and bouquets of flowers. All the traditional symbols of romance. He finished preparing the powdered milk and poured some over the macaroni.

What if she won't have you? a little voice jeered. After all, Starr didn't seem to need a man in her life. Clay scowled and stirred the cheese in so hard it flew up all over the sides of the pan and out onto his shirt.

From across the room, Starr sneaked peeks at him as she got down on her hands and knees and searched the cupboard he'd suggested. His horrendous frown and the way he was beating up that pasta spelled only one thing to her. Clay McLeod was no longer interested in having her as his lover—or, as he'd offered earlier, his mistress.

"Mistress, indeed!" She dug out a dusty checkerboard tucked deep in a corner of one shelf and slapped it down on the floor. She yanked out a box of checkers, and the lid flew off the box, raining checkers everywhere. It matched her bad mood perfectly.

The crash had Clay glancing up from placing the macaroni dish on the table. He was treated to a view of Starr's derriere in the air as she dived after a checker that had rolled under one of the daybeds.

Clay almost dropped their meal. "Leave those, for Pete's sake. Come and eat while it's hot."

Hurt by his surly attitude, Starr stood and slammed the box of checkers down on the cabinet so hard it bounced off again. "Don't take your bad temper out on me, McLeod. I don't like being here any more than you do." Feeling mutinous, she stormed over to the sink to wash her hands—missing the pained expression that crossed his face.

They sat and consumed their meager supper in total silence.

When he'd polished off the last forkful, Clay cleared his throat. "I, uh, made a worthwhile discovery. Old Paul had a sparkling wine hidden up on the top shelf—and a very good year." He rose, draped a tea towel over his arm and returned with a slender green bottle, which he placed before Starr with all the flourish of a wine steward.

Reluctant at first, she soon grasped it as a lifeline. "Bless old Paul," she joked. "And here I thought he only hung out with a blue ox. Champagne and checkers in front of a roaring fire. Why, I know people who pay hundreds of dollars for such luxury. We have it free. What more could a woman ask?"

Clay might have mentioned a few things, but didn't.

Starr read the message his eyes telegraphed and imagined the obvious addition to the picture she'd unwittingly painted. That of two lovers sharing a soft rug in front of a cozy fire.

Shivering, she said his name, half-begging, half-panicking, as she jumped to her feet. Afraid he understood the part she'd left unsaid, she murmured lightly, "I'm no good with corks. You do the honors and I'll see if old Paul has wineglasses."

She found only water glasses. But that way, it didn't seem quite so... romantic.

The wine was relaxing, the fire soothing. Their natural competitiveness soon edged out the wariness with which they'd entered the game.

After two games that both ended in a dead heat, they moved from the table to the rug. When they'd reached a three-game tie, both were feeling quite mellow. Enough to joke about skipping the tiebreaker. Suddenly a log fell, scattering sparks across the checkerboard.

The wine hadn't dulled Clay's reflexes. He bounded up, yanked Starr aside and thrust her behind him all in one motion. Then he shook the board and stamped out a few glowing embers that hit the rug.

"You didn't get burned, did you?" he asked her anxiously.

"No." She ran a hand through her hair and laughed nervously. "But that definitely decided the fate of the last game." Her teasing glance followed the flight of the checkers, one or two still circling on the floor.

Clay shrugged. "It's late."

She nodded and yawned.

He looked at his watch, reluctant to call an end to the day. "It's after eleven. Where's the time gone?" he murmured. "We haven't solved even half the world's problems."

She smiled. "I can't believe we agreed on as much as we did. I enjoyed myself. Did you?"

Clay smoothed a hand over her springy curls. "Very much."

Starr felt the quiver of his touch clear to her toes. Retreating, she knelt and began gathering the game pieces.

"I'll do the dishes while you take a turn in the bathroom," he offered. "Don't rush. I need to check on the horses and see what the weather's doing."

"Okay, but which bed do you want?"

Her husky question was almost more than Clay could handle. He turned toward the sink. With his back to her, he said, "You take the one we, uh, the one you... Hell, just pick one. Toss half the blankets on the other. I gave you most of them last night. You won't find me so generous tonight."

"Ha! This morning you had them all." Silence fell as Starr realized what she'd said.

Clay studied her as she bent over to put the board away. Abruptly, he turned off the water, snatched up his jacket and strode outside.

Starr resisted the urge to run to the door and watch his progress. She couldn't, however, take a chance on his glancing back and seeing her. Each time their eyes met, she longed to be in his arms. If she could have one more wish on SeLi's Christmas star...

Afraid to linger in case he come back too soon, Starr took a quick turn in the bathroom. Then, fully clothed, she dived under the covers. With luck, maybe she'd be asleep when he returned.

Clay stood in the doorway to the shed for a long time just watching the cabin. The horses were restless from prolonged confinement, just as he was. He tried calming them with soft, meaningless words.

Apparently the ranger was a smoker; either that, or the guy was trying to quit, for Clay had found an unopened pack stuck in a flowerpot. Clay himself had been doing so well. Now, however, he thought a smoke was just what he needed.

He tore open the pack and shook one out. Unwilling to leave the shelter, he let it dangle loose and unlit between his lips as he idly stroked the pinto's neck. A steady drip-drip of water from the eaves told him the weather was warming at last.

He went back to the door and leaned against the frame. If he could make it through the night, tomorrow they'd get back to the ranch and tie up all the loose ends. Only after the lights went out in the cabin were his hands steady enough to light the cigarette. But as a silver moon drifted between the clouds, Clay dropped the half-finished cigarette and ground it out under the heel of his boot.

If the thaw continued, allowing them to find the Drixathyon, Starr would pack up and leave. Clay didn't want that. But if for any reason they had to stay cooped up one more day, he thought he'd lose his mind.

Taking time to pull a last handful of greenery for each horse, Clay left the shed and jogged toward the cabin. He prayed Starr was fast asleep.

Inside, he navigated by a single ribbon of moonlight. The fire was down to a glowing bed of coals. He added two logs, then made short work of his nightly routine. He passed Starr's bed on tiptoe, taking note that she was curled up facing the wall.

His boots were wet and he had trouble getting them off. Once that was done, he quietly removed his jeans and shirt and crawled under the blankets Starr had left spread out on his bed. He sighed as he settled into a reasonably comfortable position.

Starr heard every move he made. She ground her teeth, forcing herself to remain silent. He'd tried so hard to be quiet she didn't have the heart to tell him she was awake. But knowing he was so close, she couldn't keep from stirring.

"Starr, are you awake?" Clay's gravelly voice came from very near her own pillow.

Blast! She'd forgotten the heads of their two beds touched. Why hadn't she slid them apart?

"Are you cold or what?" Again his soft voice floated over her. She felt his body shift, and though she kept her eyes closed, she knew he'd raised himself up on one elbow to look at her.

"Hot," she mumbled, as the flame of desire licked through her veins. "I'm hot."

"No wonder," Clay chided. "You're dressed for the outdoors, city girl. The fireplace keeps this room warm. Why don't you shed half those clothes?"

Starr flopped over onto her stomach, recalling how she'd awakened this morning nearly naked. Shifting again, she rocked his bed.

"Will you lie still?" Clay dropped back on his pillow and covered his eyes with a forearm. What control he'd possessed earlier was almost shot to hell.

Starr knew he was right; she was overdressed. But she'd be darned if she'd give him a peep show in the light of the fire. Lying flat under the covers, she shrugged out of her shirt and wriggled free of her jeans.

Both beds bounced.

"Starr—" Clay gnashed his teeth "—stand up and take the damn things off. What do you think? That I'll attack you?"

"They're off."

"Thank goodness for small favors." But he didn't sound thankful.

"I wish I had pajamas," she muttered, wriggling again to get comfortable.

Clay groaned. "Never thought I'd admit it, but I wish you did, too. Preferably those glow-in-the-dark ones with the feet."

She ignored his gibe and pulled a blanket up to her chin. The rough material scratched her skin.

"What's wrong now?" he demanded as his bed swayed again.

"This blanket itches. Maybe I'll get Paul Bunyan's shirt to wear. What did you do with it?"

"It's on the chair. I'll get it," he said quickly. "Stay where you are." The air left Clay's lungs as he considered the effect of watching her trot past in her lingerie to find that damned shirt.

"I don't need you to wait on me." Starr stood and marched directly to the chair.

Clay's brain was paralyzed. Her skin looked like mother-of-pearl in the flickering firelight. *Oh, God, it was pure torture!* Swiftly, he turned his face away and counted to ten.

He felt her climb back into bed before he gave in to his fantasies.

Starr hadn't given any thought to the fact that his scent would linger on the shirt. She was positive she wouldn't sleep a wink. However, before long she dozed off.

It wasn't nearly so easy for Clay. He could see the night sky through the uncurtained window above his bed. A single star appeared and winked brightly, as if reminding him of the night he and Starr had tumbled in the hay. He recalled hearing Morgan and SeLi outside discussing a Christmas star. Softly he repeated the words he'd heard his nephew chant. "Star light, star bright, first star I see tonight. I wish I may, I wish I might..." Clay stumbled over the ending. No way would he get his wish tonight. But what if he wished for something longer term?

He glanced at Starr and suddenly all wishes seemed possible in the stillness of the night.

CHAPTER FOURTEEN

PULLED FROM a pleasant dream by rays of sunlight dancing across the cabin floor, Starr emerged from her warm cocoon of blankets, more rested than she'd felt in days. And she'd been so certain she wouldn't sleep at all.

As she stretched and yawned, she took care to not disturb the second bed. But she needn't have worried. Clay's blanket and pillow lay neatly folded. She was alone.

And disappointed...

Just then the door opened, and his rugged form filled the space. For no reason at all, Starr felt elated. Tremors shook her suddenly nerveless limbs and sent her burrowing back under the covers.

"So, Sleeping Beauty awakes," he teased. Drops of water glistened on his ebony hair and two-day beard.

Starr found it less threatening to concentrate on his trail of wet footprints as he approached.

"I hate to rush your beauty routine, but it's warming up fast. The snow is slushy and getting slick. If we don't leave soon, it'll be too dangerous up top."

"Dangerous?"

"Avalanche." The single word was muffled by a cupboard door. "How do you feel about having crackers and canned cheese for breakfast?"

"Ugh," she said without inflection.

"Are you all right? You sound funny." Clay peered around the cabinet. Actually he didn't trust himself to go closer. It had taken every ounce of willpower he possessed to leave her asleep in that bed.

"I'm fine. Are you saying you're jumping with joy over the prospect of eating canned cheese?" Starr screwed up her face, then sighed. "Don't pay any attention to my foul mood." She reached out from beneath the blanket and picked up her shirt and jeans. "It may have something to do with not wanting to climb into these dirty clothes again. A pity Paul was so big."

Clay laughed, but his hands fumbled with the can as a sudden vision of the two of them sharing his big tiled shower at the ranch flashed through his mind.

"Just be thankful the cabin was here." Clay didn't mean to sound gruff. He only wanted her out of that damned bed.

Starr rose, wrapped the blanket around her and strolled past him into the bathroom. Talk about bad mood! He was downright grumpy. Sighing again, she stepped into her creased jeans and pulled on her rumpled shirt.

The eyes that stared out at her from the scratched mirror looked dull. No wonder he thought something was wrong. She lamented not having a comb to fix her hair, then decided no one cared how she looked anyway. Certainly not Clay McLeod. He acted as if she was Typhoid Mary.

She joined him moments later. Neither spoke again as they moved mechanically around the cabin, preparing to leave.

After the filling meal, which turned out to be cheese soup and crackers, Starr folded blankets and put them away. Then she carefully restored the kitchen to order while Clay nailed a new board on the door. When Starr joined him outside, he wired it shut.

"Shouldn't we have called the ranch?" she asked, squinting at the vast expanse of brilliant white. This was the first time she'd ventured outside since Clay had brought her here, and she was shocked to see the snow had drifted as high as the sloped roof of the cabin.

Clay placed a palm at her waist to guide her toward the shed. "I did that earlier while you were snoring away."

"I don't snore."

A smile twitched. "How do you know?"

She stopped in her tracks, frowning.

Since he didn't say anything else, she added pensively, "I would've liked a word with SeLi."

He shrugged and walked on ahead. "It was early. I talked to Hank. He said the house was still dark. We need to be quick about this side trip to look for the Drixathyon. Might be a new storm brewing. So unless you want to spend Christmas here eating beans and ham..."

A snowball struck the back of his neck. "What in hell?" He turned, hopping on one foot and brushing snow out from under his collar. Then he saw Starr bent double, laughing.

"Wanna play rough, huh?" He scooped up snow, formed a loose ball and advanced on her.

"No, Clay...please! Oh, no...ooh that's cold. It went down my blouse, darn you."

"Play with fire and you're bound to get burned. Or frozen, as the case may be."

"Truce," she called as he packed a new snowball. "I just couldn't resist. You sounded so sanctimonious."

He dropped the snowball and dusted snow off his gloves. "Well, do you want us getting stuck here over Christmas?"

Striding away in silence, she plowed a hand through her hair to shake out the lingering snow.

"I didn't think so," he said. "I just spoke the truth." Which was more, Clay thought guiltily, than he'd done in saying he'd talked to Hank. His brother had actually had the kids out in the barn looking at kittens. Harrison had mentioned that the nasty woman had called back. Apparently she'd told Vanessa that if Clay didn't return her call by this morning, she'd take matters into her own hands. Clay wished he knew what that meant. Provided they made it down the mountain before dark, he'd be able to reach the social worker and forestall any mischief she might have planned.

Sometime in the night, during one of those times he lay watching Starr sleep, Clay had made up his mind to drop the issue of SeLi's parentage. What did it matter, anyway? He'd determined that his time would be better spent convincing Starr and SeLi to add him to their family. Which could only happen after Starr cleared up this mess with Calexco to her satisfaction.

Now that Clay had his brother's family back on track, he intended to see things stayed that way. If Harrison had inadvertently gotten mixed up in something less than strictly legal, Clay wanted to know now. There was probably still time for his brother to pull back, make reparation, before doing any real damage to his career.

Waiting at the entrance to the shed, Starr saw a range of emotions cross Clay's face. He looked like a man who'd mulled over important questions and come up with answers. Did any of them concern her?

But he gave her no opportunity to ask. As he brushed past her and went inside, another more immediate situation reared its head.

"You take the gelding today, Starr," he said as he hoisted the smaller saddle onto the big bay and cinched it tight. "Patches is jittery as hell from being cooped up so long."

"I can handle her." Starr sounded defensive and knew it.

"It's not open for negotiation." Bent over the second saddle, Clay didn't see the irritation with which she transferred the dart gun to the gelding.

It was a wonder the arrogant Barclay McLeod trusted her to carry it, she thought waspishly. And just whose project was this, anyway?

The instant the pinto began to buck, almost unseating Clay, Starr hastily revised her snide comment. Instead, she watched with admiration as he rode out the stiff-legged bucking.

"Wow!" She reined in and let the bay fall in behind. "I owe you an apology, Clay. Last time I got bucked off an ornery horse, I spent my entire summer vacation nursing three broken ribs. My Christmas vacation plans don't include broken bones."

Clay flashed her a smile, although he kept a tight rein on the feisty mare. "What *do* your plans include? Have you given any more thought to you and SeLi spending the holiday at the ranch?"

When she bit her lip and averted her gaze, Clay cursed himself for not being more subtle. "No need to decide now!" he said hastily. "It's just that the kids wrote all those letters to Santa. I figured SeLi expected the old boy to find her at the ranch."

"She can write him a fast retraction, and I'll mail it somewhere on the drive back to San Francisco. I have tickets to take her to see the *Nutcracker* the night before Christmas Eve. I wanted to surprise her, but if I have to, I'll tell her early."

"SeLi at the ballet." He grinned. "It's hard to picture."

"What do you mean by that?"

"Nothing to make you come unglued," he said, shrugging out of his jacket and tucking it in a saddlebag. "I'm just being selfish in wanting you to stay. But you're right—the ballet will be a treat for her."

He faced front again, drawing Starr's gaze to the ripple of muscles that played across his broad back. That man turned her insides to mush. But with luck the pinto was giving him so much grief he hadn't noticed.

Ahead, though the trail oozed mud and needed his full attention, Clay was far too aware of the woman who trailed him. That last time he'd turned to speak, he'd been laid low by the mere sight of her windblown hair and her cheeks kissed pink by the wind. Clay didn't trust himself to turn again.

He reminded himself of the avalanche danger and pressed on.

After another ten minutes of hard riding, they arrived in the general vicinity of the stream. Clay untied a shovel he'd borrowed from the ranger's shed and channeled his restless energy into scraping away the odd mounds of snow Starr pointed out. Some fifteen minutes into the process, he stopped to catch his breath and asked, "What am I looking for?"

Starr had climbed to the top of a pile of large rocks, out of which protruded a ragged red flag. She continued to scan a rocky promontory with her field glasses.

"I told you I don't know. I'm assuming the drilling team left this flag, and that somewhere nearby is their test well. They needed access to water to run a high-speed drill."

But the mountain clung stubbornly to its secrets. The only thing that differed from her first visit, besides the warmer weather, was the sound of melting snow raining from the many branches, drowning out the stream. Starr shivered, not really wanting to remember its taste.

Clay saw her shiver. "Are you cold?" He laughed, because he'd just stripped to the waist. Digging was hot work.

Starr couldn't answer. It had more to do with the fine sheen of sweat that coated his chest than with cold. Her gaze seemed to cling to his damp chest a long time before following the natural arrow of dark hair that eventually disappeared below his belt.

Since her fantasies refused to be controlled, Starr sighed and recapped the glasses, deciding she'd help him dig.

"You know," he said, "I don't mind reshaping the landscape. But I hate looking for a needle in a haystack."

"An apt description, since Calexco gave us nothing to go on."

Starr had just climbed down from her rocky perch when a mass of snow fell from the ridge above and thundered into the ravine.

Clay felt the shudder of the earth as the snow rumbled down the mountain. "We can't stay much longer," he cautioned her.

"I understand." She pointed out two large mounds made bigger by the slide. "Those are the two ewes I found. Is that near the headwater to the stream, do you think?''

He set his shovel down and scrambled up to stand on a fat boulder. "It flows out from under a horseshoe-shaped granite cliff. I remember one time when we came up looking for stray cattle after a big storm, my dad pointed out a distinctive, wind-twisted white fir he said he always used as a landmark." Clay shaded his eyes. "For all we know, the whole works could be buried in snow."

Starr clambered up beside him. She shied away from the heat that emanated from his body. It did strange things to her equilibrium. So much so that she got down from the boulder on the pretext of checking the horses, which they'd tethered well away from the stream. Both animals had begun to grow restless.

Suddenly Clay jumped down and grabbed her arm. "Look. Over there. I think that's the tree. Let's go see," he said, slipping his hand down to circle her waist.

Starr bumped against him several times on the walk down the snowy slope, and shocks of awareness wound their way up her body.

"This is it," he announced triumphantly a moment later, startling her. She'd been so focused on *him* she'd almost forgotten why they were doing this.

"We got here in a roundabout way," he said, eyes narrowed. "This is a lot closer to that flag stake than I thought."

Starr followed his gaze. "You're right, it is. Clay," she said urgently, "you dig on one side of the head-water and I'll do the other."

"How far do you think you'll get digging with your hands?''

"I have a small shovel in my kit. Biochemists frequently need to take samples. I'm not the hothouse rose you think I am."

"Ouch. Can't prove it by me, sugar. I'm bloody from the thorns."

"Remember? Don't call me sugar," she warned as she marched back to the horses where she dug a small, archaeological shovel out of her saddlebag. It was the type of shovel that needed to be unfolded and screwed together.

Clay wisely let her handle it alone. He set about digging.

In a matter of minutes, they were both turning over snow and then rocky soil. It wasn't easy work. No talk passed between them. Because Clay turned two shovels to Starr's one, he was first to uncover a narrow opening. "Looks like a gopher hole," he muttered.

"Underwater? What do you think it is?" she asked.

"It's suspicious. Why else would it be banked by rock halfway down?"

Starr raked a curl out of her eyes and slashed a streak of dirt the length of her cheek. "This gopher subscribes to *Architectural Digest* and moonlights on the side."

"Very funny, Lederman. Dig."

Both dug faster. Their shovels struck metal almost in unison.

"Bingo!" Clay tossed his shovel aside, and although they were both grimy with sweat, he clasped Starr to his chest.

"I knew it! I knew it!" Starr hugged him back.

"Let's see what we got, shall we?" Clay asked as they simultaneously dropped to their knees in the muck. He did his best to stem the flow of water with his shovel; while using hers, Starr exposed an oblong silver cylinder.

"Be careful," she shouted excitedly. "It's leaking around the vent."

Clay eased the muddy object from the hole and handed it to Starr to hold upright as he ran to get the plastic tarp tied behind his saddle. Slipping and sliding back, he quickly secured the leaking lid.

Starr stripped off her gloves and dipped in her forefinger. Their eyes met as she tasted it and almost gagged. "This is it. A whole snootful of Drixathyon," she said, wiping the taste off her tongue.

"Damn, damn, damn their careless hides." Clay drove a stake into the ground to mark the spot, then motioned to Starr that he'd carry the cylinder back up the hill.

He propped it against a granite rock while he put on his shirt. "This must be where the stuff came from. You can see where it was connected to something with this coupling—a hose, maybe. Obviously they took the hose. Why in hell would they leave this?"

"I have no idea. What I wonder is how many more animals will die before this stream runs clean again."

"Fortunately there are other water sources up here. Bear Trap Creek cuts diagonally through the preserve up around nine thousand feet. On the backside of the mountain, down a little lower, is Deer Creek Springs."

"We're at eight thousand something here?"

"Yes. Bighorns generally stay above this level unless the snow drives them down in search of food. We could lose more if that new storm blows in."

Starr glanced at the sky. The sun was struggling to shine. She noticed, however, that high clouds were moving in. Tahquitz Peak already looked as if it wore a halo. "There's not much we can do about the weather."

"No, but something we *can* do is scoop a couple feet of snow across that stream. You said the stuff eventually dissipates. Maybe melting snow will clean it faster."

Starr stood on tiptoe and landed a kiss in the vicinity of his ear. "Clay, I swear you're a genius."

A little embarrassed and a lot pleased, he stood for a moment with his hand to his cheek, watching as she tore down the hill and began shoveling snow like a madwoman. Then giving himself a mental shake, he went to lend a hand.

"Now," he said when they'd finished and both were panting, "let's hightail it out of here."

"Okay. I don't want this stuff evaporating or something before I can get it tested." She touched the well-wrapped container.

"We'll get it tested even if I have to fly it to the lab myself."

"You'd do that?" Starr asked, sounding surprised.

"Dammit, Starr, what do you think? I'm betting Harrison will, too, when he sees what we've got," he said firmly, grasping the bay's head as she mounted.

After her last conversation with the senator, Starr had her doubts. She didn't voice them, however, preferring, instead, to concentrate on the thud of the horses' hooves as they pulled against the muddy trail.

Taking the lead, Clay was soon lost in his own thoughts—namely, how he was going to talk Starr into sticking around through Christmas. And beyond. If he did have to fly the cylinder to the lab, maybe he'd take the time to buy an engagement ring.

An opal, he thought, to match Starr's fire. Surrounded by the icy flash of diamonds. Clay knew his mother would be enchanted with both Starr and SeLi. She'd love to sew frilly things for a granddaughter. Even though SeLi wasn't exactly the frilly type... His dad would just be glad that his younger son had finally found Ms. Right.

Starr enjoyed the first half of the ride. She was glad the senseless killing of sheep was nearing an end. But anxiety cropped up during the second half, when she realized it also meant she might never see Clay again—except as her landlord. And she couldn't afford to move until that trust fund kicked in.

From the moment the two riders entered the corral they were kept busy fielding questions thrown at them by Harrison and the two excited kids.

Hank Rogers, bless him, rode in from the range about then and took over the care of both muddy horses.

"Hold on a minute, Harris." Clay placed a staying hand on his brother's shoulder. "Do you mind if Starr and I clean up and find some decent food before you continue with this inquisition?"

Starr darted him a look of thanks over SeLi's head. "A shower. I mostly want a shower and clean clothes," she said, pausing to give SeLi another hug.

"Sure, sure," Harrison muttered. "I'm sorry to press. But dammit, Clay, what's all this about a container? I won't rest until I have the facts."

"I think you're a little late with your concern, big bro." Clay picked up the plastic-wrapped cylinder in one hand and placed the other at Starr's waist as he began moving the entourage toward the house.

Tension arced between the brothers. "You accusing me of something again, Clay?" Harrison demanded.

Clay stopped. "Like what, Harrison?"

The senator glanced from Clay to Starr, then shrugged eloquently. "I don't have the faintest idea. By the way, Starr, Stanley Ellsworth called last night. Said he got our number from directory assistance when he heard about the storm. You'd better call him back. He seems to think your being stranded in a snowstorm with my brother is tantamount to hitchhiking across the country with the Marquis de Sade."

"Mom," SeLi whined, "why is that yo-yo callin' you? Don't he know we're on vacation?"

"SeLi, please. I think it was sweet of Stanley. Friends worry about friends, honey. I'll call him the first chance I get."

Clay was glad to hear her use the term *friends*. Although he thought Starr was underestimating old Stanley.

"C'mon, Morgan," SeLi said with disgust. "If that Christmas star'd just show its face again tonight, we'd take care of Stanley Stupid."

"SeLi!" Starr was left shouting at the wind. SeLi had grabbed Morgan's hand and the two were streaking toward the ranch house.

"I'm going to go shower and change in the motor home," Starr said after a long sigh. "Shall we settle now on transporting the canister?"

Clay nodded. "I'll lock it in my safe until I can fly it out. You can either write instructions to send with me or go along."

Harrison looked pensive and rubbed his clean-shaven jaw as Starr said she'd decide while she showered, then thanked Clay for keeping it safe.

Clean and turbaned, Starr took a moment before drying her hair to jot down all the tests she wanted to have run on the fluid in the canister. She wished she could go with Clay, but it wouldn't be fair to leave SeLi again so soon. If he flew it to Berkeley, by the time she drove home, the lab should have most of the results.

SeLi showed up as Starr finished dressing. The girl regaled her mother with nonstop tales about her sleepover at the McLeods'.

"Morgan's dad is cool for a pinstripe," SeLi declared as she bounced on the bed. Then, more seriously, her chin resting in her palm, she said, "He's not a stud muffin like Morgan's uncle or nothin'. But he's a rad dad for a guy that's heavy sugar."

Starr paused in the middle of brushing her hair to gape at her daughter. "Sometimes, SeLi, I need an interpreter with you."

"Whazzat?"

"An interpreter? Someone who explains what you just said in terms your poor mother can understand."

SeLi grinned. "Gotcha. For nerds and cubes," she drawled. "I said Morgan's dad is okay for a suit. For a *rich* suit. You know, *heavy sugar*. His uncle Clay, though, is—"

"Never mind! I think I got the reference to Morgan's uncle. Could we move on? How's the schoolwork coming? No tutor today?"

SeLi's head bobbed. "He's there, but I get to skip. 'Cause I missed you so much, Mom." She threw her scrawny arms around Starr's waist and buried her face below Starr's heart.

"I missed you, too, Skeeter." Starr swallowed the big lump in her throat. "Come on. Walk me over to the house. I need a minute with Morgan's dad."

"Mom, do you think they'll move back to San Francisco?" SeLi slipped her hand into Starr's as they went outside. "Morgan likes goin' to school with me and Kevin and Mike."

"Maybe not, honey. I understand his mother doesn't enjoy big cities." She squeezed the child's hand to soften the blow.

"I don't like the city, neither. I wanna stay here at the ranch. It's the greatest."

Starr slowed her steps. She'd never imagined that SeLi wouldn't want to go home. "This is a vacation. Vacations are nice, but they always end."

"But...if we stayed, I wouldn't have to see Buffy or Heather again."

"Or Woody or Trader John." Starr felt guilty using those two old fellows when she intended to wean SeLi from the dock. Sometimes though, mothers had to be creative and resourceful.

The little girl stopped at the door to the ranch house. She was teary-eyed. "I didn't think 'bout them. But Woody and Trader John, they got each other. Morgan's lonesome. Like you were when you were a kid, Mom."

"Why, I . . . SeLi, I wasn't . . ." Starr trailed off. She *had* been lonely as a child. But how did SeLi know? As she grappled for some explanation, the front door opened. Starr was relieved to see Morgan. And more relieved when the children dashed off hand in hand. Yet the allusion to her unhappy childhood took longer to shake off.

Harrison stepped out of the den and gestured her to enter. Behind him, a fire danced warmly. Starr's heart skipped a beat when she saw that Clay was present, along with Vanessa.

Just seeing Clay made her heart kick over and speed up. His stance, the way he leaned carelessly against the mantel, was reminiscent of the one in the photo SeLi had *borrowed*.

Starr simply couldn't bring herself to use the term *stolen*. Not when the reason SeLi took them was that she so desperately wanted a family to talk about in class. According to Wanda Manning, a family consisted of two parents and a child. Starr felt a surge of fear. She would do better to concentrate on the current gathering of the clan than to think about her problems with the social worker.

Clay had changed into a black turtleneck and close-fitting black jeans. His hair glinted in the firelight, and his mustache was neatly trimmed. His slow smile when he looked up and saw her made her heart turn over.

Oh, God, SeLi's not the only one who wants this man to stay in our lives.

Starr forced her limbs to move. All three McLeods had begun to stare at her oddly. She blushed, hoping they couldn't read what had gone through her mind. She realized the senator had been talking. Oh, Lord, what was he saying?

"...so you see, Starr, testing the canister is a moot point. Mere hours ago Calexco filed a lease on a thousand acres up there. It's all nice and legal."

Starr suddenly had trouble breathing. "With whom? Filing doesn't mean squat. You can't believe the Land Bureau will approve the lease when they hear about the sheep—when they know about the Drixathyon."

Harrison smiled and spread his palms. "It's out of our hands, Starr. Now it's between the Federal Bureau of Land Management and Calexco. By tomorrow every newspaper in California will carry news of a promising oil strike. Considering the ailing economy, I rather think public pressure will be in Calexco's favor.''

Starr shook her head. She looked to Clay, but found him studying his brother, his own face impassive. Turning again to the senator, she said, "If they sanction use of Drixathyon on that reserve, they'll be signing a death warrant for hundreds of bighorns. You can't let that happen. Do something, Senator!''

Harrison slipped an arm around Vanessa's slender waist. "I intend to. New Year's Day I'm taking my wife and son on a long-overdue vacation.'' His smile didn't reach his eyes. "As I said before, you and SeLi are welcome to stay and share our Christmas.'' He patted his wife's hand and she snuggled against his shoulder.

The feeling of betrayal made Starr less cautious. "How can you ignore what Calexco has done? It's murder.''

Harrison's lips tightened. "You disappoint me, Starr. I thought you were a realist. It appears you're more your mother's daughter than I'd imagined. Patrice was always one for drama.''

"*You're* disappointed in *me?*'' Starr's jaw dropped. Again her eyes sought Clay, who had straightened away from the mantel. His lake blue eyes were decidedly cool.

"Harris, you know I intend to take the contents of the canister in to be tested,'' he said. "Ask your friends at Calexco to hold off going public until we see the results.''

"Now, Clay, don't concern yourself with politics at this late date. And you don't have time to fly to San Francisco. You have to go to L.A. tomorrow to meet Mom and Dad's flight. This . . . disagreement between us will only upset them.''

"I rather think they've heard us squabble before," Clay said dryly.

"But Vanessa's dad's coming tomorrow, too. On the train. Thurgood isn't well. He has a bad heart."

"I didn't know." Clay shot his sister-in-law a sympathetic glance.

Harrison turned back to Starr. "If you and SeLi decide to stay, I'm afraid I'll have to ask you not to start one of these arguments."

Starr waited for Clay to say something more, but he only frowned and shoved his hands into his back pockets.

"Not only will SeLi and I not be staying," Starr informed the room at large, "but *I'm* taking the cylinder back for testing. After that, I'll be blowing the whistle on Calexco." Spinning away, she marched toward the door.

Harrison stepped in front of her, blocking her path. "Aren't you forgetting who hired you for this job? Even if that doesn't cut any ice with you, don't forget who came through for you when you needed help with SeLi's adoption."

Clay moved away from the fireplace. He grabbed Harrison's arm. "That sounds like blackmail, big brother. It also sounds like you're protecting Calexco. Are they holding something over your head?"

Starr felt faint. Of course Clay meant SeLi's parentage. Why couldn't he let it drop? Surprisingly, though, the outrage didn't come from Harrison, but rather from his wife. It was the delicate-looking Vanessa McLeod who stepped between the brothers with her dainty hands clenched.

"Barclay McLeod," she fumed, "how dare you take the side of a stranger against your own flesh and blood!

If you have no consideration for your brother, at least think about Morgan. Think about me."

Starr saw the woman's huge violet eyes fill with tears. Her own stomach knotted. Starr waited for Clay to see through the woman's act. When he begged Vanessa not to cry, Starr knew who'd won. Sick at heart, she hefted the wrapped canister, stepped around the senator and left the room in search of SeLi.

She didn't hear Clay take on his brother. "Have you any idea how close Starr came to dying after she drank the water from that stream? If my horse hadn't stumbled over her on the trail, I wouldn't have found her at all. What then, brother?"

The senator said nothing.

Vanessa left from the room and swept toward Starr, who was busy herding her protesting daughter toward the front door, like an avenging angel. "Family stands behind family in this house, no matter how much you interfere." Vanessa's soft-spoken Southern drawl curled around Starr like bands of steel.

This must be how SeLi felt at school, Starr thought. Like an unwanted outsider. It was plain to see that the beautiful Vanessa held both McLeod men in the palm of her lily-white hand.

The silence that rode in the wake of Vanessa's statement was broken by the shrill ringing of the phone. Starr hesitated as Vanessa picked up the hall phone. It might be Stanley calling back.

But it wasn't; it was Wanda Manning for Clay. Starr knew, because Wanda's voice boomed over the wire loud enough for Starr to identify the social worker.

Clay picked up the extension in the den. Vanessa hadn't yet hung up the hall phone, and Starr heard Wanda tell Clay she had interesting news concerning a certain birth certificate. Starr jerked open the door and shoved SeLi out.

Oh, God. How had the season of good cheer evolved into this nightmare? Starr had thought Harrison was a nice man, but he condoned death and destruction. She had given Clay her heart, yet he conspired with an evil woman to block SeLi's adoption. And then there was Vanessa. Starr had totally underestimated the woman who led the McLeod troops into battle like a warrior queen.

Struggling with the unwieldy canister, Starr caught SeLi by the hand and ran blindly with her across the clearing. Halfway to the motor home, she thought she heard Clay call for her to stop—to wait. But it only lent wings to her feet.

CHAPTER FIFTEEN

OUT OF BREATH, Starr eventually slowed down. The wind stung her face and dried her tears, but didn't come close to cooling her anger.

"Mom, are you crazy?" SeLi squealed. "What's wrong with everybody?"

Starr dropped the girl's hand to look for her door key. Her fingers shook, although the minute she stepped inside, the blast of warm air wilted her. "Pack your books and toys, SeLi. We're going back to San Francisco."

"Now?" SeLi's face crumpled. "Morgan said we were gonna stay here for Christmas."

"Oh, honey, I don't expect you to understand. It concerns the sheep. We can't stay, that's all. Don't make this harder than it has to be."

SeLi stamped her foot. "I don't *want* to leave! Last night me and Morgan saw the Christmas star. I said all the words like he told me." Tears ran openly down her cheeks. "Morgan said I'd get three wishes, so I wished for Clay to be my dad. I wished we'd come and live at the ranch. And I wished for a sister so we could all be a family. Now we won't be and it's your fault," she howled.

Starr had never seen SeLi so distressed. Not since the night her mother had died. "Oh, sweetheart," was all she managed to say. How could she explain to a nine-year-old that the McLeods' cheery fireplace, their wonderfully decorated tree and the outward picture they presented as California's perfect family was a travesty?

There was no way. She numbly shook her head. When she got back to San Francisco she had to report Calexco. The media would come. The fight would get dirty. Wanda would arrive with a court order and take SeLi away. Starr's shoulders bent under the load. What had, a month ago, promised to be the happiest Christmas of her life was about to become the worst.

"Do as I say," she pleaded. "I want to leave in half an hour." Pulling on her gloves, she took a wrench and went outside to disconnect the hookups.

Had it really only been a week since Clay showed up in the middle of the night to tease her about her neon sleepers? It seemed an eternity.

He'd saved her life. He'd helped find the canister. They'd shared laughter and passion. Didn't it mean anything to him? Because if it did, he would sweep in here on a white charger and prove to her that the promises they'd made to each other with their love-making were stronger than blood ties. Nothing and nobody would stop him.

In less than ten minutes Starr had secured everything in the motor home. It was hardest leaving behind the Christmas lights that Clay had put up. For SeLi, he'd said, who now sobbed uncontrollably.

Near tears herself, Starr coiled the colorful lights carefully in a box and left them beside the utility pole.

Nothing she said to SeLi made any difference. But then, why should it when her own heart was breaking into a thousand pieces?

Starr had had years of learning how to deal with disappointment during this season of love, peace and goodwill. Did you ever get over the pain—or the expectations? she wondered as she started the engine and pulled away without looking back. Darn it all, she'd wanted more for SeLi. Much more.

On the way down the mountain, Starr rounded a sharp corner and the lights of Riverside spread out below. And above, it was as if they'd met all the stars in heaven. But there in the distance shone one star, brighter than any other.

She squinted. Was it SeLi's Christmas star?

Determination stole over Starr. SeLi deserved the most wonderful Christmas of her young life, and Starr intended to see that she got it. Even if she had to call out the National Guard to hold off Wanda Manning.

Starr glanced around uneasily, wondering if there was indeed magic overhead.

"SeLi, honey," she murmured to the child who had stubbornly turned her face away from the twinkling panorama. "Christmas is about more than wishes and presents. It's about being honest even if that means risking something you value very much. And it's about doing what you think is right, even if it loses you a friend." Quietly she gave SeLi a simplified version of events at the ranch and ended by telling her the story of the first Christmas. When she finished, Starr thought she noted a slight softening of SeLi's tense features.

Shortly thereafter, the little girl curled up in the seat and fell asleep. The miles ticked slowly by. Los Angeles after dark was a sight to behold. Decked out for Christmas, this—the city of angels—screamed out with a commercialism that belied everything Starr had just tried to impress upon SeLi.

Here among the glare of neon lights, she lost the
Christmas star. The city of angels—where her father's
opulent home lay nestled in the hills of Hollywood a bit
northeast of the freeway—was a world of lies and fantasies. It was the world Starr had been born into. Obviously it was Clay McLeod's world, too.

No wonder Starr found it so hard to believe in
Christmas stars and Christmas miracles. In twenty-nine
years, she had yet to witness one.

Sending a last mournful glance in the direction of the
house where for years she'd dreamed of having her
parents back together, Starr pressed the gas pedal to the
floor and left childish dreams behind.

Before the cumbersome motor home had cleared the
Grapevine, Starr hardened her heart to the love she'd
held for Clay McLeod, too.

Ten hours later, sunrise was still a few hours off
when Starr crossed into San Francisco after dropping
the canister at the lab. Rain and fog had impeded her
progress for the last fifty miles. Her limbs were shaking by the time she parked outside her condominium.

"Welcome home," she muttered. The only visible
light in the dark building was the one seventy-five-watt
bulb Blevins always left on in the lobby.

More tired than she'd ever been and more despondent, Starr gently woke SeLi and climbed from the vehicle. They took nothing in with them. Unpacking now
would only make it harder for SeLi, she thought.

Still, from the minute she opened her apartment
door, Starr felt a certain relief at being home. Or she
did until she remembered that she'd have to move, trust
fund or no. Harris-Clay Enterprises owned the roof
over her head.

But she was much too tired to think clearly. Dazedly she helped SeLi off with her jacket and shoes and into bed for another hour or so of sleep.

An underlying sense of doom denied Starr the same luxury. It was four-thirty in the morning, and she didn't know a soul in the world she could call for any reason short of homicide.

Sleep out of the question, she sat in the kitchen with nothing but the light from one gas burner. She'd filled the teapot, having decided one thing that might help was a strong cup of her mother's favorite tea—Red Zinger. The name alone gave one gusto to face the day, according to Patrice Lederman.

While Starr waited for the water to boil, she contemplated everything that had happened in so short a time. December, the month when people the world over made an effort to be cheerful, had been a nightmare for Starr.

And the apartment didn't even look like Christmas.

The kettle emitted a squeal. Starr dashed to remove it from the heat, not wanting to wake SeLi.

"Mmm." The pungent aroma did lift her spirits. After a few sips, she decided the least she could do was put up a few decorations. Not that it made a lick of sense. Tomorrow she'd have to start looking for a new place to live. Yet in another way it made perfect sense. Not only would SeLi's morning be more enjoyable, but decorating was bound to keep her own mind occupied. Occupied, and off Clay McLeod's defection.

She set her tea aside while she hauled boxes of decorations from the hall closet into the living room. Once there, she saw that the message light on her answering machine was blinking. *Maybe it's Clay.* For just a moment, Starr's heartbeat matched the tempo of the winking message light.

But no, it was her mother.

"Starr, honey," Patrice began in the smoky voice that had helped make her a star. "I'm calling to cancel my Christmas Eve party. You'll never guess what. Your father phoned from Tokyo. Claims he's been thinking about old times. Says he misses me. Honey... Sam's wiring me a plane ticket." Nervous laughter trilled as the tape wound on. "Oh, tell SeLi thanks. Not that it's certain anything will come of it. But it's a start. SeLi convinced me to wish on the Christmas star one last time. I've never stopped loving your father, baby. Wish me well, huh?"

Starr reached to turn on another light as she rewound the last part of the tape and played it a second time. The news shocked her. To her knowledge her parents hadn't even spoken in the past three years. And yet Patrice had sounded more excited than Starr remembered her being in a long, long while. She sounded like a woman in love.

With mixed emotions, Starr stopped the machine. She went around the apartment in a stupor, looping garlands along the mantel and attaching huge red bows to glowing hurricane lamps. Maybe the women in her family weren't destined for lasting love. Her grandmother had been married five times. Patrice three. And now it sounded as if she'd be willing to try her first husband again.

Starr arranged a bowl of pine cones on the hearth. Well, *she* wasn't nearly so willing to forgive.

Getting into the Christmas spirit, she assembled a small artificial tree to put in SeLi's bedroom. Something about the tree created a sickening wave of nostalgia. She set the ornaments aside and went back to the kitchen to warm her tea.

The tree was so...so Hollywood. White. Symmetrical. Pink bows. Pink lights. White glittering angels, each with a cherub face and platinum hair. Compared to the McLeods' woodsy-smelling pine, strung with popcorn, cranberries and wooden ornaments, the artificial tree seemed a sham.

Decorating this condo was a sham.

After tomorrow—after she made that call to Fish and Game—Christmas would be ruined for a lot of people. Morgan, SeLi, Clay, to name a few. Not to mention herself.

But she had no choice. Had never had one.

Starr crossed the room and stood by the window. Lifting the curtain aside, she stared into the inky sky. Sometime in the last hour the fog had blown out to sea. A few stars sparkled. One stood out, winking brightly.

SeLi's Christmas star? For a dazzling, dizzying second, she thought it had followed them home.

No. That made no sense. It was a trick. A regular old star, magnified through her tears. Starr let the curtain fall. She dabbed at her eyes. Her own life might be in shambles, but she'd be darned if she'd let Wanda or anyone else ruin Christmas for SeLi.

At the table she picked up a pad and began making notes. If Patrice was on her way to Tokyo, that meant her town house, which was probably already decorated to the nth degree, would be vacant. A perfect hideaway.

Suddenly Starr felt better. Let Clay and Wanda Manning plot. She would beat them at their own game. At least until January first.

Try as she might, though, Starr was unable to lump Clay in the same barrel of bad apples as Wanda. Clay had a warm, tender, funny side that she loved. This time her tears refused to be checked. She put her head down and let them flow, succumbing in a few minutes to exhaustion—

"Mom!"

Starr jolted awake. She knocked her cup off the table. Cold red liquid splashed everywhere. Starr's nose wrinkled automatically. What was that scorched, metallic smell?

"Yikes!" She scrambled out of the chair and dashed to the stove. Her nice copper kettle was red-hot halfway to the handle. Switching off the gas, Starr swallowed a bad word as SeLi dashed into the room.

"I couldn't find you!" SeLi cried, throwing herself into her mother's arms. "I went in your room. I thought you were gone."

"Hey, it's okay, Skeeter. I'd never leave you." But then Starr remembered that Wanda Manning might succeed in separating them forever. Her hug turned fierce.

SeLi winced and wriggled free. "Ouch. Gosh, Mom, what happened? You look like something the cat dragged in."

Starr laughed and tugged on a messy dark braid. "You've been around my mother too much, young lady. That's one of her stock phrases."

SeLi giggled. "The Christmas decorations are real fresh, Mom. 'Cept you promised I could help."

"They aren't fresh, SeLi. Every one is fake."

"No, silly. Fresh is, like, cool." SeLi rolled her eyes.

"Ah, well..." Starr was still bewildered. "Turns out we won't need them. We had a message on the answering machine from Nana Patrice. She went to Japan for Christmas to be with my dad. I had all the boxes of decorations out when it dawned on me that her place is already decorated. Let me get cleaned up and make a couple of phone calls. Then we'll load up our gifts and take them to her town house. Won't that be a blast?''

"No." SeLi shook her head. "What if Morgan and his folks come back? 'Sides, there ain't nobody to play with at Nana's. And her neighbors are pure weird."

How did one argue against fact? Starr didn't even try. "I'll fix breakfast and we can discuss it some more."

"I'm sure glad it's not our breakfast that stinks so bad."

Starr smiled. "Sorry. I fell asleep with the kettle on. I'll fix pancakes if you go pick up the newspaper. I just heard it hit our door. Blevins must have seen the motor home and told the paperboy we were back."

"Pancakes. Goody, goody. Can I have peanut butter on mine?"

"Sounds gross, but yes, I suppose. If you let me read the paper in peace. I haven't seen any news in a week. I feel out of touch."

SeLi skipped off down the hall as Starr reached for the pancake mix. She had her head in the refrigerator looking for eggs when she heard the front door slam and SeLi's muffled cry.

"What is it?" Starr asked as the little girl rounded the corner at a dead run.

"Morgan's dad. His picture's on the front page. I guess he's really 'portant."

"Let me see." Starr snatched the paper from SeLi's hand. Bold headlines set her heart skipping:

State Senator McLeod
Requests Private Hearing
with Federal Judge

In smaller type below it said:

Harrison McLeod Withdraws
From California Gubernatorial Race

Fingers shaking, Starr plopped down at the kitchen table and began to read the fine print, breakfast forgotten.

SeLi slid into the nook. "What's wrong, Mom? Is Moe's dad okay?"

Starr looked up from an article that was vague at best. It was apparent, however, that someone had leaked news about the sheep. Who? Had he been sacrificed for Calexco? The oil company wasn't mentioned. Neither was Clay. Only Vanessa in one brief line saying she supported her husband fully.

"Mom?" SeLi shook her arm. "Mr. McLeod ain't dead, is he?"

Politically he was. But how to tell a child? "It has to do with his job, honey. Why don't you have microwave waffles today? I want to go see what they say about this on TV."

"Okay." SeLi didn't act too happy, but she agreed.

Starr hurried into her bedroom and snapped on the set. She caught the last of a news broadcast. Apparently the senator was slated to meet with the House Environmental Committee at ten, eastern time. Starr glanced at her watch and realized that was five minutes away. The last film clip showed a group—presumably environmentalists—waving placards that demanded Harrison's head on a pike.

Starr snatched the phone and dialed a friend in the Sierra Club. He asked pointedly whose side she was on.

"The side of the sheep, Mark. Need you ask? What about Calexco? They're as much or more to blame."

Mark refused to comment, and Starr had just hung up the phone when her doorbell rang. *Darn*. She couldn't talk to anyone until she found out what precisely had happened.

But SeLi ran to answer the door.

"Don't open it!" Starr yelled. "See who it is first." Unsettled, Starr envisioned a mob of angry reporters. But no, she thought, trying to slow her breathing. Blevins wouldn't have let strangers in. Oh, Lord! Maybe it was Wanda Manning.

Or Clay? In spite of everything that had gone on between them, Starr's heart began to gallop. She was never more aware than now of how badly she wanted to see Clay—how much she missed him.

In any case, she was too late to stop SeLi, who sounded as if she wanted to keep the visitor out. Starr's stomach lurched. That meant it wasn't Clay; SeLi would be dragging him in. It was a man, though, judging by the sleeve of a sports coat she could see.

"Stanley." His name rolled off Starr's tongue as he swept SeLi aside and marched in.

"Well," he huffed. "I'm certainly glad to find you at home and not aligned with those sheep-murdering McLeods. So far, they only have the goods on the senator, but I'll bet that brother of his isn't altogether innocent. Maybe next time you'll listen to ol' Stanley, eh?"

Starr bristled. "Barclay McLeod wasn't involved," she said in his defense. "Be careful whom you accuse of what, Stanley. I wouldn't be alive today if it hadn't been for him."

SeLi ran up and pummeled Stanley's coat. "Don't you say bad things about Moe's dad or his uncle Clay. Moe and me wished on the Christmas star. His mom and dad made up, just like we wished. His uncle Clay is gonna marry my mom. We wished that, too. We're all gonna be family, and families stick together. Why don't you just go 'way? Mom and me don't want you here." The little girl tried pulling Stanley toward the door.

"Starr?" Stanley sounded shocked. "How can you marry that ruffian?"

SeLi's words echoed in Starr's head. They pulsed outward, wrapping around her heart, crystallizing her feelings for Clay.

She loved him. When you loved someone you were in their corner through good times and bad. Like she'd back SeLi against all who'd brand her a thief and a pickpocket.

Hadn't the senator once described Clay as a sensitive man, one who listened to Vanessa's problems? A man soft on animals and children and family? She'd seen that for herself. What kind of man would he be if he *didn't* stick by his brother?

And the answer came as a shock. *Not the kind of man with whom I'd want to make babies and share my life.* "SeLi," Starr said earnestly, ignoring Stanley's presence, "it was a mistake for us to leave the ranch. Run get your jacket. We're going back. If it isn't too late, if Clay will let us help him..."

"Yippee!" SeLi shouted. She smirked at Stanley as she skidded past him and ran down the hall.

"Don't do this," Stanley warned. "You'll lose your job. Guilt by association. You'll be fired."

Starr backed Stanley steadily out the door. Just before she closed it behind him, she said, "Calexco is the guilty one. Fish and Game, among others, has let them get away with murder for years. Get used to the idea of filing your own lab slips, Stanley. I'm about to shake things up."

She hurried down the hall after SeLi, pausing to look for her car keys. She was frantically turning out her pockets when the doorbell pealed again.

"Don't answer it!" Starr shouted as SeLi scampered past. Once again her warning came too late. This time, however, when she reached SeLi's side, it wasn't Stanley who barged in. It was the man responsible for her mad scramble—Barclay McLeod. His hat was in his hand, and his nephew, Morgan, stood at his side.

"Before you toss me out," Clay said, holding up a palm, "hear me out, okay?"

Starr threw herself into Clay's arms. She clung to his neck and kissed him full on the mouth.

Shocked, he flailed wildly for a moment. Then he took control of the situation, slid his arms around her waist and pushed her gently against the wall.

Clay was breathing hard and little more than a step away from seeking a more comfortable place to continue this lovely interlude when the sound of childish giggles intruded.

He loosened his hold on Starr and gazed tenderly down at her. "I came to plead my case," he said, placing a finger under her chin, forcing her to look up.

"Does this effusive greeting mean you no longer believe I condone what Harrison did?"

She was distressed. "I realized you love him and that you're concerned about his family. About *your* family."

"The love goes without saying," he said, rubbing his thumb softly over her cheek. "Love is unconditional, but loyalty has to be earned. If you hadn't left in such a rush, you'd have heard me ask Harris if avarice and greed is the example he wants to set for his son. Fortunately, after he calmed down and really thought about it, he admitted it's not. That's why he agreed to turn himself in."

Starr feared she'd made a fool of herself again in kissing Clay. He hadn't mentioned her anywhere in that speech. So why had he come all this way? Suddenly she realized they probably wanted her to testify against Calexco. That must be what he meant by saying he'd come to "plead his case."

"I guess you two are hoping I'll make a strong statement against Calexco. I will, but I'll also have to tell what part the senator played. That's assuming the canister I dropped off last night contains Drixathyon, and I'm sure it does."

Clay frowned. "I didn't fly up here on no sleep to talk about any of this."

"Oh? Wanda Manning, then?" Starr glanced to see that SeLi was with Morgan a safe distance away.

Clay shook his head. "You won't believe this," he murmured. "The name on that birth certificate wasn't Harrison's. It was Joel Forbes."

"Joel Forbes?" Starr blinked. "Any relation to Judge Forbes?"

"His son. He died in a shipboard accident less than a year after he came back from Thailand. The judge didn't know he had a grandchild until the paperwork showed up on his desk. Apparently the birth certificate was in among SeLi's mother's things. At his age, and a widower, the judge felt the wisest thing would be to ensure a good adoption. With both parents dead, he didn't see a need for anyone to know the truth."

"How sad. I mean it's his flesh-and-blood granddaughter. I'll bet he's mad at Mrs. Manning."

"I think it's fair to say your case will be reassigned."

Starr frowned again. "Then I don't understand. Why are you here?"

"Didja come to ask my mom to marry you?" SeLi said. She seemed to pop up from nowhere.

"Well, I..." Clay fiddled with the hat he still held and shifted from one foot to the other.

"SeLi!" Starr's gasp echoed down the hall.

"That's what Morgan said. Moe, didn't you say that a minute ago?" SeLi demanded of the silent little boy.

Blue eyes wide, the boy slanted his uncle a helpless appeal. "Isn't that what you told Grandma McLeod?"

"Yes, it is."

"Then just ask," SeLi prompted. "How hard can it be to say, 'Will you marry me?'"

Clay rubbed the back of his neck with one hand. Then he threw back his head and laughed. "Listen, munchkin, proposing to a lady is hard enough without an audience. I know you want to help, but there are some things a man's just gotta do for himself."

SeLi squinted up at him.

Morgan tugged on her sleeve. "C'mon. I think he wants us to get lost."

"Well, gol-ly!" SeLi exclaimed. "Why didn't you just say so? My mom decorated our tree last night, Morgan. Wanna see?"

As the two clattered down the short hallway, Clay took a small, worn velvet box out of his pocket. "The element of surprise is gone, but since you didn't take off or call the police, maybe that means you'll accept this ring. It was my grandmother's engagement ring. She wore it for fifty years." He snapped the box open, and the light caught the blue stone nestled inside. "I was going to buy you one when I picked my folks up in L.A., but my mother suggested using this one. Do you mind?"

Starr touched the white star that radiated from the stone's center. "The Christmas star," she whispered. "Clay, it's beautiful. It's perfect. I love your mother. I love you."

He smiled. "You're beautiful. You're perfect. I love you, too. Does all that mean yes? Will you marry me, Starr?"

"She will!" two hushed voices proclaimed in unison.

Clay and Starr looked up as the children ducked back into the living room.

Laughing, Clay caught Starr close for another long kiss.

"I second that," she murmured the moment she was able. And she'd never meant anything more. For the first time in several days, she believed it was going to be a beautiful Christmas.

Was she crazy, or did the star sapphire Clay placed on her finger suddenly glow brightly?

It was magic. The magic of the Christmas star.

EPILOGUE

CLAY HEARD the commotion out in the hall and asked the caller on the telephone to hold. It was past suppertime, and the ranch house seemed strangely devoid of cooking odors. The last he'd seen Starr, she was busy helping SeLi make Christmas decorations for some event at school.

The phone call from his brother was a surprise. Harrison was due home next week, and according to the plan, he was supposed to begin picking up the pieces of his life. But he was calling to say that he'd decided to stay on in New Mexico even after finishing his five-year community-service sentence. He'd asked Vanessa to join him and she'd said yes.

Clay knew from the occasional phone call that Harrison had come to love the legal work he did in the remote Native American village, as well as the quiet, less hectic pace there.

Funny how things worked out, Clay thought. Perhaps it was fitting that Harrison end his sentence negotiating tribal water rights. Apparently the tribal council had invited him to stay. A few years ago, when Harrison's concern for the state's economy had overshadowed his good sense, Clay had doubted that his brother would ever see this particular sentence through, let alone change his ways. Especially after Calexco's fine had helped bail out the state and nothing much had happened to the men who'd been Harrison's so-called friends. He'd expected Harrison to appeal.

Wait until Starr heard the news. Clay needed to find her, anyway, because Harrison had asked if the whole family could come to Taos for a real old-fashioned Christmas this year.

As he stepped into the hall, he was hit in the knees by his red-haired, blue-eyed, three-year-old daughter, Joy.

"Whoa! Where's the fire?" Clay reached down, hoisted her aloft and kissed her soundly on her button nose. She was such a bundle of energy, and such a combination of himself and Starr, that it always made him smile.

"SeLi won't play with me," she pouted prettily. "So I tooked her ol' comb."

Clay saw that indeed she held an elaborate, jeweled comb in her chubby hand. "No way. Time you learned you can't just take things that don't belong to you. Is your sister in her room?"

Joy nodded. "And Mama."

Clay grinned. What had SeLi done now? On the way to the girl's room, he snatched up a piece of mistletoe someone had thoughtfully left on the hall table. It never hurt to be prepared. Not that Starr could be bribed. But Clay always enjoyed trying.

"Okay, princess, let's go see what's up with those two."

As he stepped silently through SeLi's open door, his heart leapt. His wife, beautiful even in her state of dishabille, was on her knees adjusting the wide, velvet skirt on a dress that made their adopted daughter look grown-up beyond her fourteen years.

His shock was audible, the message from Harris forgotten.

Starr glanced up and smiled. "You like it?" *Say yes,* she mouthed.

Clay needed no prompting. "It's gorgeous, SeLi. You look wonderfully grown-up. Twenty, at least."

SeLi floated across the room, went up on tiptoe and kissed his cheek. "Brian Flaherty invited me to the Christmas dance. Will he like this dress, do you think?" She did a little pirouette.

"A dance?" Clay's brow furrowed and he set his youngest down on the pink-checked bedspread. "Starr—a dance?" he whispered.

SeLi overheard. She rolled her eyes and plucked the comb from her little sister's busy fingers. "You didn't say anything last week when Moe asked you to help him choose a Christmas gift for Whitney Desmond."

"Yeah," Starr said, getting to her feet to unzip SeLi's dress. "You wouldn't be a teensy bit chauvinistic, would you?"

Clay held up his hands. "If that's the difference between being an uncle and a father, then I'm guilty. But hey, I know when I'm outnumbered. Speaking of Moe and Christmas, I've got to call Harrison back. He plans to continue helping the tribe file injunctions until they win. You guys want to go to New Mexico for the holidays?"

Starr laughed. "Your folks are dangling an East Coast amusement park to tempt us into going to Florida this year. My folks are doing the same with one on the West Coast—they're big on family now that they've remarried and Dad's retired. Plus, they've thrown in a studio tour for good measure." She shook her head. "After finally finishing my doctoral dissertation and everything we've been doing to bring Calexco to its knees, I just want some time alone with my husband and children. Is that selfish of me?"

"Time alone?" Clay's eyes gleamed. He waggled his eyebrows and chased after her, mistletoe held aloft.

SeLi returned from hanging her dress in the closet, tied her robe and scooped her little sister from the bed. "You guys haven't had much time alone with Mom always running back and forth between San Francisco, college and the ranch."

"I explained all that, SeLi. I was determined to get Drixathyon off the market. I thought we were all in agreement."

"We were. And we're proud of you, Mom. Wouldn't it be cool if the *whole* family did get together for Christmas this year? Including Woody, Trader John and my real grandpa Forbes? If you guys wanna talk about it privately, I'll take Joy into the den and read her one of the Christmas stories Nana Patrice sent."

Starr started to protest, but Clay picked her up and slung her over his shoulder. "It's a good idea, and a private discussion is exactly what we need." He winked at SeLi and jogged toward the master bedroom. "When you get to the den, SeLi, tell your uncle Harrison I'll get back to him later."

"Much later," Starr said, laughing.

"Whatcha gonna do, Daddy?" called Joy.

Hearing the click of the lock on her parents' bedroom door, SeLi grinned at her sister. "C'mon, squirt. Let's go see if the Christmas star is out tonight."

SeLi put her down and the two raced into the den. After SeLi had stopped to pass on her dad's message, she joined Joy at the bay window.

"Tell me again," the little girl begged, "how Nana Patrice wanted a baby and she wished on the Christmas star. Are you pos'tive my mama was borned before the next Christmas?''

"Born," SeLi corrected primly. "Don't you remember how I said I wanted a dad and I wished on the Christmas star? Starr and Clay got married, didn't they?"

"And me." The impudent child clapped her hands. "You said you wished for me."

SeLi wrinkled her nose. "I didn't know little sisters were such pests."

Joy's pretty blue eyes clouded. Her lips trembled.

"Hey, I was kidding. I only meant the Christmas star is powerful. You gotta be careful what you ask for, okay?"

"Can I ask for a brother?" Joy asked, scrubbing the faint tears from her eyes. "Then when Morgan visits and you guys play 'Nopoly, I won't hafta be alone."

"Monopoly," SeLi said absently, listening to Starr's shrieks of laughter in the other room. Then there was a soft bump as the headboard of the bed hit the wall, and all was silent in her parent's bedroom.

"A brother might be the ticket at that," SeLi said, her face thoughtful. "It won't be all that long until I go off to college. Nobody should have to be alone, Joy. Nobody."

SeLi helped her little sister kneel on the window-seat cushion. Together they searched for and found the brightest star in the sky.

"Be careful now and get this right," SeLi warned. "Repeat after me—Star light, star bright, first star I see tonight..."

BRIDE'S BAY RESORT

UNLOCK THE DOOR TO GREAT ROMANCE AT BRIDE'S BAY RESORT

Join Harlequin's new across-the-lines series, set in an exclusive hotel on an island off the coast of South Carolina.

Seven of your favorite authors will bring you exciting stories about fascinating heroes and heroines discovering love at Bride's Bay Resort.

Look for these fabulous stories coming to a store near you beginning in January 1996.

Harlequin American Romance #613 in January
Matchmaking Baby by Cathy Gillen Thacker

Harlequin Presents #1794 in February
Indiscretions by Robyn Donald

Harlequin Intrigue #362 in March
Love and Lies by Dawn Stewardson

Harlequin Romance #3404 in April
Make Believe Engagement by Day Leclaire

Harlequin Temptation #588 in May
Stranger in the Night by Roseanne Williams

Harlequin Superromance #695 in June
Married to a Stranger by Connie Bennett

Harlequin Historicals #324 in July
Dulcie's Gift by Ruth Langan

Visit Bride's Bay Resort each month wherever Harlequin books are sold.

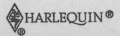 HARLEQUIN®

MILLION DOLLAR SWEEPSTAKES (III)

EXTRA BONUS PRIZE DRAWING

SWP-H1295

Let

 HARLEQUIN SUPERROMANCE®

welcome you home

Welcome to the H&H Cattle Company, near Gonzales, Texas!

Scott Hayes, he's the owner. Scott's a bit of a good ol' boy—a hardworking cattleman who's got a reputation with the ladies. Not that he has any time for womanizing *these* days. Fact is, Scott's putting in twenty-hour stretches, now that H&H is down to one hired hand. And the word around these parts is that H&H is teetering on the edge of bankruptcy.

Margaret Winston hopes like hell that's true. Because Maggie knows Scott from the old days and there's bad blood—and a good horse—between them.

Watch for *The Texas Way* by Jan Freed
Available in January 1996
wherever Harlequin books are sold.

You're About to Become a *Privileged Woman*

Reap the rewards of fabulous free gifts and benefits with proofs-of-purchase from Harlequin and Silhouette books

Pages & Privileges™

It's our way of thanking you for buying our books at your favorite retail stores.

PROOF OF PURCHASE

HS-PP82

Offer expires October 31, 1996

Pages & Privileges™

Harlequin and Silhouette—
the most privileged readers in the world!

For more information about Harlequin and Silhouette's **PAGES & PRIVILEGES** program call the Pages & Privileges Benefits Desk: **1-503-794-2499**

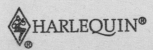